THE PERFECT LIFE

A totally compelling psychological thriller
with an electrifying finish

SUSANNA BEARD

JOFFE BOOKS

First published 2020
Joffe Books, London
www.joffebooks.com

ISBN: 978-1-78931-643-8

For Caroline

CHAPTER ONE

Heather

She knows something's going on the moment she hears the text arrive. There's a new edge to its tone: urgent, metallic, like a warning signal. She feels its power in the air, its two notes hanging, demanding attention.

She dries her hands, wet from the kitchen sink, and crosses the room to the worktop where her mobile lies. She stares at the screen for a moment, trying to ignore the feeling of heaviness in her gut.

Hi Heather, We're having a few people for dinner Saturday night — would you two like to join us? Nothing formal, just a relaxed evening. From 8.00. We'd love to see you! Victoria and Andrew x

Pulling a chair from the kitchen table where the remains of the family's breakfast are still scattered around, she sinks down, staring at the screen. It seems innocuous. To all intents and purposes it's a positive message, innocent and friendly. But her stomach clenches all the same.

Suspicion, her new best friend, crooks its finger at her, winking its knowing eye.

There's only one Victoria she can think of. Never Vicky, always Victoria, this woman is the mother of a boy called Alex, a friend of her elder son Ben who has been to their house many times to hang out in the dark, mysterious cell Ben calls a bedroom. Victoria's husband is called Andrew. Never Andy.

They live in the smart part of Hammersmith where bijou restaurants and delicatessens link hands, a peaceful haven not far from the bustle of their own road, squeezed in between Shepherd's Bush Green and White City. They've met only once or twice on the perimeter of the school football pitch.

She remembers standing next to Victoria in the rain, their umbrellas touching as they made small talk and pretended to enjoy themselves. The woman had all the right gear: leather riding boots, long oilskin coat, stylish hat and the biggest umbrella Heather had ever seen. Heather, meanwhile, had made some less than practical choices: her shoes were leaking, her coat had no hood, her umbrella had cost five pounds in Shepherd's Bush Market and wouldn't stay up properly. She felt lumpy and awkward next to this woman with her immaculate make-up and thick dark ponytail, like a country bumpkin next to a fashion icon.

And her social skills had definitely not been up to it. Victoria, establishing the proximity of their two homes, had asked if Heather and James had been to the new smart restaurant at the top of her road. They hadn't, and it was clear that Heather had never heard of it. Victoria's eyebrow had twitched upwards a fraction. Heather had felt humiliated and tongue-tied for the rest of the day.

But that was months ago, before.

She gives suspicion a little room. It's wise to be cautious, in her situation.

Studying the message again for a moment, she struggles to remember the woman's last name. Not only can she not remember it, she has no recollection of ever knowing it. More importantly, only Heather's closest friends and family have her mobile number.

The school would surely not have given it out. It's possible Victoria could have asked her son to get it from Ben, but that too would seem a strange thing to do. A lot of effort to get in touch with a woman she's spoken to once, in the rain. They hadn't even had a good conversation.

She's not going to disturb James over something so trivial. She taps in a holding message, as neutral as she can make it: *Thank you for the kind invitation. I will check with James tonight and let you know. H.* She hesitates over the sign-off. The woman has even sent a kiss — well, she's buggered if she's going to send one back. She barely knows her.

She sighs, switching the phone to silent.

* * *

Drifting around the kitchen, she wonders whether to eat. But she's not really hungry, and she might as well take advantage of the feeling and save the calories for later.

Her laptop is still open, as if awaiting instructions. She feels the muscles in her jaw tense as she clicks on the link to Facebook. With a jolt, she stares in surprise at the screen. Fourteen friend requests.

Heather is not a huge fan of Facebook, or social media of any kind. She hates to talk about herself, for a start, and can't imagine why anyone might be interested in her holidays or the supper she had last night. The only reason she has bothered is that there's a local buy-and-sell group, which can be quite useful for getting rid of old toys and gadgets. Since the boys were tiny, she feels as if she's been on an endless treadmill: buy, sell, buy, then sell, children's stuff. She sometimes wonders how much money they've spent indulging their children over the years. It must be a small fortune.

Anyway, joining the group meant setting up a profile, so she had duly done so. Her few friends, along with some of the mums at junior school, had connected with her, giving her a total audience of, well, about fourteen people.

3

Delving around in Facebook is something she's never done before, and she baulks at the idea. Though she knows the whole point of putting yourself onto social media is to see and be seen, it feels wrong, somehow, checking out strangers, seeing what they do in their spare time, following their discussions. But this is important. She needs to find out what's going on.

She checks the profiles of the people who want to be her 'friends'. A soldier from the US military, based in Connecticut — what? She declines the request. A handsome man called Jake, whose only information is a series of photographs of himself: showing off his six-pack, on a yacht in shorts and T-shirt, then dressed in cycling gear, his sunglasses reflecting a mountain view. He looks about thirty-five. Seriously? Then an ominous request from a woman called Jennifer Carter, a name that sounds familiar. Heather scrutinises the photo with no sense of recognition, then scrolls further down the profile. The woman's home town is listed as Cheltenham, and she was at the same grammar school as Heather.

She clicks 'ignore' and moves on, her unease growing by the minute. There are three more requests from women she was at school with in Cheltenham, none of whom seem familiar. The rest are people she's never heard of, but they live in London, and from the photos it seems they have children of similar age to her own. On one of their profiles, she notices the images of their friends and finds one with a mutual connection. Victoria Ainsworth. Immaculate make-up, thick dark hair falling in a swathe over one shoulder, snow-white smile. The very same Victoria who has asked them to dinner on Saturday.

* * *

By lunchtime, it's a lot worse. There are over fifty strangers trying to connect with her, not a single one she recognises. She declines them all, then sits for a moment considering whether she should delete her profile now. But if she does, how will she know when it stops? If it stops. The stirrings of panic in her stomach tell her she must do something.

Has Ben said something to Alex? Somebody must know something — and be telling others.

She should call Graham Fuller — he'll know what to do. Graham is the adviser from the lottery company, their support since the beginning. But when she picks up her mobile, she almost drops it when she sees the screen. Messages scream at her. Unlocking it, she stares in horror at the number of texts and calls she's missed. On a normal day, she might get one or two. She doesn't belong to a big social circle, just Natalie, her close neighbours Charlotte and Miles, a book club and an exercise class with groups on WhatsApp. There are only one or two mothers at school she knows and would call friends.

She glances at the first couple of messages. One offers her an investment in holiday properties around the world: 'Still in Development' and finished to the 'Highest Possible Quality'. Others are advertisements for 'The Season': Wimbledon, Ascot, Henley Regatta and more. She has never shown the remotest interest in going to any of those. She scrolls down, deleting rapidly, her fingers beginning to tremble.

The last one she looks at before she throws her mobile across the room says: *Rich bitch. You think you're so special.*

CHAPTER TWO

Heather

She's still thinking about it later, when the front door slams.

That will be a boy, then.

A scuffle in the hallway as shoes are kicked off, then a thump, thump on the stairs.

"Who's that?" she calls. If she doesn't ask, she knows what will happen. The intruder will continue to his bedroom and shut the door without so much as a 'hello' in her direction. The heavy thump of bass guitar will preclude any further efforts at communication on her part.

"'S me."

Ben. His voice is deeper than his younger brother's, gruff and monotone. She walks into the hallway and looks up the stairway to see his feet disappearing towards the top.

"Hello you. Good day?" she says, and the feet pause.

"Fine. Have you seen my football boots anywhere?" Ben's head appears, upside down, his thick hair sweeping the banister as he cranes his neck to look at her.

"No. Please don't tell me you've lost them." If he has, it will be the second time in a month.

"Dunno. 'Spect they're in lost property."

"Well, promise me you'll check tomorrow. Haven't you got a match on Saturday?"

"Probably." The head disappears, then the feet, and she can hear his bedroom door bang, the thump of his backpack on the floor.

Gone are the days when she would collect the boys from school and they'd chat on the way home. She misses that closeness — not to mention their soft hands in hers, cuddles on the sofa before bed, stories snuggled up together.

They're getting older, and she's losing them.

A scratching of a key in the lock interrupts her thoughts, and the front door swings open to reveal a second boy.

"Hi, Mum," Harry says, dumping his rucksack on the floor and kicking off his scuffed shoes, right in the middle of the hallway. "Is there anything to eat? I'm starving."

She moves the shoes to one side with her foot. It's hard to keep up with these boys — let alone James. They never seem to stop eating, and she's always shopping, cooking, and clearing up after them.

"Well, there's plenty of fruit, Harry," she says to the back of his head as it recedes towards the kitchen. "As always."

"I mean proper food." His voice is muffled and she knows he's staring into the fridge. She follows him into the kitchen. "Any pork pies? Sausages? Leftover pizza from last night?"

"No, darling, you've eaten it all. I've only just done the shopping, but I suppose I'll have to go again."

His round face appears from around the fridge door as he slams it shut. She marvels again at the blue of his eyes, the long fringes of his eyelashes.

"Can you go now then, please? I can't last until supper." He frowns and pulls open a cupboard door where the biscuits are normally kept. "I'm taking these to my room, okay?" He grabs a packet of chocolate-chip cookies and is gone before she can reply, the familiar sound of his running feet on the stairs reverberating through the house.

"Of course you can, darling, and thank you so much for offering to go to the shop for me, it's so sweet of you," she says out loud to the empty room in a sing-song voice. "I love you too, boys . . ."

Sometimes she wonders if they even notice she's there.

* * *

By the time James gets home, she's halfway through cooking supper, listening to the radio while she stirs a bubbling saucepan on the hob. The washing machine is whirring as it finishes yet another cycle, full of football gear, pungent boys' socks and underwear, and from upstairs comes a regular thump of rap music, vying with the radio for airspace.

On the radio, they're interviewing a woman about her job as a corporate lawyer. Heather has become absorbed in her description of a complex case and how she's handling it. It seems so interesting, so intellectually challenging, and so far from what Heather herself is doing with her life that she might as well be listening to a Martian describe its daily routine. She finds herself longing to be that woman, with her smart clothes, the respect she commands from her clients and colleagues, a beautiful, immaculate house, sleek sports car and a housekeeper, no doubt. Her voice is low and sexy, though commanding, and utterly self-confident. Heather has a picture of her in her mind's eye: she'll be slim, beautiful, with groomed, blow-dried hair and manicured nails. Her skin glows, her eyes are intelligent and perceptive.

Heather is so engrossed in the programme that she fails to notice James enter the room. When he materialises beside her, she's so startled that the spoon she's stirring with jerks upwards, spraying tomato sauce across the front of her shirt like an artist's flourish.

"James, don't do that! You gave me such a shock! Oh shit, look at me, what a mess . . ." She grabs a tea towel, wets it at the sink and starts to rub at the stains on her shirt.

"Sorry," James says, gazing into the fridge in an echo of his younger son only minutes before. "Have we got any wine?"

"If there's none there, there will be some in the cupboard under the stairs. I've got to go and change now. I need to nip round to the shop. I'll go in a minute, once supper's in the oven." She tries to hide the edge in her voice.

"I sense tension in the air." James knows her so well. "Are you angsting about something?"

She stops scrubbing at her shirt, which hangs wetly against her skin, the stain still stubbornly evident. "Oh no — I've made it worse now." She turns towards James, holding the fabric away from her stomach. "I'm worried that the cat's out of the bag."

James closes the fridge door, gazing at her with his frank grey eyes. "Really? What makes you think that?"

"We've had a dinner invitation from Alex's parents. Remember — Victoria and Andrew?"

"And because of that, you think the news is out? I realize we hardly know them, but perhaps they're just trying to be friendly . . ."

"Not just because of that. I've had a load of texts and missed calls. My phone was on silent, so I didn't reply to any to them, and I hardly dare look now."

James places a hand on each of her shoulders. "I think you're worrying too much. Anyway, I've been thinking. We can't just pretend it hasn't happened, not even for a few days. We're going to have to decide what to do with it pretty damn quick, aren't we? Once we've decided, I'm sure you'll feel better."

"I suppose so." She looks down at her ruined shirt. The fabric is old and tired; there's a seam gone at the shoulder and the cuffs are fraying. She should get herself a new one. It occurs to her that she can get a new one, a really beautiful one, without worrying that she's indulging herself. Though she's pretty sure she will worry. It'll take a while for her to change the long-held habit of saving money wherever she can.

"Listen," James says. "Why don't we do what they suggest and take a holiday to think it over? I was thinking maybe Mauritius or St Lucia, somewhere like that."

This is too much to think about now. "Can we talk about it over supper? I need to go to the shop now."

She trudges upstairs, pulling off her shirt and dumping it in the wastepaper basket. Yesterday's fleece will do; it's not clean, but she's only going to the corner shop. Glancing in the mirror on the inside of the wardrobe door, she pulls at her hair, trying to force it to settle down. The woman who looks back at her has serious brown eyes and a mop of wavy brown hair, silver flecks at the temples. Her face is bare, with no make-up to conceal the dark shadows beneath her eyes or lift the colour of her cheeks. She's tall and big-boned, and there's a roll of flesh around her middle that even the shapeless top fails to conceal. Her legs are long, but there's a tendency for her knees to creep towards each other. A memory flashes into her mind. Schoolgirls can be mean, and harsh words can most certainly harm you.

She scowls at her reflection, then erases it with the wardrobe door. She must get supper in the oven. If she leaves now, she can be back before it's done.

* * *

Keeping her tone measured, her eye on Ben, she says: "Alex's parents have asked us to dinner on Saturday."

Ben looks up, startled. She watches as his eyes drop back to his plate. He shifts awkwardly in his chair. "All of us, or just you?" he says. It's a fair question. Alex is his friend, and he's been to his house many times.

"Just the parents, I believe. I got a text this afternoon."

James stands, stretching his back. "What did you say?"

"I said I would ask you and get back to her. Do you want to go?"

"Good god. A bunch of stuck-up people we don't know showing off. Vying with each other for the biggest house and the most expensive holidays. I'd rather stick pins in my eyes."

She smiles. "So that's a no, then, is it?"

"It certainly is. Tell them I'm having a bath or something urgent like that on Saturday night. Tell them anything."

Ben stares at his father. "They are Alex's parents, Dad. You can't be rude. Anyway, what if Mum wants to go?"

"I don't. I agree with Dad. We really don't know them, and I'm not sure we want to."

"Well, that's not very friendly," Ben says. "What if they'd like to get to know you? Perhaps they're just being inclusive, you know?"

James, having said his piece, leaves the room, heading towards the living room.

"Listen, boys," she says. "I'm not accusing anyone here, or making any unfair assumptions, but you haven't said anything to anyone, have you?" Again, two pairs of eyes, one pair dark-fringed and wide, the other grey-blue and watchful, gaze at her. Both heads shake.

"No."

"You said not to."

"Not on social media, even? There's no way you've said something that would give it away?" The eyes stare and the heads shake again. But this time, Ben seems less certain. His eyes flick to his brother before they turn back to her.

"Ben?"

"Mum, I didn't. Well—"

Harry starts to clear his things from the table, sensing a situation building. "Mum, it definitely wasn't me. Can I go, please?"

"If you've had enough, then yes. Clear as much as you can."

They wait in silence until he's left the room. Ben slumps in his chair, his long legs sprawled under the table, head hanging.

"Well?"

"I just said . . . I might have hinted to Alex that we . . . have more money than before." His voice trails off into a mumble. He flicks crumbs from the table onto the floor.

She takes a deep breath and tries to ignore the crumbs, though her hand twitches. She holds her voice steady with an effort. "More money than before?" she repeats. "Is that exactly what you said?"

"Oh, Mum," he says, getting to his feet with a sudden movement that threatens to topple the chair, "all I said was that we'll never have to worry about money again." He picks up his plate and crashes his knife and fork onto it. "And I might have said I was going to get a car for my next birthday."

She screams a silent scream into the ceiling as he turns away to load the dishwasher, recovering herself before he turns back. But not quickly enough. She can't quite wipe the horror from her face in time.

"Mum — it's not that bad, is it? They won't know from that, they can't have guessed. Dad could have got a promotion, or you could have been left some money by a relative or something. You're so sensitive about it. I don't see why we shouldn't tell people anyway. It'll be obvious soon. It's a good thing, isn't it? How can we enjoy it if we have to keep it such a big secret?"

She can't believe it. All the care they've taken, the sensible conversations they've had, the agreements made to keep it quiet. And her elder son, albeit only sixteen — a child — is still not taking it seriously.

She rubs her forehead. "Ben. Sit down, please."

He rolls his eyes. "Mum . . ."

"Sit down." She nods at the chair.

He slumps back down.

"We've had this conversation, Ben. As a family, we've decided not to go public on this, remember? For good reasons. Do you remember?"

He nods, pursing his lips, gazing at the tabletop.

"Because it opens a huge can of worms. Because we'll get requests for money all the time, begging letters, friends and family expecting all sorts. We want to give ourselves some time to decide what we want to do with the money, without all that getting in the way. We don't want or need to change our lives. We don't want to be celebrities, to be in the papers or on TV. Do you understand?"

"I suppose so. If you say so."

"I do say so. It's important, Ben."

"Okay, okay, I hear you." He stands and moves towards the door.

"Just wait a minute," she says. He stops with an irritated gesture of his hands, his back to her. Every inch of his teenage body says he's had enough, that he wants to leave this conversation now.

"Are you absolutely sure that's all you said?" She must be certain, prepare herself for any more repercussions.

"Yes, Mum, for god's sake! Can I go now?"

"Okay. But please be careful." He's gone before she has finished the sentence.

She has a horrible feeling this is not the end of it.

CHAPTER THREE

Heather

She wakes to the sound of running water in the bathroom, the whirr of London traffic in the streets. Nothing has changed, but everything's different. That suspicious feeling still lurks at the front of her mind. She's going to have to find out if she's right, today, before it's too late; otherwise they could all be in trouble.

She waits for the creak of the floorboards on the landing, the sound of James's shoes on the stairs before she stirs. Downstairs in the kitchen he's engrossed in the paper, reading on a laptop — hers — next to his coffee cup. He peruses the business news religiously, checks the markets and then moves to the main news. She knows this because he used to give her a precis of each type of news, every morning, before she asked him to stop. She prefers to listen to the radio, but not until they've all gone, when she can sit and enjoy her first cup of tea in peace.

Her eyes still swollen with sleep, she rummages in cupboards for cereals, bowls and cutlery, banging the cupboard doors with intent. She can hear from the sounds of movement above whether the boys are up or not; today, it sounds ominously quiet.

"Boys!" she yells from the bottom of the stairs. "Are you up?" A thump and a groan answer her call. "If not, get up now, or you'll be late." More thumps, and she returns to the kitchen, satisfied that at least one of them is stirring.

James glances up at her, his reading glasses giving him an air of disapproval.

He's about to speak when he's interrupted by the arrival of the boys in the kitchen. The space seems suddenly cramped and airless. There follows a flurry of noise and activity: the crump of bread in the toaster, the rattle of cereal into bowls, the fridge door thudding, juice cartons banging onto the table.

In a matter of minutes it's over, and all three males in the family have gone, the last "Bye!" echoing eerily in the empty hall.

* * *

Her mobile, lying next to the laptop, lights up. She's relieved to see Natalie's name on the screen.

"What are you up to today?" Natalie's voice is distant, the sound of traffic in the background. She's on her way to work, then, to her job as a secretary in a local primary school. She finishes mid-afternoon, and sometimes calls in at Heather's house on her way home.

"Today? I've got quite a lot on, actually. Ben's got a match, and I've got to go over to the school . . ." Her voice peters out, because she hasn't got to go to the school, and Ben hasn't got a match, and she hates lying to her friend. But she's beginning to feel stressed and anxious, and she doesn't want to see anyone, not even her oldest friend, today.

"Oh, pity. I was going to suggest coffee."

"Today's a bit tricky. Can we make it another day? I'll give you a call. Maybe tomorrow." She feels guilty and miserable, making excuses.

"Okay, tomorrow then. You all right? You sound a bit flat. Those boys driving you mad?"

Natalie's life is quite different from Heather's. She lives on her own in a small rented flat not far from Heather and James. Her spare time is spent in the local gym, or at workout classes, or devouring detective stories borrowed in bulk from the local library. Natalie has never married and has no children, just a cat called Diva, which she adores.

Natalie is Ben's godmother. She has always spent a lot of time with the family, but still finds it hard to understand Heather's priorities. Family comes first, always, for Heather — this is non-negotiable. But Natalie has the freedom to choose what she does and how she spends her money, and until recently, when her new man came on the scene, she was always looking for company, suggesting a coffee, a drink, a trip to the cinema. Heather's life as a busy mum simply couldn't accommodate her. It's a wonder they've remained friends for so long, considering.

But despite loving her family with all her heart, and being, on the whole, deeply grateful for the joy of being a mother, Heather sometimes finds herself envying her friend's freedom, her ability to lie in at weekends, her private space. Her job, even. Heather gave up her own work at the museum, which she loved, when Ben arrived, and never went back. Now the boys are older and becoming more remote from her, she misses it more than ever.

"No more than usual. Just a bit tired. Call you tomorrow, okay?"

"Okay, don't forget."

CHAPTER FOUR

Natalie

The building I work in is an imposing Victorian mass of red brick that rises from the smooth tarmac of the playground, which is edged with a tall chain-link fence. The school is squeezed in between rows of terraced houses in the middle of Hounslow. Its only saving grace, as far as I'm concerned, is that it has chestnut trees surrounding it, which have grown tall and leafy and relieve the ugliness.

I am the school's secretary, or one of them. My boss is headmaster to a thousand children, and is as harassed and stressed as you might imagine he would be, with the huge workload, the daily crises and the carping parents. I'm not sure I can say I like him; he treats me like a workhorse and we barely converse, but I am sympathetic. I understand how tough his job is.

My work here is less than exciting. There's a constant grind of regular work to do, and though there are two of us plus two more junior admin staff, we barely get through it, because we're interrupted regularly by kids, by deliveries, by phone calls, emails, parents, the caretaker.

I throw my bag on my chair, hang up my coat and then head to the kitchen for a strong cup of coffee. There, Joanna, the other secretary, is already on the case: the kettle is rumbling as it begins to boil.

"Morning, Natalie," she says.

I grunt and reach for a mug.

"Strong black coffee for you, then." She smiles, takes the mug from my hand, unscrews a jar of instant coffee.

"Thanks."

"How was your weekend? Did you get to see that hot man of yours?"

Joanna is married with kids, and her life seems pretty mundane: school runs, soaps on TV, cooking for the family, shopping with her mum, and celebrity gossip. She takes a strong interest in my private life. Sometimes I like this. It makes me feel glamorous, interesting. As long as I'm actually dating, and I like him.

"We spent Saturday together. We wandered round the Tate Modern, walked to Soho and had a bite to eat there. Chinese." Joanna hands me a mug and I stir my coffee, watching as the last grains of Nescafé form a whirlpool in the dark centre.

"Aw, that's good. So it's going well, then?"

"Fingers crossed." She's dying to know if he stayed over, I can tell. I've been coy about this one; in the past I've said too much, gone overboard with the detail, only to have to report a humiliating dumping shortly afterwards. I know she tells her husband, she can't resist — she seems to get such pleasure from the ups and downs of my love life. But this time I'm feeling positive, and I'm not going to jinx it by overdoing it. I take my coffee and return to my desk, switching on my computer as Joanna bustles around the room.

"Sounds like you've got a good one there."

"Mmm," I say.

* * *

I met Nick online, on one of those dating sites that claims to have the perfect, scientifically tested formula for love. Of course that's ridiculous, and I'm sure everyone who registers knows it is, but still we live in hope. The websites, meanwhile, thrive on our insecurities, our loneliness, our desperate hoping that The One has signed up here, just for us.

My dating career has been less than joyful, to say the least. I've screwed up the courage more than once to put myself out there, and let's just say I've lived to regret it. There's many a lie told on those websites, I can assure you. Out-of-date photographs — and I mean *ten years* or more — or details omitted: of wives, partners, girlfriends and strange sexual proclivities I really don't want to go into.

But Nick seems different. I thought so the minute I saw him in the flesh. He looks like his photo, for a start. He's a young fifty-eight, which works very well for me. Nicely dressed, slight tan, well-groomed hands. I like clean hands on a man. He also has hair, which is always a bonus in an older man. It's greyish, but pretty thick, and it has that nice salt-and-pepper effect. Soft when you run your hands through it, which, yes, I have done.

He has been married, once, and was divorced a few years ago. He has two grown-up children, one in Australia, the other in Scotland, who he sees when he can. He's funny and charming, and he makes me feel good. He's an antiques dealer, though without a shop, so I'm a bit vague on how he actually does his job. But it seems to keep him solvent, anyway, and he's busy with it, always travelling around doing some deal or other. He's pretty self-sufficient, too: looks after himself well, is a good cook, doesn't need to rely on a woman to take care of the household drudgery.

I'm doing my best not to assume too much, this time. I have, in the past, made the wrong assumptions and been let down badly; I've also been guilty of overwhelming a man with my enthusiasm. It's interesting how men seem to get put off by a woman showing she cares; you would think they would enjoy it, that it would be good for their ego.

I'm going to be careful not to overdo it this time. I'm delighted to have found someone I like, and that it's going in the right direction.

* * *

19

On the way home, still a little disappointed about our coffee, I get to thinking about Heather and friendship. Specifically, about what a 'best friend' is.

Some people talk a lot about friends, but they use the term loosely. A 'friend', to them, might be someone they work with, or somebody they've seen at the pub a few times and said 'hello' to. An online connection, who has become a 'friend' at the click of a button. Friends of friends, or perhaps people they know of, rather than know personally — but they still call them 'friends', as if they have a special relationship with them.

My opinion, for what it's worth, is that these are not real friends. To me, real friends are people you've shared experiences with, good or bad, over time. They know you and understand you. You have a connection with them, through interests, values, your world view. History. It's a form of empathy between two individuals who enjoy each other's company and know they can trust each other.

A best friend is someone who has and does all these things — and who has your back, whatever happens. They know more about you than anyone else, including parents and siblings, because they know the things you're not going to tell your family, ever.

Take Heather, for example. She is my best friend. You might argue that she's my only friend, and I suppose she is, in the truest sense of the word. I do, of course, have other friends, but Heather has been with me since we were frightened young girls on our very first day at senior school, our shirt collars stiff against the pale skin of our innocent necks. We grew up together through those terrible, formative years, sharing our worst fears, our darkest secrets. And one or two better times as well, I suppose. I can't remember that many.

We know more about each other than we know about ourselves.

Is it possible to know too much about someone? Or, to put it differently, do we ever really know another person? Perhaps a person is always holding something back, never sure enough of another human being to give everything — absolutely everything — to them.

Maybe you would if you were in love. Perhaps I've come to this conclusion because I've never actually been in love: truly, deeply, all-consumingly in love with someone, not like Heather was with James when they first met. I've never experienced the desire to surrender everything, to bare the very core of my soul to another individual. I can't imagine ever feeling that way. It must be frightening, a huge risk, and you must be absolutely one hundred per cent certain that this person will never betray you. I'm not sure that's possible, ever, with anyone. Not for me, anyway.

CHAPTER FIVE

Heather

It happened almost a week ago, on a grey Wednesday morning that started the same as most other days. Heather had been to the supermarket for the weekly shop and arrived home laden with groceries, already exhausted. Household shopping was a chore she hated, and that day was worse than usual. She'd driven the Range Rover to the big Tesco on the Talgarth Road, hoping the car park wouldn't be too busy. But as soon as she drove through the entrance, she knew her luck wasn't in. Already a line of cars was cruising around between the crammed parking spaces, every driver peering out in the hope of seeing the next shopper leave and nipping in before anyone else. It took a full twenty minutes to find a space, and even then she had to perform contortions to get out of the driver's seat without showing her underwear.

She cursed James for getting such a big car. She hadn't wanted it, and for good reason: she couldn't gauge the size, she couldn't park it, and it was too slow, too lumbering. Though it was old and they'd bought it third-hand, it was one of those models that smart people buy. She disliked giving the impression that they were well off — they were not. James worked as a financial adviser in his own business, which paid well enough — just — to send the boys to private school (he insisted) and live in West London. Because of this, they lived modestly and were careful with money. It was no hardship for Heather, brought up to be thrifty, but she would rather not pretend to be something she wasn't.

The store was full of mothers with buggies and small children, slowing down Heather's progress. Her long shopping list meant she had to visit almost every aisle, negotiating a trolley that behaved like a recalcitrant child, weaving to the right at every opportunity and refusing to follow a straight line. It took hours.

Back at home, unpacking a multitude of bags, she realized that she'd forgotten the key ingredient for that evening's supper: the chicken. They always had roast chicken on Wednesdays, James being a man of habit, and though she longed sometimes to create some mad concoction to surprise him, there were advantages to a regular routine. At least she knew where she was.

She had got to the aisle, but there'd been a woman with a loaded trolley in the way, so she'd been unable to reach the organic chicken she wanted, got distracted while she waited for the woman to move, and forgotten to go back. She cursed. Now she'd have to go out again. Fortunately, there was a butcher within walking distance of their house: good, though expensive. She put the rest of the shopping away, grabbed her bag and keys and left the house for the second time that day.

It was a stroke of luck that he had a chicken the right size, and organic, too. One small nugget of good fortune in a frustrating morning.

As she left the butcher's, the chicken weighing heavy in her shopping bag, she paused at the newsagent next door, where she stopped sometimes to buy odds and ends. For once, she was going to reward herself with a magazine and a bar of chocolate. When she got home she was going to ignore everything else and have a break, like other women seemed to.

She gazed at the confectionery counter, a dull ache in her gut. She struggled to control the urge to buy not just the large-size chocolate bar, but the contents of an entire shelf. It was one of those days.

Picking up the smaller bar and a glossy women's magazine, she went over to the counter. In front of her, a man was buying a lottery ticket.

"If I win, I'll buy you a drink," he said to Sanjay, the owner of the shop, whom Heather had known since they first moved into the area.

"I don't drink," Sanjay said, with a smile.

"Well, okay, I'll buy you a cake then." He seemed determined to offer the man something from his imaginary win.

"Thank you, very kind. What will you do with the rest of your huge win?"

"I'm going to travel the world, buy a Ferrari and live in a chateau in the south of France." With a grin, the man proffered a ten-pound note.

"Man, you'll need to win a lot then," Sanjay said, with a wink at Heather. He handed over the change and waited for the customer to leave. Heather put her purchases on the counter.

"Lottery ticket for you, lady?" he said. "Ferrari? Chateau in the south of France? It's a rollover, so you can have it all."

Heather had never bought a lottery ticket in her life. She knew the odds: you were more likely to be killed by a jumbo jet landing on you in the middle of Shepherd's Bush than you were to win the lottery. Or something like that.

But on that day an urge took hold of her. In that small moment of wanting to pamper herself for a change, she felt different, almost reckless.

"Sorry — what's a rollover?"

"Nobody won the last one, so you get that money plus the new jackpot. Twenty-nine million, in all. Two for the price of one, only two pounds a ticket. It's a bargain!"

"Go on, then. Though I wouldn't give you tuppence for a Ferrari — far too flashy for me. What do I have to do?"

As she left, dropping her change into the charity box on the counter, she wondered what on earth had got into her.

* * *

It wasn't until the following day that she remembered the ticket. Fumbling in her bag for her keys, she felt the crackle of paper in her hand and pulled out the slip, thinking it was a squashed receipt. For a moment she was bemused; the colour was wrong for a receipt. But then she remembered. Her first-ever lottery ticket, bought on a whim. Of course she wouldn't have won anything. She never won a thing, not on the tombola at school fairs, not in the raffle, nowhere, never. But she felt she should check, nonetheless. A win of even ten pounds would be fun.

She had asked Sanjay what to do, never having paid the slightest attention to the lottery before. It was something other people did. Mugs, James would say. People who dreamed of boats and holidays and flash cars, like Lottery Man ahead of her. She'd thought she needed to choose the numbers, and when Sanjay handed her the ticket with the numbers already in a line across the middle, she felt slightly ridiculous. But she had no idea what to do next, so she asked him, and as a queue began to build up behind her, she started to get flustered, so she listened to his explanation with only half her mind.

Did he say look in the newspaper? Half expecting not to find anything, she typed '*Lottery result this week*' into Google. The first listings gave her the answer.

At first, she didn't understand what she was seeing. Lotto? But was that the same as the lottery? She examined the ticket. It said clearly, at the top, *Lotto*. It must be right, then. She checked the date. All the numbers seemed to match, so she must have done something wrong. Was this some kind of sample ticket she was holding, and her real one had gone missing? She checked the numbers again. They were a perfect match — every number the same as the ones on the screen in front of her. She scrabbled about in the bottom of her bag again, in case there was another part of the ticket lurking there. Nothing.

She went back to Google and clicked on a different search result. The numbers were exactly the same. What was going on? She'd clearly misunderstood. Checking her watch, she realized it was close to four o'clock, and she was due at the dentist at four thirty. She'd have to get going if she wasn't going to be late.

Later that evening, supper done and boys in their rooms, she remembered the ticket again.

"James," she said, "have you ever bought a lottery ticket?"

He glanced over his reading glasses at her. "No, and I don't intend to either. No one in their right mind would do it. Why?"

"Well, I bought one yesterday, just out of curiosity. And for a bit of fun, really," she said, avoiding his glance. "Now I'm trying to find the results. I think I must have done something wrong. Could you try, and see if you get the same result, please?"

An irritated look passed over his face.

"Come on, it's worth checking, isn't it?"

He said nothing, harrumphing a little as he got out his mobile and started to jab at the screen.

"Got it, I think," he said. "Yesterday's result. Eight, twelve, twenty-one, twenty-seven, thirty-nine, forty-one. With seventeen as the bonus ball. Did you win?"

She swallowed. Handed him the ticket, so he could see for himself. Watched as his mouth dropped open and his eyes widened, flicking to and from the ticket to the phone, over and over, like he was watching the tennis at Wimbledon.

"Well, I'll be . . ." he whispered.

They sat looking at each other for a few minutes, though it felt like much more. James moved first, letting out a long puff of air. She realized they'd both been holding their breath.

"What?" she said. "Is it right? It can't be right, surely?"

"It certainly seems like it," he said, his face relaxing into a more normal expression. "Any idea how much it is?"

"Give it to me," she said, holding out her hand. "Are you sure?" She closed the window on the website and started afresh. The same numbers, the same date — yesterday. It was all there, exactly the same. "Oh my god, James. Do you really think I've won the lottery?" She felt a smile start to creep across her face, and immediately wiped it off.

"Yes, I think you probably have," he said. "But let's not get too excited, in case we've got the wrong end of the stick. Let's see what you're supposed to do if you think you've won." He reclaimed the mobile. "Yes, you need to give them a call. Oh, and sign the back of the ticket, straight away."

The slip of paper seemed so fragile. She held it as if it was red-hot, by the tips of her fingers, and gently turned it over. As she wrote her name in the small orange box on the back, her hand was shaking.

"It's a bit wobbly, do you think it'll matter?" she said, her voice cracking. Then she remembered.

"What is it, what's going on?" James said as she leaped from her chair, her hands flying to her mouth.

"Twenty-nine million. This week. He said . . . the jackpot . . . it's *twenty-nine million*."

"Oh my good god," he said, each word enunciated with precision. "Heather, come here, sit down with me." Her body felt like a firework ready to be lit, but she sat down anyway, on the edge of the sofa, clasping her hands together to stop them shaking. He put his own over hers. "We mustn't get too excited. We might still be wrong."

"Do you think anyone'll be there now? Shall we try? I don't think I can wait till morning. What should we do? Oh, James, what if it's true? Twenty-nine million? It's not . . . I can't . . ." She could barely breathe. She started to laugh, and then, to her horror, she wanted to cry.

"Hang on, I'll see if I can find out if they're open late. Where's your laptop? I can't see properly on this thing."

He typed in '*National Lottery opening times*' and the results flashed up immediately. He clicked on the first and there appeared a long page of text about the different types of lottery games and how to claim the prize. Scrolling down, he frowned at the screen for a couple of minutes while Heather tried to resist wrestling the laptop from his hands.

"Nothing there," he said at last. "Frustrating. But it does seem to say that you can take the ticket to a shop and get them to check it. Where did you buy the ticket?"

"The newsagent on Goldhawk Road. They stay open pretty late."

They stared at each other, their eyes wide.

"Let's go," he said.

CHAPTER SIX

Heather

They almost ran the short distance to the shop. It was a strange shuffling gait, half-walking, half-running, that would have made Heather laugh if she hadn't been so wound up. James was holding her hand with a grip so strong the bones were crushed together, but she said nothing, because it was comforting, and it stopped her from breaking into what would have been an ungainly sprint. Her heart was thumping so hard it hurt. Her other hand, in the pocket of her jacket, held on to the ticket as if it were alive and would escape and run off down the Shepherd's Bush Road if she let it go.

She was relieved there wasn't a queue of customers waiting at the counter. Sanjay was still there. He smiled at her as she stepped towards him, barely trusting herself to speak. She drew a trembling hand from her pocket and placed the ticket face up on the counter. The numbers seemed huge, as if they understood the gravity of their situation.

"Ah — did you win something?" Sanjay said, retrieving his reading glasses from below the counter and picking up the ticket. She almost snatched it away from him — but James's hand was on her arm and she managed to control the urge.

Sanjay seemed to be moving in slow motion, peering at the ticket, then at the machine on the left of the counter, then back at the ticket again. He turned it over, studying her signature. Then, with a solemn face, he handed the flimsy slip of paper back to Heather. She felt her eyes widen; she held her breath.

James rescued her. "Well, did she win?"

Sanjay's eyes dropped to the counter. He rubbed gently at a mark on the glass top with his index finger. In that moment, Heather wanted to climb up and over the counter and squeeze the answer out of him. But then the skin around his eyes started to crinkle and his lips parted in a huge smile. Afterwards, she remembered his teeth — discoloured, crooked — and thinking he should visit the dentist and get them cleaned. He glanced at the mirror above his head, the one that showed the aisles. The shop was empty.

"You better buy some champagne, now," he said, leaning forward over the counter with a conspiratorial air. "And go and reserve that Ferrari. You won the lottery!"

* * *

They had indeed bought a bottle of champagne that evening. Sanjay urged them to buy more than one bottle: "Because you can, now, eh?" but James said one would be quite enough, though he bought the proper stuff, not the Prosecco they usually chose.

Sanjay, smiling broadly, shook their hands. He gave them the number to call to claim their win and wished them luck. They returned home in stunned silence, Heather still clutching the ticket in a clammy hand in her pocket. She would never forget that short walk: the lights, the traffic, the drab cluster of people at the bus stop outside the shop, the noise of London, the stink of diesel fumes tickling the back of her throat. Everything was so normal, so familiar. Everything seemed the same. But at the same time, everything was different. She wanted to jump and leap and dance in the street, to yell and scream, because nothing this thrilling had ever happened to her before. But she knew she couldn't, shouldn't do all those things — certainly not with James there, his feet solid on the pavement, holding her down, keeping her safe.

Once inside, they took their coats off, hung them neatly in the hall. Heather retrieved the ticket from her pocket and without a word they retreated to the kitchen, closing the door quietly behind them. The soft thump of bass and periodic yells from upstairs signalled the boys' presence in their rooms, engrossed in computer games.

They grinned at each other and hugged, James lifting Heather right off her feet, which made her laugh and protest that he was going to give himself a heart attack. It wasn't the same as screaming, but she felt the tension lift a little.

She had to stand on a chair to retrieve the barely used champagne flutes from the top cupboard: a tricky business, as her legs had gone numb and didn't seem to be working properly. In a strange moment of lucidity, the last one she was to have for a while, she took the lottery ticket with her and rolled it neatly into another of the glasses, pushing it to the very back, out of sight.

As she placed the delicate flutes on the worktop next to James, a warm flush of realization rose from her centre like an electric current, leaving her scalp fizzing.

"James," she said, grasping his arm, her voice sounding distant, shaky. "Is it real? Twenty-nine million? Oh my goodness." She shook her head, trying to order the torrent of thoughts pouring through her mind. Later, she remembered thinking: *This must be what it feels like to be on drugs.*

James, seemingly oblivious to the enormity of the situation, stood at the counter, focusing on opening the bottle, a slight frown puckering his forehead. His fingers, she noticed, were not shaking.

"Oh my god, James!" Her feet wouldn't keep still, as if an electrical surge had just reached them. "It's so much money! I can't imagine what it looks like — and I've won it! I've never even bought a ticket before. How did this happen?

What . . ." The words faded away, as if she'd forgotten how to form them, and her mouth didn't seem to want to close anymore. The room felt too hot, too bright, stifling her.

James placed his hands on her shoulders and guided her to a chair, where she sat in complete bewilderment until he placed a glass of golden liquid before her and she heard the gentle crackle of bubbles from the surface. He sat in front of her, a huge smile creeping over his face. She laughed.

Champagne had never tasted so good.

•

CHAPTER SEVEN

Heather

When the doorbell went, they froze.

Heather glanced at her watch: it was only seven thirty. Aeons seemed to have passed since they last opened that door.

"I'll go," James said, jumping up from his chair.

"Wait . . ." she said, but he had already gone. "We need to . . ." *We need to tell the boys, decide who else we're going to tell, we need to talk about this, just you and me . . .*

She peered round the kitchen door, straining to hear the voices at the door.

"Come in," James was saying. "Heather's in the kitchen—"

What was he doing? Didn't he know they needed to talk right now, before anything else happened? She stood for a moment with her back to the wall, her eyes closed, the champagne glass still clutched in her hand.

"It's Miles," James said, in his most cheerful voice. She gathered herself and managed a smile as their neighbour, tall and smart in a business suit, stepped into the kitchen. His eyes flicked immediately to the open bottle of champagne, the glass in her hand.

"Aha," he said. "Are we celebrating something?"

"Ah, yes, actually." James flicked a look at Heather, who tried to glare at him without Miles noticing. The result caused James's eyebrows to rise. Calm and collected, he reached into the cupboard for another glass.

"Come on then, what's the news?" Miles took his jacket off and draped it over a kitchen chair, smoothing his hair back in a characteristic gesture.

"Well." James gave the word considerable dramatic emphasis, a mysterious smile on his face.

Miles's smile broadened. "Come on, do tell . . ."

"James!" Heather said, horrified at the speed of events. "We haven't even told the boys yet . . ."

"We will, it's fine — Miles, have a drink." He poured the sparkling liquid into another champagne flute. It threatened to spill over the edge, but Miles scooped it up expertly, sipping at the white froth, halting the flow. "Heather and I will have a quick chat in the other room . . . then we'll explain."

Miles's eyebrows rose even further into the lines of his forehead as James guided her to the living room, his hand at her back.

"What are you doing?" she whispered, once the door had closed. "We can't tell anybody! We don't even know if it's true, not properly, yet."

"Yes, we do," James said, taking her fluttering hands in his. "We do, Heather, it's confirmed."

"But — we need to decide how to handle this. Who to tell . . . we certainly need to tell the boys before we tell anyone else! They would never forgive us if we didn't . . ."

"I know, I know, let's think about this. Wouldn't it be good to celebrate with someone else, though? Miles is one of our best friends, and even though we wouldn't have actually invited him, he is here at just the right moment. Let's suggest he goes back and gets Charlotte and while he does that, we'll tell the boys. Then we can all celebrate together. This will never happen to us again, Heather! Let's enjoy it. Breathe deeply for a minute, and think about it."

She breathed. As always, James's was the voice of reason. It was perfect to have friends celebrate with them, as long as the boys had been told. "Okay," she said. "But we must swear them to utter secrecy, James. We can't have it getting out before we've even — I don't know what happens next, but before we've even told the family. If we want to tell anybody! Oh Lord, what about the papers?"

"It's all going to be fine. We'll swear the boys, and Miles and Charlotte, to absolute secrecy, on pain of — I don't know what — until we've decided how we're going to handle the news. And the papers . . . we'll request absolute anonymity. I'm sure the lottery people will help us on that score."

She nodded, her shoulders relaxing a little. Thank goodness for James.

"Here, give me a hug," he said. "Don't worry, I won't let anything bad happen. Now, let's go. I'll tell Miles to get Charlotte, you get the boys down. Oh, and . . ." He thought for a moment. "Let's just say we won, not how much, eh? Best to be a little bit cautious."

* * *

Miles and Charlotte were the first people they'd met ten years before when they moved into the row of terraced houses that line the short street off the Uxbridge Road. James had taken a couple of days off work to help sort the house out, and they were busy humping boxes, unwrapping and finding the right place for things. It was exhausting work, and they'd been at it for hours when the doorbell rang.

Heather, dishevelled and bad-tempered, opened the door to find Miles and Charlotte standing there, a bottle in Miles's hand, flowers in Charlotte's. "Welcome to your new home," Miles said in a booming voice, his large frame filling the doorway. It would have been rude not to invite them in.

She made a pointless effort to tame her wayward hair, smoothing it down with grimy hands, and led them to the kitchen. She felt dusty and unkempt beside Charlotte, slim and immaculate in white trousers and a tailored blouse. She looked as if she'd just emerged from a salon, her hair shiny and smooth. Alongside her, Miles was big and ebullient: a country gentleman in chinos and a checked shirt, with polished brown lace-ups and yellow socks. She was glad James was there; she would have felt overwhelmed on her own. She was acutely aware of the horrible mess in the house.

The men made small talk while she rummaged around in packing crates, searching for glasses. It was almost impossible to sit down for boxes, scraps of newspaper and piles of pots and pans waiting to be put away, so when she eventually found the glasses, they stood around rather awkwardly toasting their new home and making apologetic remarks about the mess.

As it turned out, Miles and Charlotte were the only neighbours they got to know socially. This was mainly because James became friendly with Miles, sharing an occasional pint at the pub and a similar interest in rugby. Miles was a property developer with his own business, recently started, while Charlotte didn't work. She seemed happy to stay at home, though there were no children to look after, and she kept their home immaculate.

Heather felt from the start that she had nothing in common with this polished woman. Her own life was different — hectic and chaotic by comparison, filled with organizing the new house and running around after the boys. She rarely saw Charlotte on her own. But a neighbourly friendship was struck, more from circumstance and proximity than choice.

* * *

With Miles on his way to get Charlotte, they told the boys. A few minutes of chaos followed while the boys whooped and danced around the house, screaming with excitement. Laughing at their antics, Heather and James gave them a short time to celebrate, then sat them down and explained firmly how the family was going to behave. There was to be no publicity, no media storm, no photographs, no fuss. Absolutely no talking about it on social media. The boys were disappointed, already longing to tell their friends, but they reluctantly accepted the reasoning.

Or so she thought, at the time.

Heather took a few deep breaths as she approached the front door to let Miles and Charlotte in. The rest of the evening went by in a blur of champagne, laughter and clinking glasses, and soon Heather relaxed, her anxiety fading with each sip.

She went to bed that night telling herself, and almost believing it, that everything would be fine.

CHAPTER EIGHT

Heather

The man from the lottery company arrived with a full briefcase and a big smile. He introduced himself as Graham Fuller.

He shook their hands and invited himself in. He was a large man, filling their spacious kitchen with his presence. She would never forget the delicious aura of normality he brought with him. His suit was wrinkled, his shoes needed a clean, his tie was awry. She almost wanted to hug him. Despite the champagne, she'd barely slept, rising early to distract herself with housework, but it hadn't helped, and the tension in her shoulders had got worse as they waited for him.

Just having him sit at their kitchen table seemed to relieve the stress. They drank coffee and got down to business. The last vestiges of doubt were dispelled when he confirmed the win. Before Heather could take it in, he'd set up a private bank account in their name so that the money could be transferred securely. He advised them to take a holiday.

"You need time to let it sink in," he said. "Take the boys with you, spend some time getting used to it. Start to make plans, if you like, but no rush — you've got all the time in the world. If you want to go right now — today, even — we can arrange an advance. Just let us know."

She watched James as he nodded. She could almost see the picture in his mind transmitted through his eyes: sandy beach, luxurious hotel, beautiful view, being waited on hand and foot. That was the sort of holiday he loved. All she could think was that the boys had some weeks to go before the summer holidays. They couldn't take them out of school now; it would look suspicious. Anyway, they disagreed with children missing school for almost any reason other than serious illness.

"I don't think—" she began, but James broke in.

"I think it's a great idea," he said. "Though we can't go until the boys have finished school."

"Good," Graham said. "Most people do take a holiday. It helps with the transition. You can take the time to talk it through properly. No point making snap decisions you might regret later, eh?"

Heather was about to object: she didn't need a holiday, and lying on a beach was not her thing. But she didn't want to sound like a misery. Perhaps she should go along with it; Graham was the expert, after all.

It was all so quick and easy. And unreal. Within an hour, the meeting was done. Graham handed over a sheaf of leaflets and a business card. "Call me any time," he said. "It all seems a bit strange at first, doesn't it? If you can't remember something from this meeting, don't worry, I'm happy to go through it again."

They walked him to the door in a daze. He turned to shake hands. "Oh, by the way," he said, glancing around. "One more thing before I go. You might want to take a look at your security — just a precaution. It's as well to be cautious. Get something done before you travel. Then you'll know everything's safe while you're away."

Heather was left with the feeling that their lives had just been overtaken by creatures from outer space.

* * *

"I'll do some research this evening," James says. "The world is our oyster!" He's fond of clichés. "How about it, Heather? I've always fancied Mauritius, myself. Or what about Fiji? It's supposed to be stunning. Or, I know where you'd like — Capri, somewhere like that, with some history for you to look at. Listen, I've got to get to work. Have a think and we'll book something later."

He leaves her sitting alone in the kitchen with the empty coffee cups.

Heather's beginning to understand why people go public. The knowledge, the scale of it, the weight of all that money sitting in the bank, in a new account, earning as much in interest every week as some people earn in a lifetime, is a huge burden. It feels like a simmering pot with the lid on, popping open every so often to release great puffs of pungent steam, threatening every time to reveal the contents.

She researches 'lottery winners'. Pictures of people spraying champagne everywhere, talking about their new fancy cars and homes, the places they've travelled since they won. Huge cardboard cheques being handed over. Much bigger wins than hers, and much smaller. Some people saying they wished they hadn't won the money; it ruined their lives. Family break-ups and feuds, friends won and lost. Gossip and bad feeling. One story describes how years later, a family is still dealing with begging letters from all over the world, getting abuse when they refuse to give away their money. Another story shows how much a charity has benefited from the generosity of a winner. It's all bewildering, to the point she can't read any more.

They've kept the secret for two days. Her mum doesn't know yet, nor James's sister. Natalie doesn't know yet, either.

But now, it seems, someone else has got a whiff from the pot, making it all the more urgent to come clean.

She picks up her mobile. She needs Graham's advice. She feels wobbly, uncertain all over again, vulnerable to the old urge. She needs someone to calm her down, give her practical advice.

* * *

"Hello, Heather! Graham speaking. Good to hear from you. How's it all going?"

She swallows. It's comforting to hear his voice, amid all the madness. "I'm not sure, to be honest."

"Has something happened?" His voice sounds solicitous.

"I think — well, it seems the news has got out. I'm getting a huge number of messages on Facebook, calls, texts, all sorts. Mostly from people I've never even heard of. Some of them are — quite abusive."

"I see," he says. There's a pause.

"I don't know how it happened. It could have been the boys, but I'm not sure."

"Any calls from the media — newspapers, TV?"

"Not that I know of. But there have been some numbers I don't recognise. I didn't listen to the messages, there were too many. But there was at least one text calling me a rich bitch, and it does seem to be escalating. It's pretty nasty."

"Sounds like you're right — you've been rumbled." He sounds cheerful, too cheerful for Heather. She needs advice, not confirmation of the situation.

"So what should we do?"

"I think this is the time to take my advice and fly away," he says. "Come off Facebook for a while, change your phone number. Have the calls been to your home? Anyone on your doorstep?"

Unable to help herself, she glances through the hallway to the front door, with its coloured Victorian glass panels shedding rainbow lights on the floor below. Then she absorbs what he's just asked her and steps back, out of sight of the door. Her breath catches in her throat. "No! I don't think so . . . is that what's going to happen?"

"It may, it may not. But it's as well to be prepared. If the media hear about it, and it sounds like they might, you could get some uninvited visitors. I know the boys are at school, but is there somewhere else the family can stay for the moment? You might want to go to relatives, or book into a hotel, just until the news dies down."

She sinks into a chair and leans her elbows on the kitchen table to steady herself. *This is terrible — it's all going too fast.* A voice deep inside her screams: *I don't want this! I don't want it!*

CHAPTER NINE

Before

I stare at him, my belly cramping. "How much do you need?"

"It's only for a short time, just to pay the salaries. A week or so, not longer, I promise." He turns away, unable to look me in the eye.

"How much?"

"Twenty-five thousand . . ."

"Twenty-five thousand." The words drop like stones onto hard ground. I will him to look at me, but his eyes are glued to the table.

"It's only a delay in payment. Two clients owe us at least that much. We're chasing, but they're being slow. It happens . . ."

"But it shouldn't happen, right?"

He turns to me then, a muscle twitching in his left cheek, dark patches in the armpits of his shirt. "Of course it shouldn't happen, do you think I'm an idiot or something? I know how to run a business. It's just a setback, it's early days. Nobody makes a profit in the first year. I warned you we'd have to be careful, but you just carry on spending as if there's a bottomless well of cash at the bank."

I try to keep my voice level, though the unfairness takes my breath away. "So it's my fault, is it?"

A dangerous glint appears in his eyes, his lips curling into a sneer. "I'm working all the hours I can, you know that. I'm exhausted. You can't possibly understand, how can you, with your little job, your girls' nights out . . ."

So now girls' nights out are sinful? My job's worth nothing? It takes a huge effort, but I don't want this confrontation, not right now.

He lifts both arms, drops them, taking a deep breath. His voice softens: "Look, as I said, it's only for a week or so. Do you want me to beg?"

"No, I don't want you to beg. But you know why I'm saving it. It's the money from my dad, it's all I have. It's my security, that's all."

"I know, I know. I hate asking for it, you must know how humiliating this is for me. But I promise you'll get it back. Really. The business is solid, it just takes time. Take pity . . ." He folds me in his arms, kissing the top of my head. "You know I love you . . ."

And once again, I feel my body relax against his, the curve of his smile against my hair.

He knows he's won.

CHAPTER TEN

Heather

"Are we fixing a date for coffee?" Natalie's voice is distant, muffled. She must be on her lunch break, the only time she's able to talk while she's at work.

"We are indeed." Heather had intended to tell her on the phone, like she had done with her mother. But now, suddenly, at the sound of Natalie's voice, she wants to see her best friend in private, tell her all, share the good news. And her worries and her anxieties.

Though they've been forced, by the possibility of a leak, to rush the discussion about who they will help with the money, it wasn't difficult deciding. The same people they're sharing the news with. How much they'll give away, they still don't know.

Heather's mum was delighted at the news. In her mid-eighties, she has managed on her widow's pension and a small pot of savings for a few years now. It was a good feeling, being able to reassure her that they'd all be fine, financially, for the rest of their lives. She'll be comfortable into her old age, with no worries about care should she need it. She had begun to worry, of course, especially as a number of her friends were now infirm and needing full-time help.

She's more worried about how to tell Natalie. Struggling through school, university and her twenties, for many years Natalie fought the twin battles of excess weight and low self-esteem, leaving her vulnerable and prone to depression. The one thing that gave her hope in those days was knowing that one day she'd inherit her parents' grocery chain. But before she was grown, the supermarkets came along and small independent grocers were engulfed. The business failed faster than they could ever have imagined. Her dad, a proud man, never recovered from what he saw as the family's shame. He'd wanted to leave his only child with a worthwhile inheritance, and it had all gone. He was broken, losing all his energy for life, and died soon after. Natalie's mother was already suffering from bad health, and it wasn't long before she too passed away, leaving Natalie with nothing, only debts which would take years to pay off.

Heather would never call Natalie happy, exactly, or even content. She hates her job and has done for years. She should have left that school years ago, found something she enjoyed doing, but now she seems resigned to carry on until she retires, though that's still a good few years away.

Heather's not at all sure how Natalie will react to their news. She sometimes seems envious of Heather's life: the career she loved — albeit on hold — the loving husband, the boys. Though as a family they've always tried to include Natalie, inviting her to gatherings, celebrations, even their holidays, every so often there's a wistful look in her eyes when she's with them.

How will she react to Heather winning so much money? If the playing field seemed tilted from the beginning, it will certainly seem badly skewed now. It could all seem very unfair to a person like Natalie.

"Can you come over after work today? I know it's short notice, but . . ."

"I can, but wouldn't you rather go to that new coffee shop? Their cappuccino is delicious."

"Not today, actually. There's something I need to talk about."

"Oh dear, nothing bad, I hope? Now I'll worry all afternoon."

"No, don't worry, please. It's good, it's all good. See you later — come as soon as you can."

* * *

By mid-afternoon, it's pouring with rain, gusts of wind slapping water onto the windows. Natalie arrives dripping on the front doormat, her umbrella bent, her fringe plastered to her forehead beneath the hood of her raincoat.

"Honestly, why do we live here?" She shakes her head, unzipping her boots. "Sometimes I just want to pack up and go to Spain for the rest of my life."

"Not such a bad idea," Heather says. "Come in and dry off with a nice cup of something. Coffee? Hot chocolate? Good for days like this. Or a cup of tea?"

"Strong coffee, please." Natalie scrubs at her wet hair in the hall mirror, fluffing it up, then giving up with a shrug. "I look like a drowned rat."

"Only a bit." Heather smiles and ushers her in. "Come and sit down. Dry off and get warm while I get the coffee."

Natalie sinks into a sofa with a sigh of relief. "It's so cosy in your kitchen. I wish I could get a sofa into mine — if the cat's having her supper, I'm lucky if I can squeeze past."

"It is nice to have the space," Heather says. "Although when the boys are at home it seems to shrink to half its normal size."

She brings a tray over to the coffee table, settling down next to Natalie.

"That's better," Natalie says, sipping her coffee. "Work was doubly tedious today. We've got an inspection coming up next week and everything has to be exactly right. I don't think they realize how false it all is — we just get everything right for the day, and then it all goes back to normal."

"I wish you had a job you enjoyed," Heather says, not for the first time.

"I know, and I should do something about it. But the holidays are good, and it pays the bills, just. Anyway, enough of my boring life — you have some news?"

"I do." Heather puts her mug down and shuffles forward, turning towards Natalie. She's thought about how to say this the most sensitive way she can, but now she's here, it just needs to be said. "It's big news, and I can still hardly believe it, but the other day, on a whim, I don't know why, I've never done it before, but I bought a lottery ticket. And guess what?"

Natalie's eyes widen. She sits bolt upright, almost spilling her drink. "What — you won?"

Heather nods, smiling.

"How much? A lot?"

Heather nods again. "Quite a lot, yes."

"Wow, Heather! Come here . . ." A huge smile spreads across Natalie's face and she leans over to Heather, hugging her tight. But when she lets go, the smile begins to fade. It's almost imperceptible, but the hint of a shadow sweeps across her face she leans back into the cushions. Anybody else would probably not have noticed, but Heather has known her for so long, she can almost tell what's in her mind.

She moves a little closer. "Natalie?"

"It's okay, I'm just . . . taking it in."

She waits, sipping her coffee, while Natalie gathers herself.

"That's amazing," she says at last. "You probably don't want to say exactly, but . . . was it millions?"

"It was. Quite a few."

Natalie blows out, a rush of breath that seems to hang in the air between them. "Incredible," she says, her voice breaking. "Lucky. That's . . . so lucky." All of a sudden, her face crumples, a fat tear escaping, rolling down her pale cheek. She turns her head away, brushing at her face with a shaking hand.

"Hey, what is it? Come here . . ." Heather pulls her into a hug, one arm around her damp shoulders.

"I'm so sorry, I didn't mean . . . horrible of me. I'm so happy for you. I am, really. It's just—"

Heather grabs a box of tissues from the table and gives it to Natalie.

"Listen," Heather says.

Natalie's eyes brim with tears, her forehead marred with deep lines of anxiety.

"No need to be sorry, Natalie. I think I know how it feels — no, I do—"

Natalie is shaking her head, ready to deny the unsaid words.

"It must all seem terribly unfair, that I've won so much money, when I have . . . all this. And you've struggled financially for so long. But listen, you're part of the family — you are. We're going to look after the family first and foremost. That includes you."

There's a long pause while Natalie wipes her tears away. For a moment, Heather thinks she hasn't heard, but when she lifts her eyes, Natalie's face is transformed.

"Heather, I — you don't mean it. Really? That's the nicest thing anyone's ever said to me. Thank you, thank you." Now the tears roll freely and she sobs, her fingers grabbing at the tissue box. "Sorry, sorry, I'm just . . . it's a bit overwhelming. I don't know what to say . . ."

"I know." Heather waits a moment while Natalie blows her nose. "Now, take a deep breath."

Natalie does as she's told, her shoulders relaxing.

"Better?" she says, standing.

Natalie nods, her eyes still swollen with tears.

"Enough to have a celebratory glass of champagne with me now? Because we can, you know."

CHAPTER ELEVEN

Natalie

I can still hardly believe it. Nobody ever wins the lottery, to my mind. It's as if the papers have concocted the whole story of the lottery to make us buy tickets, knowing there's never a pot at the end of the rainbow. The odds are terrible, as James has told me many times — you'd be crazy even to consider buying a ticket. The fact that Heather went to a shop and actually went through with buying one is almost incredible, with a husband like James and her background of practicality, frugality and everything else I would say about her: cautious, sensible Heather.

But she did — and, blow me down with a feather, she won. Good on her.

I couldn't help my reaction though. I suppose I was feeling pretty sorry for myself when I arrived, what with getting soaked, the relentless rain, and the day I'd had. The job is really getting me down, and with the inspection next week, the tedium is almost unbearable. I knew I should have been delighted for her, for them, deliriously happy.

But I wasn't. I'm not an 'emotionally generous' person. Probably why I've never had many friends. It takes someone like Heather to get close. She knows the background, understands why I'm like I am.

I felt terrible, reacting like that. All sorts of emotions hit me, one after the other, and there was nothing I could do about it. Shock, surprise, joy, jealousy, self-hatred, shame. Also greed, that terrible vice, when she said she'd look after me. How could I? Why couldn't I just celebrate with her, enjoy the wonderful, impossible thing that had just happened to my best friend and her dear family? She deserves it just as much as anyone else.

But not as much as me. I can't help it, as I said.

Of course I was delighted when she said I'd be treated as one of the family, and 'looked after'. But I couldn't help thinking, even as I was laughing and drinking champagne in celebration: *How much? How much will you give me? Will I be able to give up work?*

I'm really not a nice person. Although perhaps I can be forgiven for that — surely anyone would think the same, without wanting to? I don't even know how much she won, so speculation is useless.

Anyway, she said they hadn't had time to think it through, or even to tell everyone they needed to yet. It's all been so sudden. They're going to take a long holiday (luckily it's school summer holidays soon) and make some considered decisions. 'Considered decisions'. That's so like them.

But I'm still impatient to know how much I'll get.

* * *

I know I shouldn't have done, but I couldn't help myself.

I think I was probably still in shock when I went to work the next day, my emotions still in turmoil. I was excited, upset, happy, envious, all at once. Joanna could tell straight away that something was on my mind.

"You're quiet today," she said as she opened the pile of post just delivered to her desk. "Anything wrong?"

"No, not at all." There must have been something in my voice that alerted her. And I couldn't stop a small secret smile from creeping onto my face.

"You sure?"

"Quite sure. It's the opposite of wrong, actually."

As I said, I couldn't resist.

"Oh, do tell," she said, her eyes widening. "Is it something to do with your man?"

"No, nothing to do with him. I can't tell you, but something has happened. To Heather, not to me. Something rather good."

"Go on, you can't stop there, it's not fair. You can tell me . . . I promise, I won't tell a soul. Cross my heart."

She actually did cross her heart, like a child.

I was so full of it, my mouth brimming with words, bursting out of me, beyond my control. With nobody at home but my cat, I'd been unable to share my news with anyone.

"Well," I said, the word full of promise.

"What — tell me!"

I almost laughed at her face. Her eyes were so wide they looked as if they would pop, her eyeballs about to shoot across the room.

"You really mustn't tell anyone. Really, it's important. If it gets out, she'll be furious with me."

"I said, cross my heart. Not even at home, promise faithfully. Promise, Natalie." She looked ready to explode with excitement.

I looked around, to make sure nobody was close. No sound from the corridor, the classroom doors closed. The headmaster was holed up in his office with the door firmly shut.

I took a deep breath. "Heather won the lottery."

It was worth the risk just for her reaction. Her cheeks turned a livid red, her mouth forming a perfect 'O'. Her feet jerked out in surprise, her chair rolled back at speed and collided with the desk behind her, whipping her round and almost tipping her off.

"Steady on," I said, delighted. "Are you okay?"

"I — r-really?" she said, stammering with excitement. She righted herself on the chair and scooted back to her desk. "How much?" she whispered theatrically. "She actually won? Was it big — what, millions?"

I nodded and nodded again.

"It was millions?"

I made a zipping motion across my mouth, and winked. "I really couldn't say."

"My goodness, amazing! I've never met anyone who's won more than ten quid! Well, I've never met Heather either, but she's your best friend, so I feel like I know her. Wow. Fantastic. What's she going to do with it all? Is she going to be in the newspapers?"

"Absolutely not. They don't want any publicity. None. That's why you really must keep it to yourself. Just you, okay? I mean it. I don't want to lose her as a friend."

"Especially now." She winked back at me.

I opened my mouth to object, but closed it again when she carried on.

"Is she going to share her good luck with her best friend, by any chance? If I was her, I would, knowing you're always broke, and in a job you hate. And your rent is ridiculous . . ." Now she was in her stride, I was going to have a problem stopping her.

"Listen, I don't know yet . . ."

"Well, she jolly well ought to give you some, especially if it's millions." Her voice began to rise. "But I don't know, you see it in the papers all the time, people win loads of money and spend it all on themselves, selfish bastards. You'd think they'd at least share some of it with their friends, but no, they blow it all on holidays and cars . . ."

"Hang on, Joanna. Heather's not like that . . ."

"I'm sure she's not, but you never can be sure what money will do to people, you know. They can be so thought-less. Anyway, I thought they were pretty well off? It seems wrong, doesn't it, that the people who really need it get noth-ing, and the rich get all the luck? I've always said . . ."

I sighed. Joanna was probably the wrong person to tell. It was going to be hard to stop her now.

* * *

I lived to regret that moment of indiscretion. All through the day, Joanna made barely veiled references to it, winking at me knowingly every chance she got, and almost giving it away to everyone who walked into the office.

"Natalie's had some good news, you know," she said. "Top secret." This made everyone think I was getting married. Mortified, I was forced to deny it. Or: "Think we might be planning a fabulous holiday soon, eh, Natalie?" However much I gesticulated, giving her throat-cutting signals, telling her when we were alone to stop talking about it, she persisted.

Because of the way she was, influenced perhaps by the papers she read, she got it in her head that Heather was a snob, a selfish woman who didn't deserve her good luck. Joanna wasn't the brightest spark, and she believed anyone with money was right-wing, arrogant and immoral. Which possibly some people were, but I didn't have the same inverted prejudice she seemed to thrive on.

By the end of the day, I was so fed up with her I wanted to scream. When I left the office I told her in no uncertain terms that if she told anyone, including her husband, I would find out and there would be huge trouble for her. I think she believed me, because by then I'd had enough and I was close to hitting her. I stood over her and made her promise, again, to keep her big mouth shut. She actually looked a little scared as I stamped out of the office, slamming the door behind me.

Joanna and I are friends, but in truth I have little choice in the matter as we work so closely together. I doubt if we would be friends under different circumstances. She enjoys her job, for a start, while I hate mine. Our jobs are the same, the same tasks, the same boss, the same boring repetitive work, the same mind-numbing routine. She has next to no ambition, is happy to be working and bringing in enough to have an ordinary family life, happy to stop work when school closes and go home to her family. But she has a vicarious interest in celebrities, the rich and famous, the privileged, as if it's her right to know what they wear, how they live. There's always a copy of *Hello* and *OK!* on her desk — she reads them religiously, believing all the chat about love and broken hearts and cheating, exclaiming over the beautiful homes, the clothes, the handsome men. I dislike this in her, though I try not to show it; I think it's distasteful.

But I'm being judgmental; I am as much to blame as she is. I should have known better than to have told her a secret that wasn't mine to tell.

CHAPTER TWELVE

Heather

At the V&A there's an exhibition of Regency clothing. Normally, Heather would avoid any kind of fashion collection, but today all she wants is a safe place to wander, somewhere she won't feel challenged. It's as good a place as any to be lost in thought, to pursue an inner calm. The mannequins are frozen in time, in their graceful garments, the rooms cool and quiet. She starts to feel better, venturing further into the museum, strolling through vast collections of Renaissance art, the Medieval rooms, the sculpture rooms where marble faces stare at her with cold, unseeing eyes. She sits on a stone bench for a while, staring into the distance, oblivious to the passing groups of tourists, the wandering couples, the chattering schoolchildren.

In the café, with its soaring ceiling and intricate windows, there's a low hum of conversation and plenty of free tables.

She orders an Americano and carries it to a table in the corner, where her mind once again starts to wrestle with the enormity of her problem.

It's only been a week — a week! Such a short time, and yet so long — since the win, and already she's wishing it hadn't happened. Her life was good, before: not perfect, admittedly, but good. They had enough money, a house in Shepherd's Bush, their boys at a good school, a holiday every year. She never expected even that much from her life.

But now, with millions in the bank, it all feels wrong. She doesn't want to be super-rich, with all the baggage that implies: the possessions, the invitations, the fame, the bling. The jealousy. The utter ridiculousness of having so much more than the man in the shop who sold her the ticket. Or the homeless girl she saw this morning, huddled in a corner near the Tube station, sitting on a flattened cardboard box. Her eyes were blank; a red carbuncle marred the china-white skin of her cheek. The fingers of her hands were too thin, the bones almost visible beneath fragile skin. Heather had fumbled in her purse for some change, and finding none, ended up giving her a ten-pound note, knowing as she gave it to her that it would probably fuel an addiction.

But she's never been able to resist. It's one of the few things that James criticizes her for, and she admits she's a pushover. The down-and-out in the street, his mangy dog by his side, the 'chugger' with her collecting box, the glass jar full of coins on the bar at the local pub, all benefit from her small change, sometimes more. She weeps at the charity appeals on television, the starving children in Africa, the homeless children here, the deprived, the sick, the disabled.

She doesn't need this money; she doesn't deserve it. It doesn't make her feel special at all, as the mystery text abuser said. Guilty, inadequate, off-balance, more like.

It occurs to her now that her instinct has always been to give it all away.

* * *

She stares at the garish collection of food piled onto the kitchen table, the pounding of her heart drowning out the voices on the radio. Packets of biscuits with mouth-watering pictures on the sides, cakes beckoning from transparent windows, fat bars of chocolate with gleaming wrappers. Why has she bought all this? The visit to the museum was calming, she felt better for it, but still she stopped off at the big Tesco and piled the trolley high. Is this comfort food? Will it help to sit with a pot full of tea, or a jug of water, and feed her face on this mountain of sugar? Probably. But this is dangerous.

The Heather of today — more than middle-aged, settled, dedicated mother, wife and homemaker — doesn't do this anymore.

She opens the cupboard, telling herself to put it all away. But the cupboard is already bursting. She'll have to make some space. Examining the contents, she starts to throw out-of-date items onto the worktop, finding stale biscuits, empty packets — boys! — and a large multipack bag of Walkers crisps containing only cheese and onion, which nobody in the family likes. Grumbling under her breath, she throws all the stale and unwanted food into the food bin, separating out the recycling into different boxes under the sink. She fills a black bin liner with the rest of the discarded packaging and puts it by the back door to be taken out later.

But when she's finished clearing out, there still isn't enough space for all the food she's bought. She gazes at the pile again. She'll just have a taste of the chocolate; it certainly won't last long in her household, and she needs to claim some while she can.

* * *

In the en-suite bathroom that leads off their bedroom on the top floor, once the attic space but tastefully converted into the master suite, everything gleams. She's polished the taps, the plugs and the plug holes until she can see her face in them. The glass walls of the shower unit are glossy, unsullied by water stains and blobs of shampoo. The toilet bowl, the main offender, is now shiny and snow-white where she's wiped and scrubbed and fumigated until she could do no more. The floor is polished to a high shine; the air is freshened and perfumed so that no trace remains.

In the kitchen below, the table is clear. The packets and boxes and foil-wrapped items are all stashed away in the cupboard, which swallowed them up quite happily once she'd rationalized them.

She lies on the bed, her eyes closed, her stomach bruised with the effort, her mouth parched and sore despite all the water. The hair around her face is damp; she had to rinse it afterwards to remove any trace of the smell, though she had been careful to tuck it behind her ears before she started. She should change her clothes, just in case, but she's too tired now. It will be a while before the family gets home, so there will be time.

Guilt and self-loathing have taken up residence again. It's been a while, and they're both delighted to be back.

CHAPTER THIRTEEN

Heather

"I'm scared, James."

She lies beside him, her head nestled on his shoulder, his arm curled around her. A book on economics is propped on his knees. Sometimes his choice of bedtime reading confounds her — she can't think of anything less relaxing.

She feels the surprise in his body before the book goes down.

"Scared? What of?"

James is never frightened of anything. He seems so . . . *settled* in himself, so certain. Nothing ever fazes him.

"It's the money. I'm scared it will change everything. Us, the boys, our friends. The way we live. Our attitudes, values even."

"Why would it do that? We're still the same people we were before you bought that ticket, and we're still going to be the same in a year's time — ten, twenty years' time."

She props herself on one elbow and gazes at his face. His dear, middle-aged face with its deepening shadows and lines, framed by an ever-shrinking bonnet of greying hair. James is very much 'what you see is what you get'. No agenda, no chip on the shoulder, no baggage. That's why she loves him. He has a way of making things simple.

She flops back onto the pillows, stares at the ceiling, where a spider's web has spiralled into a long, dusty straggle. "Oh, I don't know. It's what money does to people. All this online stuff, the abuse. I'm beginning to see what celebrities have to put up with, how frightening and uncontrollable it is. It's horrible, so unnecessary — they don't even know us. Not to mention all those people trying to be my friend, our friends, it's so — disingenuous . . ."

"Good word." James nods with approval.

"It's not funny. People are so hypocritical. I was never flavour of the month before, when we didn't have a shedload of money. They couldn't give a toss about me. Now all of a sudden they can't wait to invite us to all sorts. They're like wasps to a plate of jam tarts — pesky, snarky, a sting in their tails."

"That seems a little unfair."

"It's not, though, James. I can't even look at my phone any longer, in case I see some horrible comment about myself. Envy is a terrible thing. And it's not just that. This kind of money brings with it a lot of bad stuff."

"Like what?"

"Come on, James, you must have thought about this too. Graham skirted around it a bit, he obviously didn't want to scare us, but I knew what he meant. We have to be ultra-careful. People kill for a lot less than we've got in the bank, right now. Twenty-nine million pounds! It's huge. People murder, and steal, and lie for a fraction of that."

"Okay. Yes, I have thought about that. We'll go away, as soon as the boys break up, make some decisions."

"It is what the lottery people want us to do. But that's my whole point. Already we'll be changing things, doing things differently, going on fabulous extravagant holidays. I'm not sure I want all that."

"Come on, Heather. I know it's a shock to the system. It'll take a while to get used to it. But — it's just a holiday, which we can easily afford, to give us some time to think, to get used to having the money to do the things we've always wanted to. Our boys' future is safe — that's great, isn't it? That's reassuring, for me, anyway."

She sighs. He's so damn practical. "You're right, of course. Me too."

"And listen. Having this much money may well change what we do. But it doesn't have to be in a bad way. Let's make sure it's good, hm?"

He is right. He always is. But her own words hum around in her head.

People kill for a lot less . . .

* * *

It's Saturday and the boys are yet to emerge. Heather wonders, as she often does, if they were up all night on their laptops or gaming consoles. She should check on them more, control their use. It can't be good for them: the late nights, the screens, the contact with complete strangers. The zombies and the guns and the killing.

It's yet another thing that makes her uneasy, fuels her feeling that she's not doing a good job as a mother, though she knows that all the boys do it. Other mums make the same remarks, though some are stricter than she is. And some less so.

The house phone rings — and in the same moment, the doorbell jangles. Her entire body jolts with the shock of the noise. From the kitchen she can just make out a dark figure standing up close to the stained glass. As the phone is closer to where she is and there's nobody else downstairs, she picks it up, distracted by the doorbell and the fact that she's still in her dressing gown, uncombed and unkempt.

"Hello," she says softly, inching down the wall of the hallway, trying not to be seen by the visitor at the door.

"Mrs Jessop?" The voice in her ear is harsh, confident and male.

"Speaking." The figure at the door raises an arm, knocks loudly. She can hear James moving upstairs.

"My name is Kevin Spears. I understand you've had some good news."

Her stomach does a backflip. "I'm sorry — do I know you?"

"I'm from the *Daily Mail*. I wondered if we could have a chat about your—" She takes the handset from her ear and stares at it in horror, glances towards the door and back to the phone. She cuts the call with shaking fingers and stands frozen to the spot as the strident notes of the doorbell cut through her again.

James appears at the top of the stairs, his face puckered with irritation, about to say something, but she holds up her hand to stop him. She points to the phone and to the door, mouthing "Daily Mail" as clearly as she can, then passes her fingers across her throat in a slicing motion. James's eyes question, then widen, his foot hovering over the top step of the staircase. She shakes her head emphatically and to her relief he nods and starts to back away, his bare feet soundless on the carpet. She tries to do the same, terrified any movement will alert the stranger at the door. She freezes again as the letterbox rattles. A white business card flutters onto the mat, then after a moment the dark figure moves away, the silhouette fading to a ghostly cloud in the rippled glass of the door.

She breathes again, but her whole body is shaking, tears not far away.

Dread, suspicion's big brother, has its heavy hand on her shoulder.

They sit, weak with shock, at the kitchen table, both still in pyjamas and dressing gowns. Thankfully, the boys have not stirred. James has unplugged the phone and stuck brown cardboard over the windows in the front door. The doorbell is disabled, their mobiles silenced. Heather's has been in the drawer for some time now, face down. She feels as if they're battening down the hatches in case of attack.

"This is terrible, James! We have to go away, right now, I can't handle this." Her eyes follow her hand with fascination as it lifts her mug of tea, the liquid slopping near the lip as her fingers tremble. She puts it back down abruptly, brown liquid pooling on the table. Ignoring it, she folds her hands into her armpits to stop the shaking.

"Please, James — let's just up and go. We can, it doesn't matter what it costs . . ."

"Steady," he says. "I agree, we have to do something. But let's think about this. When do the boys break up?"

Her heart sinks. "Still five weeks to go." She knows this, because only yesterday she did a diary check, adding in the multitude of end-of-term activities: the sports day, the art exhibition, Speech Day. "We can't take them out yet, not until lessons stop."

"How much do kids actually learn at this stage in the summer term?" James says. Logical, analytical as usual.

"The exams are done, but they're still being taught. The school won't be pleased if we take them out early. You know how much Mr Crampton disapproves; they get such short terms anyway." A heaviness has settled in her stomach, an ominous, dragging feeling that won't go away. She can taste the bile at the back of her throat.

"Chances are we'll be besieged by journalists now, which won't be good for the boys either," James says. "How can we even get them to school, and be sure there won't be reporters at the gate? And who knows what will happen if — when — their classmates find out? If we go now — disappear — by the time they're all back in September after the summer holidays, nobody will remember anything about it — or at least we can have our story straight. And we can avoid a furore with the media."

"Oh god, James, I hate this." She puts her head in her hands, elbows on the smooth surface of the kitchen table. "I hate it, it's going to ruin everything."

"Hey." He enfolds her in a blanket of arms and warmth and masculinity. "It's not going to ruin anything. Listen to me . . ." Gently, he removes her hands from her face. "We won't let this ruin our lives. It's going to be fantastic, I promise you."

CHAPTER FOURTEEN

Heather

"Right — here's what we're going to do," James says, pacing around the kitchen as if he's presenting to a meeting. "We're going to talk to the school, straight away. Mr Crampton, if possible. I know it's the weekend, but I agree, this has got to be done right now. We can't live with these crocodiles on our doorstep. We're lucky the boys are at a boarding school. They'll have to board for a few weeks — I'm sure the school has room. They'll love it, especially as it's the lead-up to the end of term. They can join in all the activities, and we won't be taking them out too early. We can ask Crampton to increase the security at the school. We can even pay for it if necessary, if we feel it's not good enough. You know him best: is he up to it?"

"He has plenty of experience." With James taking charge, the knot in Heather's stomach starts to ease. "There are some super-wealthy parents at the school," she says. "I think there's even a boy prince, from the Middle East. Mr Crampton is used to being discreet for him. His family is ushered through the back door when they visit, including their bodyguards. That's how careful they have to be."

"Right. Let's talk to him today. We'll tell them it's urgent. Then we'll get the boys over to the school straight away. Hopefully, we can get away from the house without too much attention."

"Okay . . . what will we do, you and me?"

"We'll go to a hotel for a night or two. We'll ask Graham for his advice on where we can go that's discreet. He'll know, he must have done this loads of times. We'll get a car to pick us up, drop the boys at the school, us at a hotel."

"And then go away?"

"Yes. I think we should find somewhere we can stay from now until the end of the summer holidays. Three or four months. A villa, or a house somewhere warm, where there's plenty to do for the boys: water sports, activities, whatever. We can really settle in, and all this will have died down by the time we get back."

"But what about your work?"

She knows there's no question of James giving up work. Building a business is what he's always wanted to do, and he's intensely loyal to his two business partners. He looks thoughtful for a moment. "I can take some time off over the summer, certainly, but I can't just abandon Bill and Jane, leave them with all my work as well as theirs. I tell you what, if we don't go too far, say somewhere in southern Europe, it won't be a problem for me to fly to and fro if I need to. We have the money."

Bill and Jane are partners in James's business. The three of them have worked together for years, growing the company to over thirty people, with solid profits. It would be wrong of James to abandon them, and Heather is relieved that life, in at least one way, will continue as before.

"I just need a bit of time to tie up a few things before I leave," James goes on. "Two or three days, then we can go. You'll feel better then, trust me."

She does trust James. But the dull, heavy feeling that she never wanted to return is weighing her down more each day. The sooner they get away, the better.

* * *

The school couldn't have been more amenable. When they explained that they needed an urgent conversation with the headmaster, he agreed straight away, and they set up a Skype call. He reassured them that their news was safe with him, the school's security up to the challenge. In less than an hour, they had agreed on the details. The boys were to move into the boarding house that night and stay until the end of term. They were delighted to be making the move.

Heather starts to pack her things in a daze until James reminds her that she can buy anything she wants, at any time, without worrying. Which is intended to reassure her, but only makes her feel more unsteady. The speed of it is breathtaking, and it's happening anyway, outrunning her feeble attempts to understand it. Their lives are changing, and she feels the ground under her feet falling away.

A driver arrives minutes later, and they dash around the house, turning off appliances, locking windows and setting the alarm before leaving, emerging into the street with hoods up, their eyes firmly on the waiting car. Heather is dimly aware of someone walking in their direction as they are handed into the back of a large Mercedes, its tinted windows reminding her of the limousines lined up outside the hotels in Park Lane. She doesn't know if the person is interested in them or just happens to be there, but she doesn't dare glance back, or remove her hood, until they have left the street and are safely on their way. It's not a good feeling that settles over her as she stares out at the London traffic.

* * *

"Well, this is pretty okay, don't you think?" James says, striding to the window of the enormous room. Sumptuous drapes fall in neat folds to the soft carpet, the view across the street softened by delicate gauze. "Not a bad little place."

"I don't know what to say." She shakes off her shoes, noting their shabbiness against the pristine cream of the carpet, then lies back on the bed, running her fingers over the soft silk cover. "Is this what being rich feels like? Because I just feel weird."

"Enjoy it, darling — you've won the lottery!" James starts to unpack, opening an enormous wardrobe and hanging up his two suits. They dangle, forlorn, on a long shining rail.

She looks around. The room rates here are eye-watering, the decor extravagant. Those drapes alone probably cost more than she would spend furnishing an entire house.

James chuckles as he comes to sit beside her. "It's just a hotel, darling," he says. "The money comes mostly from business people, plus a few of the seriously rich. Don't be intimidated by it, just enjoy it. A couple of days' relaxation will do you good. The next thing we need to do is decide where to go for the summer. That will be fun."

"Yes, I'll get on to that while you're at work." It will help to be busy, to have something positive to do while she feels so strange.

"I've had a couple of thoughts, actually. Miles has offered to help us find somewhere. It might make life easier if he does the looking for us, on a business basis, of course."

In the past, Miles has tried to get them to invest: a time-share in Barbados, a golf course in Spain. But they were never in a position to get involved, and they knew too little about property to risk the meagre savings they had.

"Are you sure?" Heather's surprised — there was a little awkwardness the last time they turned down a proposition from Miles. "Now he knows about the money, I'm sure he'll be thinking we'll change our minds about investing. We don't want to get into that again."

"No, we don't, I absolutely agree," James says. "But he does have the contacts. If I brief him properly about what we want, I'm sure he can come up with something. And time is of the essence. He's a good friend, and he'll be keen to help."

"I know he will. Okay, but please, don't get dragged into that again, especially right now, before we've had a chance to breathe."

"I won't, I promise. Why don't you have a look for somewhere as well? Then we can get a second opinion, too. There must be good travel agents in this area." He sits beside her on the bed. "Listen, I've had a thought. If we're taking a house for three months, we can invite family, close friends to join us. Your mum, Natalie, Liz and Steve and the cousins, we can celebrate with them, talk about how we're going to help them. All on us, we can pay for everything! We can even invite Miles and Charlotte if we want to, as they already know. What do you think?"

She's not entirely sure what she does think. Liz is James's sister, who lives in North Wales with her husband, Steve, and their two children, Joshua and Cara, who are similar ages to Ben and Harry. Liz is not at all like James. In fact, she's about as far from him as a sibling could be — and she and Heather have had their moments in the past. But of course James wants to include them. They're his only other family.

"That would be a great thing to do. Not sure if Mum will want to come, though I'm sure she'll appreciate being asked. And Natalie will love it. But, James—" A thought occurs to her. "I'm probably being alarmist but . . . I've read all these stories about family fall-outs because of big lottery wins. I'd hate to think that might happen to us. Not that our families are like that, but you do hear terrible things. It would be best if we can decide what we're going to do for them before they come, so that we can present it as a decision, don't you think?"

"Good point. We'll make sure we have a few days together before anyone else comes, and the boys should come as soon as they finish school, so we can have some family time. I'll fly back and bring them over myself at the end of term."

She walks over to a stunning display of fresh flowers — peonies, roses and some she doesn't recognise — on a side table, dipping her head to catch the fragrance. She breathes deeply, giddy with the heady aroma. She can't help thinking how much this one display must have cost. She doesn't need to think like that anymore. But does she want to start taking extravagance for granted? All her life she's been frugal, and proud of it; is it right to change that mindset now?

"Are you going to work right up until we go?" she says, turning back to James. The prospect of being on her own, remembering that she's incognito, dealing with the sophisticated staff in this mini-palace of a hotel, alarms her. Already, she feels like a fraud. This is the first time they've behaved like wealthy people, and it all feels so unfamiliar. So . . . wrong.

"I think I'll have to, if we're going to be away for most of the summer."

She inspects the room. "Well, it could be worse, I suppose," she says. There's a bottle sitting on ice on the dressing table, and she wonders if that's what they're meant to do, as rich people — drink champagne all day. A pulse in her temple starts to drum, a gentle ache that threatens to grow.

"Come on, Heather." James follows her gaze, smiling. "This is the beginning of something, not the end. You'll get used to this in no time, trust me. In the meantime you can relax, pamper yourself, enjoy having enough money to do exactly as you want."

"You're right, of course. I suppose it's all happened so quickly. I'll be fine."

But she doesn't feel fine. She feels shabby, ugly, and out of place. So far, she's not enjoying this at all.

CHAPTER FIFTEEN

Heather

A short distance from the hotel she finds a mobile phone shop and tries not to appear too dim-witted as an enthusiastic young man explains the features of the latest technology to her. She buys two handsets, one for herself and one for James, and asks the lad to set hers up.

Her first call is to the school, where she leaves her new number with the office. Five minutes later, it startles her by ringing, the new tone strident in the studied calm of the hotel suite. She answers it, her tone cautious.

"Mum, is that you? You sound different."

"Oh, hello, Ben. Telephone voice. I wasn't sure who it was."

"Is this your new secret mobile? Did you get a good one?"

"Seems good to me. Apparently it's the latest version of — well, of whatever it is. You know I don't really care about these things. You'll see it soon enough. Anyway, don't give the number to anyone, please. We have to be careful about these things now. How are you getting on?"

"Fine. Boarding is even better than I thought it would be. We played pool for about three hours last night."

"Sounds . . . educational. Are you on a break?"

"Just a few minutes before next lesson. Mum, can we get a boat?"

"Whoa, where did that come from?"

"There's this boy here called Ahmed, and his dad has a huge cruiser. They take it all over the world, and it's got a plunge pool and jet skis and its own crew. It's even got its own chef—" His words come out in a rush of enthusiasm, tumbling over themselves in a torrent, as if he's been saving them up and he wants to make sure they all come out, right now.

"Hold on a minute, Ben." Her heart has begun to slide, on a slippery slope within her. "Just because your friend's dad is rich enough to have a boat, doesn't mean we need one too. Might I remind you we live in London, miles from the coast — and we've hardly set foot on a boat in our lives?"

"But we can move, or buy somewhere near the sea, and keep it there, then when we go on holiday we can just get the crew to pick us up . . ."

"Ben, stop it. This is getting ridiculous. When Dad asked what you boys wanted, he didn't mean for you to start thinking up ways to spend it! Listen, we'll talk about all this when we go away. In the meantime, you need to go to your lesson. And try to keep your feet on the ground, darling, won't you?"

"Okay, Mum. But can we add it to the list?"

"We'll talk about it," she says, firmly, though her heart is now somewhere near her boots.

* * *

"So, did you have a good day?" James says, removing his tie and opening the top button of his shirt.

They sit side by side on the oversized sofa in their suite, an open bottle on the table next to them.

"I went shopping, and bought a few things . . ."

"Good." James nods approvingly.

"But then I sat in a café thinking about all the people who can't even afford the basics like food and shelter. Like the homeless girl I saw the other day at Shepherd's Bush."

James shakes his head, a wry smile curling his lips. "Maybe now we can help some of them."

"I hope so," she says. "I was thinking about how we don't really need it, do we, after all? Not compared with those people. And then Ben rings and says he wants us to buy a superyacht! I can't get my head round it, it's all so crazy. I just want it all to go away."

James takes her hand and smiles. "Heather, my poor darling. You are suffering, aren't you?"

She nods and he draws her to him. If she speaks, she might cry, and that would be stupid. She's the luckiest woman in the world. She has a loving family, a bank account with more money than most people can dream of, and all she can do is complain.

"I know what you're saying, but it's early days, and it's a big adjustment," he says. "Try not to agonize too much about it. That's why we're going away, to put it all in perspective, to plan. Tomorrow, why don't you spend a bit of time finding a holiday? You can talk it through with a travel agent, let them do all the work. I'll talk to Miles tomorrow too, and we can compare ideas. You'll feel much better once we have a plan, believe me."

She leans her head against his shoulder, wishing she could believe him.

* * *

"Some expert help with travel plans, of course, madam," the sleek man on the desk says. "I can direct you to an excellent company not far from here. Superb service, ultra-professional, I'm sure they will find you the perfect solution to your needs. Business or pleasure?"

"Pleasure," she says. "With the family."

He smiles his perfect smile. "Wonderful. Sun, sea and sand?"

"Probably. We have two boys, so it's got to be somewhere where they can work off some energy."

"Marvellous," he says. "I'll call the agency now and tell them to expect you. It's about five minutes' walk, unless you'd like me to get you a car?"

A 'car'. He would mean a chauffeur-driven limousine, then, to drive the two-minute journey to premises around the corner.

"No, thank you, I'll walk," she says stiffly.

* * *

She pauses at the discreet doorway, where a shiny steel sign indicates that she's found the place. A thick glass door pings open when she presses the button and she finds herself in a wide hallway, a soft cream carpet underfoot. The walls are hung with large photographs of exotic beaches, wildlife, sapphire-blue seas, colourful markets and eastern architecture. She heads for the reception area in the open-plan area beyond, wondering what she should expect.

A young girl stands to welcome her. She's impossibly pretty, her glossy brown hair drawn back into a ponytail which reaches almost to her waist. She wears an immaculate grey skirt suit with a pale-pink satin blouse; her heels sink into the carpet without a sound.

"Mrs Jessop. Welcome, let me take you through." The girl leads her through a tall wooden door into a room furnished like a sitting room, with sofas and armchairs arranged around a coffee table consisting of a huge square of glass balanced on chunks of white marble.

The girl indicates the sofa and offers Heather a drink before disappearing through a side door.

On the table in front of Heather lies a large square book, with the logo and name of the agency in gold lettering on the cover. Inside, golden beaches stretch into the sunset, snow-topped mountains soar above green forests, beautiful couples smile from the decks of luxurious yachts.

Suddenly Heather doesn't want to be here. Her hands start to shake, her heart thumping. Terrified she's about to have a panic attack, she leaps to her feet. She needs to get out before the girl comes back, before anyone else arrives to see her.

The glass door clangs behind her; she runs, her bag drumming on her back, until she's out of sight.

CHAPTER SIXTEEN

Heather

She walks and walks, her heart rate dropping, her breathing settling with each step. Her throat aches with the effort of running, her top is damp with sweat, but she carries on walking, her feet taking her towards Regent's Park.

As she reaches the outer circle, she remembers why she loves it here. Like an oasis in the centre of the city, the park welcomes the stressed, the oppressed, those in need of quiet and calm. A precious piece of harmony in the cacophony of the city. Strange, exotic whirrs and chirrups of the birds in London Zoo fill the air — or perhaps it's the troupe of energetic monkeys. At any rate, it's an incongruous sound in the tranquillity, but it's one of the reasons she loves the place.

She walks until her feet ache, then finds a quiet place to sit, where few people go. Only the regular dog walkers come to this corner, and as it's late morning, there are few people around. She sits and stares at nothing, exhausted by her chaotic emotions. Why did she run? She wonders if she would have done the same before. Before the money, before she started to feel like a fraud. But of course, she wouldn't have dared open that expensive door at all, before.

A robin flits into the green canopy of the chestnut tree that spreads its shade close to the bench where she rests. Its ecstatic song soars above her, a glorious celebration of sun, nature, summer. For a moment she's able to forget, to luxuriate in the beauty of the sound. She closes her eyes and listens, the sun warming her face as she turns it to the sky.

A dog barks nearby. The robin flutters away and the moment has passed. A shadow falls back over her, her mood darkens. She can feel her muscles tense as the anxiety returns. Why can't she deal with this? She's a woman in her fifties, with all the wisdom and maturity that that brings. She's had a good career, raised two lovely boys, has an enviable family life. This . . . this extraordinary, freakish turn of events wasn't something she dreamed of, but surely she can handle it, turn it to her advantage, make it wonderful, instead of treating it like some kind of terrible burden?

What she needs to do is focus on all the good things she can do with the money. Yes, that's what will help her out of this hole she's dug for herself. She squares her shoulders and stands up, breathes in the fresh aroma of newly cut grass and turns back towards Marylebone. She can handle this. She will sort this out in her head. She just needs time, and some space.

And maybe some cake, on the way back.

* * *

As luck would have it, there's a cake shop on the walk back to the hotel. Its windows display a mouth-watering range of gateaux, in colours from deep, dark chocolate through raspberry pink to zinging lemon yellow. There's even one the colour of sapphires, dripping with blueberries, oozing juice. Individual tarts boast shiny red strawberries, grapes, and loganberries, while apples sliced in perfect symmetrical designs decorate an array of tartes Tatin sprinkled with dark splashes of cinnamon. There are doughnuts of all kinds, thick slices of rich fruit cake, cookies embellished with enormous chunks of white and dark chocolate. Cupcakes tempt from tiered stands, their domes adorned with sprinkles, generous whirls of rich cream, grated chocolate and fruit jellies in bright colours. It's a sweet-toothed dream.

Her mouth waters and she swallows as she gazes longingly at the voluptuous display. A smiling woman waits patiently for her decision.

"I'll take a box of mixed pastries, and one of cupcakes, please," she says. "And one of those apple tarts, and the one with the blueberries, as well." She's grateful that the counter is busy; the woman is less likely to want to talk. She can't handle lying to her as well. Making up stories about why she's buying so much cake would be a step too far, today.

"A slice of apple tart?" says the woman, her cake slice hovering.

"No, the whole thing, please." Heather keeps her eyes down, pretends to be lost in thought.

"The same for the blueberry pie?"

"Yes, a whole one, please."

"Having a tea party?" the woman says with a smile as she secures the cake boxes with tape.

"It seems so," she says, forcing herself to be friendly. "Last-minute decision. You have a great selection."

The total bill is enormous, as much as she used to spend on the weekly shop. *But now things are different,* she tells herself as she gathers the loaded bags from the counter. *I don't need to worry.*

* * *

The guilt is the same, though. It follows her back to the hotel, fills her with shame as she hurries through the lounge on her way to the room. It makes no difference that she can afford the best cakes, that she has a pot of gold in the bank, getting bigger every day. She's wound up, angry with herself, elated, ashamed and defiant, all at the same time.

She eats straight from the boxes, using tissues to wipe the globs of cream from her chin, the trail of jam from her upper lip. She gobbles the luscious slices of apple pie, destroying their beauty, cramming in as much as her mouth will hold, followed by pastry after flaky pastry, the crumbs drifting onto her trousers to land on the floor around her like golden confetti. She washes each mouthful down with water until her stomach feels like the inside of a washing machine, the contents sloshing about when she moves. She saves the blueberry pie until last, savouring the sweet burst of summer on her tongue. The zip of her trousers will no longer close, so she removes them and stumbles to the bathroom bare-legged and barefoot. She locks the door behind her, grabs a towel and tucks her hair behind her ears. A brief inspection of the room establishes that there's no toilet brush. The bathroom is huge — almost the size of her bedroom at home, with cupboards fitted flush to the walls so you'd barely see them, no handles to destroy the line. In one, she finds a toilet brush. She has everything she needs.

She kneels, reverent, at the porcelain bowl, lifts the lid and opens her mouth.

CHAPTER SEVENTEEN

Heather

For a while, in her teens, bulimia was her friend. When she reached the age of thirteen, when everything was so confusing, it provided a feeling of control where none existed elsewhere in her life. At school she couldn't tell who liked her and who didn't, why they treated her kindly one minute and cruelly the next, why someone would one minute let her sit next to them, only the next to cringe away from her and laugh, making out she smelled. The lessons, at least those where the teachers were able to keep some semblance of order, were an escape of sorts, because bad behaviour could be detected and sat upon. But though she worked diligently, she knew that being good in class, behaving as the teachers expected, doing her best, would compound her problems.

Games lessons and breaks were the worst. She lost count of the times she asked to be excused from games — for her period, for a stomach ache, a headache, a bad knee. Her mother did her best; she wrote the notes of excuse, though sometimes she questioned whether Heather was really too unwell to join in. Heather always was.

The teachers tried to encourage her, but it did no good. During games lessons she was supposed to sit quietly, doing her homework or reading, but the fact was that there were no free staff to supervise. Sometimes she would sneak out of school to the grocer's shop around the corner. There she would tell them she was buying food for her classmates. Biscuits, cakes, sandwiches, sweets; her entire allowance was spent on food. On the way back from the shop she would sit on the bench at the bus stop and eat, hurling the empty packets one by one into the nearby waste bin. Back at school, she would creep into the nearest toilets, start up all the hand driers, and run to the nearest cubicle to vomit.

It became more frequent, daily if she had the money. She bought laxatives and diuretics at the local chemist. Purging became her obsession. With the food inside her, she felt disgusting and bloated. No wonder the girls called her names; she deserved it. But when she'd purged herself, it was like taking a shower, feeling clean all over, only this was clean inside rather than outside. It felt good — at least it did until the self-loathing kicked in.

She would pin her hair back to ensure it didn't get in the way; her pockets were always full of pins and tissues, in case there was no toilet paper. She washed her face and hands obsessively afterwards, scrubbing away the smell. She found excuses for the little cuts and grazes on her knuckles, caused by her teeth as she shoved her fingers as far down as she could. The only thing she couldn't help was the state of her teeth, which turned yellow and raggedy. She endured numerous fillings as she grew, as the regular presence of stomach acid in her mouth took its toll. But even the dentist was too busy to question why this tall, awkward, seemingly healthy girl had such bad teeth. He muttered about sugar and diet, but her mother assured him that Heather ate a good diet with lots of vegetables. Luck of the draw, she said. Genes must have skipped a generation; her own teeth and her husband's were strong and healthy and had lasted well, though Heather's grandmother couldn't have said the same.

She stopped smiling; her teeth gave the bullies another reason to snipe at her. She worried about bad breath; she would stand in front of the mirror and try to smell her breath as it steamed up the patch of glass, but she couldn't tell. She brushed her teeth anyway. Her gums bled often.

At the beginning, when Heather realized she was becoming addicted to the cycle of bingeing and vomiting, she almost wanted her mum to find out, stop it happening, tell her she didn't need to do this. But then it became too important.

It was easy to conceal from the adults. Her weight hardly fluctuated, so nothing for her parents to worry about there. She was a good girl, perhaps a bit shy and quiet, but well behaved and polite. She was working hard at school, passing her exams with good results. As she grew older, her mother began to wonder out loud why she didn't have a boyfriend, but she and her father assumed it would happen one day, once she'd got a bit more confidence in herself, so they didn't worry too much.

Nobody knew how bad it was. Not even Natalie, who knew more than anyone about her suffering. Heather was too ashamed to tell even her best friend how badly she was abusing herself.

Thrown together by dint of being isolated by the rest, their bond was stronger than that of their other classmates. They stood up for each other, covered for each other, tried their best to protect each other from the bullies. Once or twice the teachers intervened, suggested every so often that they separate, make new friends and join in with the others. But the girls knew that wouldn't work. There was nobody else prepared to stand up to the bullies and openly be their friend. The teachers had no idea. In those days, there were no anti-bullying policies. You just had to survive, somehow.

It was a strange friendship, though. At times, it seemed that Natalie resented Heather simply for being the only friend available to her. Certainly they didn't have the same interests. Natalie liked cookery classes and physics, Heather swimming and history. Natalie's clothes, outside school, followed the latest fashions — when she could get a big enough size. Heather used clothes only to cover herself, to disguise her shape. Natalie watched endless soaps on TV, while Heather was more interested in historical dramas and museums.

But somehow it worked. Though they had their moments, the odd hour or so when they had a falling out and weren't speaking, they stuck together like glue. Safety in numbers, however small.

* * *

There was only one time she might have been discovered.

One day when she was seventeen and in the sixth form at school, she'd gone to the shop round the corner during a free period. The sixth-formers had special privileges — they were allowed out at break times and could eat their lunch in their own common room. Natalie was in class, so she wasn't around, and Heather was in the grip of her addiction, vomiting every day, sometimes twice or three times in twenty-four hours.

She had bought the usual array: jam tarts (a favourite), chocolate brownies, a whole lemon tart, a bagful of fresh doughnuts, chocolate muffins. When she was in school, she preferred the soft, spongy food that she could get down quickly; there was never much time to hang about. On the way back from the shop, taking the long way around so she wouldn't bump into any other sixth-formers, she stopped at a park bench and stuffed as much in her mouth as she could, swallowing hard. She could feel the sweetness travelling down into her stomach, the waist on her skirt start to feel tighter, her stomach distending. She was running out of time to get rid of it, so she discarded the empty wrappers in the bin and walked fast back to school. In her bag were still a large bag of chocolate muffins and the rest of the doughnuts. She would keep them for later, see if she could find a moment to get them down.

She slipped in through one of the side doors, which was closest to the quietest toilets. There was nobody around; the school was in full session and the corridors were eerily silent. She entered the washrooms as quietly as she could, checking that the doors on the cubicles were open and nobody was there. She went right to the end, where the last cubicle was set slightly apart from the others. Though, like the others, its door and flimsy screen walls ended inches from the floor at top and bottom, she felt safe there. Dumping her bag on the floor, she pinned back her hair as fast as she could, knelt on one knee and rammed her fingers down her throat once, twice, three times.

Sometimes afterwards, if there was nobody around, she would wash her knees as well as her face, scrubbing them as best she could with soapy hands. Often she would walk around with wet tights. She always wore the thick black ones so it wouldn't show.

A tiny sound outside, the squeak of rubber on the floor.

She froze, still kneeling, the rancid smell of the toilet making her gag. Had someone come into the washroom? She vomited one last time, flushing the toilet at the same time to mask the noise. Wiping her face with toilet paper and checking for splashes on her jumper, she picked up her bag with the remainder of her stash, unlocked and opened the door.

She was so startled she almost dropped her bag. There was a girl standing right outside, a shocked expression on her face. Heather didn't know her name. She was probably a couple of years younger.

"Are you all right?" she said. "I heard someone being sick." As she spoke, her eyes flicked to the bag in Heather's hand. It was still open, the bag of doughnuts visible on top.

With shaking hands, Heather zipped it closed and swung it onto her shoulder. "No, I . . . yes, I felt a bit sick and I had to throw up. I'm better now though. I'll just . . ."

She went over to the row of basins to wash her face and hands, avoiding the girl's stare. To her horror, glancing in the mirror above the basin, she saw that there was still chocolate around her mouth and a sprinkling of sugar on her chest. She scrubbed at her skin with her fingers. She could see in the mirror that the girl was still there. Heather wished she would go, but she seemed determined to hang around.

"Are you sure you're okay? Do you want me to tell Matron?"

Matron was a perspicacious woman who knew all too well what young girls got up to. She was the last person Heather wanted to see.

"God, no. I'm fine, just forget it, okay?"

* * *

After that, she managed to restrict herself to once a day, at home, for a good few months. She decided it was too dangerous to do it at school; she had probably been lucky to get away with it for so long. She avoided the girl after that incident, stopped buying food at the local shop and only took the laxatives at home.

On one occasion, when Natalie was on yet another of her strict diets, hoping to lose weight for the summer, they had a disconcerting conversation about anorexia that left Heather taut with anxiety. Another girl at school, in the year below them, had lost so much weight she'd been admitted to hospital; her parents were frightened she might die. Apparently at mealtimes she would eat no more than a mouthful or two, and her mother found her vomiting after supper one day when she'd had no more than a sprig of broccoli and a couple of peas. It had shocked the school. The headmistress talked about it in assembly, and Matron was on the alert for other sufferers.

"Sometimes I wish I could fast like she did," Natalie said as she sat down to her frugal, calorie-counted packed lunch. "If I could just lose the first couple of stone, I'd feel so much better." Natalie had done a calculation, and she reckoned she needed to lose three stone to be a size ten. Heather, for whom this subject was too painful to contemplate, kept silent.

"Do you think she was throwing up everything, and that's how she lost so much weight?" Natalie continued. "I mean, I know she was exercising all the time, but if she ate and then got rid of it, she would definitely lose weight, wouldn't she?"

There was an awkward pause as Natalie waited for an answer. Heather had to say something, if only to avoid suspicion. She shook her head, her eyes down. "I don't know. But it sounds really dangerous — she was basically starving herself. She could have died."

Natalie sighed. "I suppose you're right. But dieting is so boring. And I so want to fit into a nice dress."

"I'm sure you will," she said.

* * *

James doesn't know about the bulimia, either.

At the moment when she'd thought she could tell him everything, after he'd asked her to marry him, when her happiness felt new and undeserved and unimaginable, she faltered. Shame and low self-esteem had shadowed her for so long. They'd filtered into her mind, crept under her skin, inveigled themselves into every part of her life. They were entangled in her very essence, and though she wanted to banish them for ever, getting rid of them was not so simple.

It had taken years to get to where she was when she met him. At twenty-three, dragged to a point so low by her addiction to vomiting that she considered the ultimate solution, she at last sought help. Her GP, an overworked man with sagging bags under his eyes, gave her two minutes to explain herself, checked her eyes and her throat and palpitated her stomach. He questioned her about her home life: fine; her work: it's good; friends: well, I have one. She left the surgery with a prescription for Valium and an irresistible desire for chocolate cake. Three whole cakes later, the shower running to disguise the noise, she had her head down the toilet in the bathroom. That day, she felt nothing but contempt for herself.

86

There followed a long and dispiriting search for help. A new GP, referrals to a string of NHS therapists, months of waiting for an appointment. Agonizing sessions when she cried and sobbed to a stranger, every appointment leaving her drained and depressed. The group sessions were, if anything, worse. She could hardly bear the tears of the other women (they were all women), the sad stories. They all seemed to have more reason than her to be hurting, to be punishing themselves. Every single day she battled the urge to go home and fill her stomach. Holding her job down was as much as she could manage, though the strain of hiding her secret was exhausting.

But she persevered, somehow, and in the end determination and time paid off. She reached her thirties and, whether it was the result of maturity or the many hours of baring her soul, the urge seemed to diminish. Her career was taking off, she had a job she loved, and she'd become, if not used, then resigned to the idea of never getting married or having children.

It was a hard-fought battle. And she'd thought it was for good, that she'd grown out of it, won the fight and moved on.

But now, in her fifties, when life should be sorted, when she should be wise, and mature, and responsible, she seems, to her horror, to be slipping backwards, feeling that pull once again. It seems that her grip on her new self — so hard-won, so important to who she is now — was more fragile than she'd ever imagined.

She has to deal with this now, before it takes hold again.

CHAPTER EIGHTEEN

Natalie

My friendship with Heather was the backbone of my childhood. When I think back to my teens, I try to block out the days sitting in the classroom or suffering on the playing field. Instead I remember the hours after school when Heather and I would dawdle our way into town before splitting up to get our separate buses. Sometimes we'd laugh so much we couldn't stand. We'd be bent double, clutching our tummies, tears running down our cheeks. I don't remember any of the reasons for our giggling fits, but they were fun.

At the weekends, we would often hang out together, wandering around town, in and out of the shops. We'd sit and eat ice creams on a bench in the park in the summer, watching the families go by, averting our eyes from the kids we knew from school.

Because of her height, Heather was clumsy and awkward, and she always looked as if she was trying to be smaller. Her shoulders would hunch into her clothes, and she always wore flat shoes. But the openness in her face was real. She was honest and loyal, and there wasn't a mean bone in her body.

Which all, of course, made her life at school much more difficult than mine.

While Heather was open, I was closed. Where she was honest, I made up stories. She was easily hurt, whereas I pushed back — not that it did me any good. Don't get me wrong; I'm not criticizing her. I loved and trusted her implicitly. I stuck with her, and we were inseparable friends. But she never really knew me. She was — is — a much better person than me, and I consider myself lucky to be her friend.

I mention making up stories because that has always been my thing. It has always defined me. As an only child, with working parents too busy to notice, I lived in a fantasy world that other siblings would almost certainly have knocked out of me. In some ways, I was spoiled, given everything I needed and left to my own devices.

In others, I was neglected.

From a very young age, I believed I was special. For this I don't blame my parents, particularly. From story books, I took on the mantle of a princess, or sometimes a fairy, ruling my subjects from a sparkling throne in a luxury castle on top of a mountain. In my fantasy, I was always slim and beautiful, my fair hair falling in shiny curtains of gold down my back, my waist ankle-thin. Though real life told me I was kidding myself, I always believed that underneath, the pretend me existed, and one day the swan would emerge from the ugly duckling that I saw in the mirror.

I don't suppose I was that unusual, for a little girl growing up without brothers and sisters. But probably most little girls grew out of it.

* * *

It was lucky for both of us that we joined the grammar school at the same time, although we didn't know it at the time. Fresh from junior school, we were in the same class from the first day, both nervous and excited, innocent of the trials ahead of us. By chance, we sat next to each other, and I liked her immediately. She spoke to me, for a start; I was used to being ignored because of the way I looked. And I liked her face, which was open and friendly.

At break time, we found our way to the dining room together, and over the months that followed, we stuck together like glue, a small unit outside the inner ring of the popular girls.

We were both only children, used to being solitary, and we found the big class sizes of the school intimidating, if not overwhelming. That was one of the similarities which brought us together. But in other ways, we were quite different.

My family comes from a long line of shopkeepers. My parents owned three big grocery stores in the suburbs of Cheltenham and Gloucester, and my mum and dad worked in our shops for as long as I can remember. I was brought up with the sound of the cash register ringing in my ears and out-of-date (though edible) food on the table. We weren't posh, like Heather's family, but we were comfortably off, with a big house in a new housing estate on the outskirts of Cheltenham and a collection of smart cars which were my dad's pride and joy. As an only child, I had everything I wanted, except brothers and sisters. Perhaps for me, Heather filled the role of sister — we were certainly as close as siblings might have been.

Heather's family was middle-class, religious and buttoned-up. They lived in a modest seventies semi-detached house and they never seemed to have much money.

Her dad was an educated man. He read books about Winston Churchill and the world wars, which would always rest on his favourite chair in their sitting room when he wasn't around. He was a civil servant, whatever that meant; in Cheltenham at that time, you didn't ask. I later learned that he was one of many people who worked for GCHQ, which I understood to be the government's intelligence service. But you couldn't ask what they did, and they weren't allowed to tell. Heather's mother was a stay-at-home mum; she'd met her husband while working at the same place — but in those days, married couples were not allowed to work there, so she gave up work and looked after Heather.

Like Heather, I didn't fit in with 'The Set', that group of know-it-all, have-it-all girls. I wasn't tall, as she was, but in my teens I was horribly overweight, with hips that blended into waist into chest in a continuous curve. My legs, my worst point, were inverted triangles from top to bottom, barely acknowledging a curve at the knees. They scraped together when I walked, and when I wore tights they made an odd whooshing noise that caused me even more embarrassment. My school blouse, straining over my ample bosom and protruding stomach, would gape between buttons, so that I developed a habit of pulling it down at the waist in an effort to straighten it out. My cheeks were round, my hair thin, mousy and unruly; it always seemed to slip out from the plastic clip I used to hold it back. I hated my body all the way through school.

Heather was overweight too, but tall, so she carried it well. Better than I did, anyway. She had thick, dark hair that fell in shiny curls which I envied, and her face, though not pretty, was almost beautiful. But like me, she had no confidence. She didn't fit in, and the other girls knew it.

* * *

It was our lack of prowess in the gym and on the sports field that really melded us together. The teachers were relentless. We all had to change into our sports kit in a matter of minutes, and woe betide any girl who lagged behind. Together with the other girls who hadn't made the grade with The Set, Heather and I, both painfully ashamed of our bodies, would change with as much decorum as we could manage in an open room. But still we had to counter a barrage of taunts and derision as, hanging our heads, we trotted out to play hockey or netball or stumble around the athletics track, trailing behind the pack. Thank goodness we had each other.

Neither of us had proper boyfriends at school, though I had more luck than Heather. Well, not luck exactly — rather, the odd tussle in the long grass at the edge of the park with a spotty boy who wanted to see how far I would go. Of course I made out that I was 'going out' with the boy, and kept up the pretence for a few weeks at a time. I couldn't spin it out for long, though, without being found out. You need people to see your boyfriend to believe you have one, when you're a teenager and fat.

In class, fortunately, we held our own, which was a bit of a double-edged sword with the meaner girls. Though Heather always had more enthusiasm than me for studying. She was lucky, too, to find a subject she loved. I never did. I did my homework, was diligent enough in class. I even revised for exams, but I was never really engaged in it all. I was away with the fairies, imagining how my life was going to be once I became luscious and gorgeous and all the magazines would want me on their front cover.

My parents couldn't have been prouder when I went to university. Nobody in our family had ever done that before. They told everyone, even strangers who came into the shops, to my huge embarrassment. I was their clever girl, going on to great things, a proper job — perhaps even in an office. But I only went to university because I didn't know what else to do, and because Heather was going. I even tried to get into the same university, unbeknown to her, but I wasn't good enough. I chose sociology because I'd heard it was easy, not through any lofty moral values or desire to give back to society. I didn't harbour any ambitions to be a social worker, or an aid worker, or anything like that. It was easy enough, and it was a means to an end. I wanted to get a degree. I wanted to keep up with Heather.

At university, where I was like a fish out of water, a small miracle happened, though. I was pretty miserable there, to be honest, and all the other students seemed so self-assured. They were all hooking up with each other like mad, except me, the fat ugly one who sat on her own in the Union bar like a loser.

I don't think I was aware that I wasn't eating, or perhaps it was the distances we had to walk every day to get to lectures, but I started to lose weight. By the end of the first year my clothes were no longer fitting and I had to go and buy new ones. By the end of the second, I was down to a size fourteen and I had a boyfriend — for a couple of months, at least.

At last, I felt, the butterfly was beginning to emerge. Of the two of us, I was going to be the one with the boyfriends, the husband, the kids.

I left university in size twelve jeans with no idea what to do next. I went back to my parents feeling like a failure, and was forced to endure their misplaced admiration all over again. Of course, I hoped that Heather would return home too, and that we could carry on as before, finding work locally and spending our spare time together. But Heather was on another, loftier path than me. Heather was embarking on a career.

She was off to London, to get work experience at the British Museum. She loved history, adored archaeology, and was passionate about her work. For her, university had been a joy: at last she'd been able to focus on what inspired her and forget the dark days of school.

I did envy her that — while, of course, still being happy for her.

I jumped at her invitation to share a flat, though I had no job and no prospects. My parents were dubious, but they decided it was up to me — I had proved I was clever, after all — so off I went. Once we'd found a flat-share, I had to find work, and there followed a series of short-term menial positions — bar work, waitressing, even cleaning — that paid just about enough to keep me off the breadline.

I had hope, then. I was young, slim and, if not beautiful, I was growing into my looks. I had a degree, of sorts. There was still time for me to evolve into a princess.

CHAPTER NINETEEN

Before

I didn't want to do it. I wanted to keep it, save it for the future, in case of emergencies. It would be a buffer, in case I was one day left on my own. Or if we had children and we needed a cushion for their education. That didn't happen, and I'm glad now.

Or, if I'm completely honest with myself, in case he got us into serious trouble. Which isn't far off being true right now. I love him, but he's not good with money. We live well beyond our means, in a house far too large for just the two of us. Heaven knows what the mortgage is costing. We entertain too much, with champagne and the best cuts of meat. Our holidays are in the most fashionable, luxurious places.

I was always happy to let him run the house, the finances, make all the decisions. I liked being looked after, not having the stress of dealing with the bills. I enjoy my job, love working with small children, but it doesn't pay well. When we married, he was in a good job that paid well, and he took it for granted he would look after the finances. So when he resigned from the corporate world to set up his own business, I assumed he knew what he was doing. At the beginning, he was full of energy, so ambitious. Many others have tried and failed, in that business, but his plans were incredible, and I admired his passion.

But then the cracks started to appear. He came home later and later, looking washed out, too tired to talk. I would ask how things were and he would snap back at me that everything was fine. His moods swung from sky-high to the floor in moments. He soon started to complain about the cost of everything: the bills, the help we had in the house and in the garden. They had to go. Even then I didn't mind; my financial contribution to the household was so small, it was the least I could do to take on the cleaning.

I knew things weren't going well, but I hadn't realized the scale of it until he asked to borrow my father's money. I was shocked. He knew how much it meant to me. I'd locked it into a three-year savings account, with a penalty to pay if I withdrew any of it early.

I gave in to him in the end, I couldn't help it. I felt sorry for him. He was working so hard to get the business off the ground. For his sake, for the sake of our marriage, I had to support him. So I handed over the twenty-five thousand, and believed him when he said it would come back four-fold. That's what he's like: so confident, so sure of himself, it's hard not to ride on the wave of enthusiasm along with him.

I hated giving away even part of Dad's inheritance like that. I was scared it had gone for ever.

CHAPTER TWENTY

Heather

All traces of cake have been removed and sanitized. Though she's showered and changed, she still feels unclean, shocked at the return of her illness and its power over her. Her worst fear is that the demon will take hold once again, grabbing her with greedy fingers, and she'll be helpless to escape. In the middle of her life — no, a stage on from that, even — she is catapulted back to being a teenager, with all the angst and uncertainty that sent her into a spiral of self-harm when she was fifteen.

She's consumed with shame. No one must know, not even James. Though he would be kind and supportive, he would also, though he'd try to hide it, be shocked and horrified, and she can't bear that.

The sooner she can get away, make the key decisions and start living a normal life again, the better.

But when James starts talking, she realizes that's not going to happen.

"Right," James says, setting out some glossy brochures on the coffee table. "Miles has come up with some suggestions — quite good ones, I'd say. What do you think about the

French Riviera? Monte Carlo, say? Or Saint Tropez? Though I imagine both are quite busy in the summer months. Or we could go to Italy, somewhere like Lake Como, which is beautiful; we've never been there. Or what about Montenegro? He says lots of wealthy people go there to avoid the crowds. Or southern Spain, somewhere like Puerto Banús, which is glitzy and glamorous and sounds like fun. Heather?"

Heather opens her mouth, then shuts it again. Swallows, then buries her head in her hands.

"Darling — what is it?"

She removes the hands, managing a wobbly smile. It's not James's fault. "I — it's all too much for me." She picks up one of the glossy brochures, puts it down again. "Honestly, I don't think I want to be around wealthy people, or glitz and glamour. I think I need quiet, and peace, and a beautiful view. Space to think, and plan, and come to terms with it. And ordinary people around me, who don't know us or what's happened. It's just not — us, James, all this."

James hesitates, nodding. "I see what you mean — you're right. Miles is so keen and enthusiastic, I think he's allowed his imagination to run away with him. I'll tell him we'll sort it out ourselves."

* * *

She pauses for a moment outside the unassuming travel agency. The window is splashed with garish signs: 'Special offer!' 'Lowest price!' 'Children go free!'. This place seems much more her style. No pretensions here.

Inside, it's shabby in a comforting way. There are the usual posters on the walls, a rack of brochures from tourist companies, a couple of desks with computers and chairs for customers. A woman glances up from her screen as Heather enters, smiles a welcome. The contrast with the intimidating travel agent's in Marylebone couldn't be greater.

"Can I help you with anything?" she says. "Looking for a nice holiday? There are lots of good offers at the moment."

She waves her arm at the stack of brochures beside her on the desk. "Please, sit down."

"I'm looking for something a bit different."

The woman has a motherly air about her. Her hair is pulled back from her face into a clip at the back, and though it's a warm day, she's wearing a bright blue cardigan, which gives her a jaunty appearance. Her nails are painted a bright, shiny red, to match her lipstick. "Where were you thinking?"

"Somewhere relatively close to home. No jet lag. Warm, sunny, and quiet. Definitely away from the popular tourist destinations. It's just for the four of us at the start, though we'll be joined by a bigger group after a couple of weeks, so it needs to be pretty spacious, with six or seven bedrooms. A house or a villa, detached, with a pool, lots of outdoor space and a beautiful view. Preferably of the sea, so somewhere on the coast, if possible. Water sports locally for the kids, all teenagers. We want to rent it for probably three months over the summer, starting as soon as possible. And the security needs to be good."

"I see," the woman says, turning to her screen. "That is quite unusual, you're right. What budget do you have in mind?"

"I have no idea what it costs. Let's see what you've got — start high and work our way down. Does that sound okay?"

"Of course! I'll do my best. Let's start by narrowing down the country, shall we?"

* * *

So, Spain it is. After an hour or so searching, Heather and the woman in the blue cardigan settle on an area in the south-west corner, not far from the Strait of Gibraltar, where the Atlantic Ocean meets the Mediterranean Sea. There, they focus on a small town called Zahara de los Atunes, on the Spanish Costa de la Luz. The travel agent, who seems to understand what Heather wants and doesn't ask too many questions, knows it personally, having visited by chance a couple of years previously. Zahara is popular in the summer months with the Spanish, many coming from nearby Seville, but it doesn't attract many British tourists. It has the attractions of beautiful unspoiled beaches and countryside, and it's close to the Mecca of kitesurfing, Tarifa. To Heather, it sounds perfect.

They find a large villa to rent, located on a hillside overlooking the ocean a couple of miles from Zahara, in an area called Atlanterra. The price would have made her hyperventilate before, though it isn't the most expensive, and looks quite modest on the exterior. Its simple contemporary architecture is the opposite of their house in Shepherd's Bush; it's like a building made of square blocks, no curves to be seen. But inside, it opens out into beautiful sunlit rooms with huge balconies, luxurious bedrooms with cool marble floors and palatial bathrooms.

Heather falls for it straight away. The pictures show a stunning view of an azure sky reflecting on a calm sea, a huge expanse of windows tinted to keep the interior cool without dulling the natural light. It has multiple sun decks with furnished seating areas, a wide terrace under cover, and an infinity pool that falls away seamlessly towards the ocean. Though there are other villas dotted around on the slope down to the sea, the house is secluded, surrounded by tall cypresses and lush foliage. Tall, electric front gates protect it from prying eyes, and it has a private path leading down to the curve of the beach, where the golden sand is smooth and unspoiled.

For the first time since the day she woke up with twenty-nine million pounds in the bank, Heather feels a pleasant tingle of anticipation at the prospect of the weeks to come.

CHAPTER TWENTY-ONE

Heather

The cashmere touch of warm air settles on the skin of her arms as they walk from the plane into the terminal at Gibraltar. The runway at this tiny airport seems to run right into the glistening sea in both directions, while the Rock juts unexpectedly into an expanse of clear blue sky. It couldn't be more different from West London.

This was the first time she'd travelled business class in her entire life (the museum's budget barely stretched as far as economy to Scotland), and it seemed strange to be on a journey without the boys. But, though the fare seemed extravagant for such a short flight, prompting deep-set feelings of guilt, the feeling of calm in the cabin was soothing. The forward section of the plane was quiet, the seats spaced far enough apart to accommodate her long legs. She dozed for a while as James read the newspaper, allowing herself to relax as the plane rose from Heathrow.

On the other side of the terminal building, they soon spot their name on a sign among the drivers waiting at the barrier. A smiling man takes their bags and leads them to an immaculate white limousine, ushering them into its cool interior. Heather feels the last vestiges of stress trickle out of her as the car eases onto the road, its engine humming softly as it gets into its stride.

Gibraltar is soon behind them. The sea, sparkling in the dazzling sunlight, disappears behind a sprawl of high-rise apartments, cranes and warehouses as the busy main road takes them through Algeciras on the route towards Cádiz. The traffic eases around roundabouts and crawls through a landscape bristling with industrial buildings.

But as the road starts to climb, the scenery changes without warning. The sea comes back into sight and a huge bay spreads out ahead of them, its long sandy beach reaching onto the hills above it in a splash of yellow sand dunes, like careless brushstrokes on an oil painting. Beyond, an army of colourful parachutes draws her eye, hovering over the bay like a flock of seabirds waiting to dive-bomb their prey.

"Is this Tarifa?" she asks the driver.

"The town is just a bit further," he says, indicating ahead of them. "You see the kitesurfers? They're on the beach at Tarifa."

Once they're past the huge bay, the landscape changes once again. An army of white wind turbines marches across the land, turning and whirling in the powerful wind of the Atlantic Ocean. They seem to beckon the road towards Zahara, and as the car approaches the town she can still see a few of the tall soldiers signalling in the distance.

It's not long before they're climbing a narrow road on the Atlanterra hill, where the ocean wraps the land in a soft shawl of golden sand. The views to Heather's right are breathtaking, the sea spectacular, unfolding in stripes of turquoise, green and grey as it stretches away to the horizon. In the distance, they can see the dark land mass of Africa.

As she steps from the car, stretching her aching back, she feels lighter, more free than she has done for months. They're met by a smiling property agent who opens the villa for them, hands them the keys and leaves them to explore.

Dropping her bag on the cool marble floor, she slides a door to one side and walks out onto a broad balcony edged with glass balustrades. Today, the sea is calm, two tiny white boats in the distance standing motionless on its glassy surface. The air smells of seaweed and salt and she breathes it in, her eyes closed, enjoying the warmth of the sun on her face.

Gazing at the spectacular view, she feels hopeful at last. Here, on the edge of the Atlantic, perhaps she can find the space to breathe, to make some plans.

And to step back from the cliff-edge of her addiction.

* * *

Carrying only money, sunglasses and keys, they take the path down the slope to the sea. It soon transforms into a line of steps with a sturdy wooden rail on one side. At the bottom, they go barefoot, the wet sand cool beneath their feet. Ahead are huge rocks linking the beach with what could be an old pillbox or a disused lookout shelter at the very furthest point of the headland, reaching out into the sea.

The tide is on its way out; gentle waves foam and splash, pulling and pushing at the water's edge as they walk. On the hillside to the right are more villas, partly hidden by lush vegetation, and a terrace of three or four identical houses with colourful fronds of bougainvillea clambering along their balconies.

A little further on they reach the wider part of the beach, where families gather in tight knots of coloured towels, pop-up tents and angled umbrellas, small children shouting and playing in the shallows. In the far distance lies a low hill before the bay curves round to a cliff, with another lookout at the end. Straight ahead, at the end of a long stretch of golden sand, the town of Zahara shimmers in the heat, its low-level buildings white against the dark hill beyond.

It's late afternoon by the time they reach the town, the heat still beating down in a shimmer of sunlight. Heather doesn't mind; she loves to feel the warmth, the clean air on her arms and legs, too rare a thing at home.

At the heart of the town, the buildings are older and smaller than those on the outskirts. The houses huddle together, their terracotta roofs at different levels and odd angles, divided by streets just wide enough for a car to pass. Many of the narrow streets are dotted with the tables and chairs of restaurants spilling out onto the pavements.

The shops are still mostly shut; they'll open when the heat begins to fade, staying open until late in the evening. She wonders if she could get used to taking a siesta in the afternoon. Perhaps you can't help but slow down in the heat, slipping gently into the rhythm of Spanish life. It sounds like a good way to live.

At a small café, they take a table in the shade and order drinks. Heather studies the menu idly, challenging herself to work out what the dishes are without checking the English translation.

"Shall we eat?" says James. "It's early, but I'm starving."

"Why not? We can do anything we like . . ." Heather grins at him, and he smiles back.

"That's the first time I've seen you smile in days," James says. "This was a great idea, coming here."

"I hope so. It does feel instantly relaxing, doesn't it? The sun, the sea, no pressure. Beautiful villa and plenty of time to ourselves. Just what I need."

A waiter recommends the tuna salad, the café's speciality.

The food tastes fresher than anything at home. Rose-pink chunks of raw tuna melt in Heather's mouth and the green leaves of the salad are the colour of summer gardens.

As they walk back along the beach, families are beginning to pack up for the day. Their arms loaded with fold-up chairs, beach bags and towels, they trail back to their homes in small groups. People walking along the shore nod and smile; dogs play in the foam and run barking up the slopes towards the houses and apartment blocks above the beach.

This time, rather than following the steps to the back of the house, they turn off the beach and walk up the road, noting the discreet frontages of the other villas and the front doors of the row of modern townhouses they spotted earlier. These will be their neighbours, if there's anyone there. Outside are only one or two cars, though they all have garages. Perhaps they are rental properties, unoccupied until high season when the schools are out.

Nobody takes an interest in the pale-skinned couple strolling along the road.

CHAPTER TWENTY-TWO

Heather

Heather eases herself into the pool. It's like being on the edge of the world, the water at the rim dropping into the sea in a strange, dreamlike illusion, deliciously cool on her sun-drenched skin. She dips and dives, her scalp contracting at the sudden change in temperature, and stands at the edge for a while, letting the water lap around her, her mind drifting.

As the sun starts to dip over the horizon, she emerges, cool and dripping, and she and James sit together in comfortable silence gazing at the view. The only sounds are the gentle lap of the waves on the beach, the odd cry of a seabird. Even if there were traffic on the small road that leads to the house, it's unlikely they would hear it over the swish of water on sand.

Later they might wander into the village to explore the shops. But there's no rush. It's a good feeling, having that empty expanse of time ahead of them.

* * *

The electronic tones of the entry phone slice through the calm. Startled, they stare at each other questioningly. They're not expecting anybody. Who is there to expect? With a stab of irritation, Heather ties a sarong around her damp costume and pads barefoot to the hallway. The entry phone shows her a woman at the front gate, small, blonde, and from the look of her, British. In one hand, she holds a bottle of what looks like cava, in the other a plate of cakes.

"Hello?" Heather says, into the handset.

"Hi!" The woman raises her face to the camera and grins. She holds the bottle high, waving it from side to side. "Welcome to Zahara. I'm Julie. We heard you were staying a while, so we thought — I thought — I'd come and say hello. We're neighbours. We live over there." She flourishes the bottle in the general direction of the town.

"That's so kind. Come in, please." She presses the button and the gate glides across as she opens the front door, smoothing back her hair, still damp and uncombed since her swim.

"Nice to meet you, Julie. I'm Heather," she says, holding out her hand. Julie's hand is cool and tiny in hers, and it rests there only a moment before she's heading through to the living room, following the sunlight and the view. "My goodness, that is beautiful." She turns around, inspecting the room. "This is a stunning house."

Julie's dressed in tiny white shorts, a pink vest and flip-flops, her skin a deep tawny brown that suggests she's been here for a while. She surveys the room, nodding her approval, then heads towards the kitchen area and starts opening cupboards. Heather can see James staring from the balcony, bemused, reaching for his T-shirt.

"Where's your husband? Oh, there he is. Will he . . . ?" She points to the bottle and Heather nods. "Where are the glasses? Ah, here they are." Triumphant, she holds three champagne flutes high, then busies herself with the cork. Heather is nonplussed. It's like a whirlwind has blown into their tranquil space.

Glancing at her, Julie stops abruptly. "Oh god," she says. "I'm so sorry. I'm doing it again. I'm always like this — so rude of me. I'll slow down. Are you okay with me . . . ?" She indicates the glasses and the bottle and Heather, smiling, nods.

"Hello!" James steps into the room, removing his sunglasses and holding out a hand to Julie.

"James, this is Julie, a neighbour. Julie, this is my husband, James."

"Good to meet you both," Julie says. "I was just saying to Heather, I have a habit of blowing into people's houses like a hurricane. I apologise. Roger says I'm too much for people; I take over. Hyperactive, that's me. Here you go. Do you have an ice bucket?"

Feeling a little shell-shocked, Heather searches around, eventually finding an ice bucket, and soon the bottle is cooling in a bed of ice. Julie keeps up a stream of chatter, mostly directed at James, whose expression is one of amused disbelief. Heather wonders how old Julie is: she could be anything between early forties and late fifties, at a very rough guess. The deep tan could be disguising her age in either direction.

Julie picks up the glasses, indicating the cakes with her eyes: chocolate Rice Krispies cakes, like the ones Heather used to make for the boys' birthday parties when they were small. Not her normal choice, and so British.

"Come on, then," Julie says. "You bring the cakes and the bottle, James." Her flip-flops beat a gentle rhythm onto the terrace. As they follow her, they catch each other's eye, and James shrugs and smiles. There's not much they can do in the face of this whirlwind woman. She's only being friendly, after all.

"Isn't this fabulous? What a view, you're so lucky — though ours is pretty good, too, I must say." There's a slight northern tang to her accent, and Heather wonders where she's from. But she daren't ask, for fear of too much information.

"Where are you from? Do you have children, are they going to join you? How long are you staying?"

Heather runs her finger around the rim of her glass as James fields the questions, answering some honestly, blocking others with a vague reply. He looks as if he's enjoying himself. Heather hopes Julie will run out of steam soon. And that she won't visit too often.

"Oh god, there I go again. I'll shut up, shall I?" She makes a zipping motion across her mouth, and Heather laughs. Though she feels overwhelmed by this woman, she can't help but like her.

"We've taken the house for three months, the whole of the school holidays," Heather says. "We're getting some peace before our kids and the relatives arrive."

"And there I go, disrupting your peace, causing mayhem again." Julie jumps up, refills her glass and picks up the plate of cakes before Heather has even opened her mouth to reply. "Have a Rice Krispies cake. About the pinnacle of my baking skills, but though I say it myself, they're scrummy." She picks up one of the paper cases and tips the contents straight into her mouth. "Best way to eat them. Otherwise you get all the bits down your front and the chocolate gets all over your fingers."

"Do you live here?" James says. Julie seems to be settling in for the evening.

"Yes, been here for a couple of years. Roger — my husband — inherited a house in Scotland from his parents when they died. I hate the weather there, it's too cold for me, so we sold the house and bought this place. We love it, though it can be a bit quiet in winter. That's when I need to get away, go to the city, get a bit of nightlife, you know?" She takes another cake and for a moment is silenced, her mouth filled with Rice Krispies. Heather takes her opportunity.

"As you're practically a local, where would you recommend for dinner tonight? We're going to wander into Zahara as soon as the sun goes down . . ."

The heat fades as Julie rambles on, the sky touched with cloud high in the atmosphere. A plane far away is a single silver dart across the blue.

* * *

108

Heather feels the effects of the cava in her legs as she and James walk along the cooling sand towards the town.

It wasn't something they were expecting, to be approached by the neighbours. In London, you barely see the closest ones, let alone those further down the road. It's rare to become friends with them, as they have done with Miles and Charlotte. Everyone's too busy, working too many hours, or juggling childcare, school runs and kids' activities, to socialize with anyone but their best friends.

As Heather suspected, Julie had a wealth of information about the local bars and restaurants, which ones are good and which overpriced. She was happy to offload it all, but Heather stopped her with a smile when she moved on to her favourite shops, hairdressers and beauty salons. She risked overload if she tried to absorb any more after two glasses of wine.

When they reach the town, they find Julie's favourite eating place without difficulty and book a table for later. They still have time for a wander, to get their bearings in the town in the cooler air of the evening.

CHAPTER TWENTY-THREE

Heather

Daylight seeps around the window blinds, forming golden stripes across the bed. It's quiet but for the gentle swish of the breeze in the trees and the waves beyond. And the gentle snore of James lying next to her.

Heather stretches and relaxes back into the pillow. They have nothing to do, no time constraints, a whole day ahead of them, and there are a full ten days left before James has to return to England to fetch the boys from school. It's a strange feeling, being so free, knowing that the boys are fine, happy even, where they are, and they don't need to worry about money ever again.

Then, with a sudden twinge of anxiety, she remembers Julie. In the row of villas nearby, the owners, all British, have formed a close friendship. It sounds to Heather as if they spend the summer in and out of each other's houses, drinking, barbecuing and partying. The other neighbours, in the bigger, more secluded villas, are mostly Spanish, excluded from this close-knit group.

She is wary of getting too close. The last thing she wants is to join a social group that expects to entertain and be entertained.

One other thing troubles her about Julie. She seemed to know they were here for a long time, not just a week's holiday. Did she guess, or has someone told her that the couple who arrived only a couple of days ago was going to be a fixture for the summer? It's strange. Surely she wouldn't arrive on the doorstep of every tourist with cake and a bottle of bubbly? And she seemed to know Heather was British before she'd even opened the door. It's odd, and ominously familiar, reminding her of what happened at home. She wonders again how it happened, how the story got out. Perhaps she'll never know.

There goes suspicion again. It keeps popping up when she least expects it.

* * *

"Hey, Mum." Harry's freckled face grins at her as the picture wobbles on the screen. "Woah, Ben, stop pushing me. I'm talking to Mum!" Behind Harry's mop of hair she can see posters — motorbikes, guitars — on an expanse of white wall.

"Are you in the dorm?" she says. The boarding rooms at school have been a mystery until now.

The picture makes a sudden lurch, turning down to a dark blue carpeted floor and Harry's bare feet, then to a bed with a tangle of pillows and duvets, to Ben's face, peering into the top of the screen.

"Hi boys, are you missing me?"

Harry's face reappears. "Yes, Mum, of course." His brow crinkles a little and she feels the tug of love in her heart. "But it is good being a boarder. Last night we swam for a bit, then we played pool for two hours. What's it like over there?"

"It's brilliant, I think you're going to love it. Beautiful sunny weather every day so far. We haven't checked out Tarifa yet, but on the way we saw lots of kitesurfers in the distance — it looks fantastic. We'll have a look and get some lessons organized before you come over."

Harry grins and gives her a thumbs up. Ben's arm waves from behind him and makes bunny ears above his head. "Cool. What's the house like?"

"I'll take you for a tour . . ." Heather pads around the house with the laptop, giving the boys a running commentary, then takes them to the balcony to show them the sea and the beach.

"Can't wait, Mum. Is it hot?"

"Might be a bit too hot for you, especially in the middle of the day. But Dad and I are getting into the Spanish siesta. A sleep in the afternoon, then wander into town and eat late. It's still so warm at ten o'clock in the evening, you don't want to go to bed too early."

"When's Dad going to come back?" Ben's face, upside down, takes over the oblong screen.

"I'm not sure. A few days before the end of term, I think. He's got some work to do, then as soon as school's out, you'll fly over with him. Hope you've got your passports with you — it'll save having to go back to the house."

"I think so. Can we kitesurf every day? Can we buy our own?"

She smiles at Harry's excitement. "Let's see how you get on first — you might hate it."

"We won't!" Ben shouts from the background.

"Okay, boys, I'm going to sign off now. I'll call tomorrow, or maybe Thursday, about the same time. Look after yourselves."

"Will do. Bye, Mum!" The image wobbles again and Ben's face appears. "Bye, Mum, love you!"

"Love you, boys!"

* * *

There's something about a mother's love for her children. She's tied to them in a way that never stops, never lets go. An invisible ribbon of love connects her to them. When they're happy, the ribbon hangs loose, gently swaying in the wind.

When they're not, it's like a steel band that pulls at her heart and squeezes until she's breathless. It doesn't seem to work both ways, at least not as far as Heather can see. Children do love their parents, and the ribbon connects them, but for them it has a loose bow in the middle that gradually unfolds until, when they're adults and can take care of themselves, it gently parts.

She knows that soon, too soon, the ends of that ribbon will flutter to the ground. Childhood seems to fly by, just a few years of soft chubby hands in hers, of hugs and tantrums and cuddly toys. These teenage years, when the bow starts to loosen, are the prelude to adulthood, when, if she and James have done their jobs, those ribbons will fall away, no longer needed. That's how it should be, and she should be proud.

But the knowledge makes her sad. She walks onto the balcony and stares out at the long stretch of sea. The band of turquoise at the shallowest point turns into a dusty green further out. Beyond, where the ocean hides its deepest secrets, it becomes a dark, looming grey. She wonders how much of it is unknown, undiscovered by humans, and she hopes there are still vast areas where creatures live and thrive in peace.

But she can't look for too long. It's too bright, for a start, without her sunglasses, and her eyes are beginning to water. More importantly, she's getting morose. She can't afford these self-indulgent moments. She's too close to the edge to risk it.

Luckily, James has no such worries. He appears at the glass door of the living room bearing a tray of drinks, a sun hat perched at a jaunty angle on his head.

"Fresh lemonade, madam?" he says with a smile, heading for the shade, where the loungers await. "It's a tough life, being multimillionaires, eh?"

With an inward sigh, she smiles back. It's a good thing one of them can see the funny side.

CHAPTER TWENTY-FOUR

Heather

A light breeze rustles the bougainvillea that trails over the pergola above, its flowers a vibrant shade of pink against the morning sky. Heather drags her gaze away.

Today they're going to plan what to do with the money.

Twenty-nine million. Heather still can't quite believe it. She tries to visualise it piled up in a vault. How much space would it take? Do they even keep millions in bank notes? Or is it an illusion, money that never really exists in the material world?

They will never, ever need that much money, even if they buy new houses for themselves and the boys, an array of holiday homes and a fleet of luxury cars. Quality art on the walls, sculpture in the manicured gardens. If James chooses never to work again, they will still have more than enough, even if they live an extravagant lifestyle for the rest of their days.

"Okay," James says. "I'm going to set up a spreadsheet." He taps away at the keyboard, his glasses slipping down his nose in the heat. While she's in a tangle of anxiety on one side of the table, he's the picture of relaxation. Heather feels a surge of affection for him, this calm, ordinary, lovable person.

"Let's do the boring bits first," she suggests. "The stuff you know all about. Investments, securing the future, university fees, houses for the boys . . ."

"Care home fees . . ." James continues.

"Care home fees? I wasn't thinking that far ahead, but I suppose you're right. Couldn't we afford care at home?"

"Of course — I meant cost of care generally, for your mum and for us. I'll fill it in, I know the kinds of amounts. Though the costs rise all the time, so I'll add thirty per cent, to be sure."

There's a pause while he taps away at the keyboard. A seagull's cry adds an eerie note to the swish of the ocean below them.

"Number one: pay off mortgage and debts," he says.

"Debts? Do we have any, apart from the mortgage?" she says, surprised.

"The car, and the odd credit card bill, nothing much. But the mortgage is quite a lot. Though maybe not, in the scheme of things." He winks at her. He's enjoying this.

She lets him carry on, her mind wandering. Her head is full of possibilities: things they can do that they've only ever thought possible in their wildest dreams. That doesn't mean spending it all on Ferraris, superyachts or palaces. She wants — needs — to find a way to make it all mean something.

When they've imagined every possible scenario in which the immediate family might need the money, they turn to everyone else. For Heather's mother, they provide for a new house, in case she needs to move when she's older. They add in a considerable amount to cover the best care available, should she need it, and an income, through investments, to keep her comfortable for the rest of her life.

"She'll be absolutely delighted," James says.

Liz and Steve are more difficult. Do they want to give them an income, or a lump sum to do with what they wish? Steve seems flaky, unable to hold down a job for long, and James wants to secure Liz's future and that of their children independently, just in case.

"What do you mean, 'just in case'? Are you assuming he might leave her, or die?" This conversation is getting more complicated.

"I'm going to be cautious," James says. "You see, this is where families get it wrong. We have to consider Liz over and above Steve. We should imagine she's left on her own, however that might happen, and ensure her financial stability for the rest of her life. And for the children, too, of course. If we look after her, Steve will benefit from it, but he won't be able to take it from her."

"I see what you mean. When you put it like that, I'm relieved there aren't more relatives to think of."

James fills in some more figures. "Right, that's them sorted. What about Natalie — what do you want to do for her?"

"Oh, Natalie." Strangely, the thought of Natalie makes her sad.

James glances up from the screen with a puzzled frown. "What do you mean, 'Oh, Natalie'?"

"She's such a complex person. Her life has always been . . . a bit of a struggle, you know? She's never been really happy — though she would hate me to think it, she's quite proud."

"I know she was bullied at school, but so were you. You've both come through all that now."

Heather doesn't want to think about the truth of that.

"I think I've been luckier than her, though," she says. "I had a career I loved, and I have you and the boys. She's never had that, probably won't now. Just saying, it makes me a bit sad."

"So how can we help her, without appearing to be pitying her? We can be as generous as you like. It is your money, after all . . ."

"It belongs to the family . . ."

"But you won it, so you should have first say. I mean it, Heather. Look, it's enough for you to do almost anything you want with it, and still have plenty left."

She hadn't thought of it like that, but his words trigger something in her mind. It's like a window opening slowly, light flowing through it. She stands and walks over to the parapet, leaning into the wind, allowing the glow to creep into the dark corners.

Perhaps she can make this money do something incredible.

The back of her neck starts to tingle. This is a heaven-sent opportunity, one that most people can only dream of. She — they — can choose to make a life-changing difference somewhere: to a cause, or multiple causes, that they really care about. Not just a few pounds here and there, but an injection of money that will make dramatic change happen. And she's going to start with Natalie.

"I know what I want to do for her," she says at last, kicking off her shoes and returning to her seat. "Brace yourself, James, I think I've had an epiphany."

He gazes at her over his glasses.

"I'd already been thinking, long before this happened. I need to work, now the boys are older, I need to feel worthwhile," she says. "So . . . I'm going to create something wonderful with the rest of the money. A cause, a charity, something to change people's lives. I don't know exactly what it will be yet, but I have the germ of an idea. Natalie can work with me if she wants to, give up her job for ever. If she doesn't want to, that's fine, we'll give her enough in the bank to give up work anyway. And buy her somewhere to live — her own place. Chelsea, Kensington, Holland Park even, somewhere she'll love. What do you think?"

A slow smile creeps across his face. He stands, removes his glasses and comes round the table towards her. He takes her face in his hands, kissing her gently on the lips.

"I think," he says, "you're beginning to get the idea now."

As he returns to his seat, a feeling not unlike joy washes over her. Not laugh-out-loud, jump-for-joy emotion, but a settled, satisfied, warm feeling inside.

"I think I've realized how good this could be."

James removes his glasses and smiles slowly. "At last. I told you it would all be okay. It's a good thing, this money, not the terrible, frightening demon you seem to think it is."

"No, I don't mean for us. What I mean is . . . we've been lucky, yes. The money has come to us, but it's not meant only for us. We can make it work for others, too, not just our families. It's as if we've been given the responsibility, the wherewithal, if you like, to do something . . . brilliant. Not for us, but for people, for the environment, for a thing that needs profound change. This money, James, it could be transformational . . ."

Suddenly, her feet need to move. She jumps up and opens her arms, letting the wind pull at her dress, tangle her hair. She lifts her face to the sun and laughs.

"You're going to start dancing in a minute!" James says.

"I might! I feel so much better now. Come on, let's go and celebrate over lunch . . ."

* * *

A small dog runs up to them over the sand, its tail wagging. It's some kind of dachshund, with large paws and a shiny brown coat. Heather bends down to stroke it. It licks her hand and bounds off again, ears flying, barking with excitement, stopping every so often to sniff the air. She loves how it races, carefree, living in the moment. Perhaps she can be more like that now — perhaps this is what the money can do for her.

"I like it here," she says to James, as he bends to pick up a tiny, perfect shell from the line of broken pieces that gathers at the point where the waves foam and fade. "It's not just that it's beautiful, and the weather's fantastic. I love it that nobody knows us, no one has any idea of the state of our bank balance, or what's just happened to us. I think the boys will love it too."

James puts his arm loosely around her shoulders as they meander along the shallows, dipping their bare feet in and out of the water. "I like it, too. We should try and keep it this way, incognito, nobody interested in us."

"Except Julie," Heather smiles.

"Except Julie," James says. "I rather liked her, actually. She seems fun."

"She does. I just hope she doesn't pop by every day."

"Hm. Me too."

They stroll in comfortable silence towards the huddle of whitewashed buildings in the distance. Heather breathes in deeply, feeling a new calmness settle on her. It's going to be all right. She's going to be all right. And she's going to use the money to create something spectacular.

CHAPTER TWENTY-FIVE

Heather

"Do you feel ready to invite the others yet?" James puts down his fork, leaning back in his chair with an air of satisfaction. His sunglasses reflect the scene before him like a distorted mirror. Across the shimmering sand, the shoreline stretches for miles both left and right. "I know they'll be keen to get a date."

"I'm sure they will," Heather says. "Wouldn't you be, if you knew you were going to get a share of the millions?"

She smiles, but she's not really joking. She's thinking of Liz and Steve. She wouldn't admit it to James, but she's glad they live so far away. There's something about Liz that she can't quite put her finger on. Nothing negative, particularly, but she finds her a little . . . dizzy. Liz's tastes are bohemian while James's are conventional; she's scatty while James is organized; she loves to party, which is James's idea of hell. Plus, she talks all the time. Perhaps she'll get on well with Julie.

Steve, her husband, is loud, very Welsh, and loves a joke. It can get rather wearing. Entertaining them, even for a few days, could be challenging. Fortunately, their children,

Joshua and Cara, are good-natured and funny. They'll be great company for Ben and Harry.

"Have you sorted out collecting the boys?" she says, side-tracking James while she thinks how to answer his question.

"All booked — my flight home on Wednesday, and all three of us back on Friday. I'll have a day in the office and some time to pack."

"It'll be lovely to have them here. I'm looking forward to their faces when they see this place. And then, the others afterwards — are you thinking we'll get everyone here together? Might be a bit much . . ."

"Really? Your mum, Liz and family, Natalie? It's not a huge number."

"And the boys," she says.

"And the boys, of course." He nods. "And then Miles and Charlotte a bit later. I'm sure it will be fine — we have loads of space. Do you think your mum will come?"

"I'll ask her, but I don't think so. It'll all be a bit much for her. She seems perfectly happy not to travel, these days, with her bad hip. But I'm cautious about the others — having them all here together, I mean. I just . . . don't want any tensions. We need to be careful how we tell them, try to keep it confidential." She sighs. "Though it seems to me it's almost impossible to keep things quiet these days."

"No more nasty messages, though, I hope?"

"Not since I changed my number. I'm hoping that's the end of it. It made me suspicious of everyone. I don't want to feel like that for the rest of my life."

"It'll all have died down by the time we get back, I'm sure. Look, here's what I suggest for our house party."

"House party?" Heather makes a face.

"Okay — for our guests. We'll have a week to ourselves with the boys, then get the others over. Liz's family and Natalie together will be fine. Your mum too, if she comes. Miles and Charlotte can follow in a couple of days, after we've done the money discussions."

"Okay," she says, though her mind is whirring through what the visitors will need: food, clean bed linen, drinks, entertainment . . . The tension begins to rise again. She hopes some of them won't be able to come.

"Let me talk to Mum first, see what she thinks," she says. "She may not want to come at all, or she might prefer a couple of quiet days with just us and the boys."

"Good idea. I'll get an agent to do the bookings, once we know. Don't look so worried, darling. I'll organize it all. Once all the money stuff is done and dusted, we can relax and enjoy the summer. Call your mum when we get back, and then I can get started on the others, okay?"

"Okay," Heather says, summoning up a smile. But she doesn't feel okay.

"You don't look too happy about it," James says, leaning forward, covering her hand with his. "Listen. The brilliant thing about the money is that we don't have to angst about the little things. Remember, there's a housekeeper on call to do all the cleaning and shopping, and we can get her to cook for us when the others come. It'll take all the strain out of having guests. We'll get the kitesurfing sorted for the boys, and have some day trips out, all first-class, just for us. You really can relax, you know."

"I know." She does know. But she can't shake the uneasy feeling that seems to follow her everywhere. Though being here has eased the strain in many ways, the fear of the bulimia returning hasn't left her. She's still shocked at how fast her resistance crumbled when things got on top of her. And she's terrified that if it takes hold again, she'll never rid herself of it. It doesn't bear thinking about.

In her twenties, during the long period of disentanglement from her addiction, Heather tried to identify what it was that made the difference. She wasn't so interested in why it happened in the first place, but how she conquered it. What were the things — or, more likely, what was the combination of things — which took her from helplessness to control?

Her work helped her recovery most. She'd begun to understand that this was something she was good at, that others respected her for. She was not prepared to risk her job by becoming too ill to work, and she was determined to deny her illness a foothold inside her workplace. Her colleagues, whom she liked and admired, could not glean even a hint of her condition, or that part of her life would be tainted. She had found her bottom line.

Once she'd become more comfortable in her skin, she finally achieved some balance, and the bulimia stepped away — with it, the indignity, the shame and the helplessness. At last, she could dare to be proud of herself and the life she'd battled for.

Then James stepped into her inner sanctum and saw her for what she had become: a happy, secure, well-balanced person with an interesting job and a stable life. To her surprise, she found herself in a warm, supportive relationship.

It was inevitable that Heather would come across James eventually. He had been accountant for the museum for some time, but it was a while before she put a face to the name she saw from time to time on the monthly accounts, or heard mentioned in passing by her boss.

At the time, she'd been working on an exhibition of Italian glass. It was a delicate job in more ways than one. Many of the pieces came from private collectors, and handling the owners required patience and diplomacy. The exhibition was due to start in only a few days, and Heather found herself working late into the evening to be ready in time.

It was November, dark and dismal. Huge raindrops drummed against the windows of her office like the fingers of children pleading for entry. Although the room she worked in was small and well lit, the rest of the museum took on a mysterious character once the lights were dimmed and the visitors had gone. Any sound echoed and boomed in the cavernous rooms, causing her to start and glance at the door nervously.

So when the phone on her desk rang, a loud chirping sound that she hated, she dropped the book she was holding in alarm. But it was only the security guard asking what time she would be leaving. He mentioned that the accountant, too, was working late, and asked her to let security know when she was leaving.

Though she still had plenty to do, her train of thought had been interrupted, and after the call she was fidgety, unable to settle back into her task. Deciding to finish it off the following day, she collected her bag and her coat, turned the light off and locked the door behind her, fumbling with her key for a moment in the dimly lit corridor.

"Finished for the night, too, then?" The voice came from right behind her. She nearly jumped out of her skin.

She turned to see a tall, middle-aged man in a dark suit, holding a briefcase in one hand and smiling. "I'm so sorry to alarm you. The security man mentioned you were still here and I should let you know when I was leaving. I was just coming to tell you that."

He held out his hand. "I'm James — James Jessop. The accountant?"

"Yes, of course. I'm Heather." She took his hand. It was warm and comforting.

"Shall I walk with you to the door? It can be quite spooky on a night like this."

He seemed pleasant enough, so she agreed. She hated that long walk through the shadowy rooms to the side door of the museum.

But when they got to the door, they found it locked, with no sign of the security guard. They went together to find a phone, called the main number and the after-hours number without success. At the security office towards the back of the building where the deliveries came in, the door was firmly closed against them. They listened, but could hear nothing. They decided to wait there for half an hour, and if the guard hadn't turned up by then, Heather would call a key-holding colleague.

So they sat on a bench and got talking, mostly about the museum and her job, which was the subject she felt most comfortable with. He was a good listener, this well-spoken accountant with the gentle voice and the polite manner. When the security guard arrived an hour later, they were both surprised to see him.

The following day, James called and asked Heather to lunch.

CHAPTER TWENTY-SIX

Natalie

I can hardly wait for the end of term, and for once it's not because I hate my job.

I've been dreading the long summer holiday, with nothing booked, no money to do anything and that long stretch of time when people are still working or away. There's nothing quite so lonely as having time on your hands when everyone else is busy with kids or sunning themselves on a warm beach somewhere.

But then Heather won the lottery! And suddenly I'm going to Spain, everything paid for — I leave the day after I finish work. I can't quite believe it. She said she'd look after me, but I wasn't expecting this. It's all organized and paid for by them, and I can stay as long as I like. She's even given me some money to buy myself some summer clothes, bless her. I'm so excited!

Last night she called, and we talked for almost an hour. She told me she and James had had a long session and decided, in principle anyway, what they were going to do with the money. As well as me, they're asking a small group of close relatives over to Spain: James's sister, her husband

and children, Heather's mum. They're going to tell us their plans. Then Miles and Charlotte, their neighbours, are coming over. I presume they're coming later because they won't be part of the money discussion, not being family. I've met them before; they seem pleasant, easy-going people.

To be honest, when Heather invited me and said they were paying for everything, I wondered if the holiday was all they were going to give me — but then I thought, no, that would seem a bit mean. If they've won millions, they'll be more generous than that, surely. But you never know what money does to people.

It was exactly what Joanna thought, too, when I told her. "What, a measly holiday, for her best friend? I hope she's going to do better than that," she said. "And only to Spain? I'd have thought they'd have gone for Mauritius, or Fiji, or the Bahamas, at least."

I explained that James wanted to be able to get back to London easily for work. That started her off on another rant. "Surely he's not going to carry on working? Some people don't know their luck. I'd be off, I tell you, quick as a flash, sunning myself somewhere exotic, where all the celebs go. Now that would be fun, rubbing shoulders with the rich and famous. Palm trees, white sand, cocktails . . ."

I said, mildly, that I didn't think Heather and James were interested in joining the jet set. She harrumphed a little and went back to her work.

But I couldn't help wondering what they might be thinking, Heather and James. About me, that is. Although Heather says I'm part of the family, I'm not related to them, however long I've known them. Some families stick together and never let anyone else in. Heather's generous by nature, but I'm not sure about James. They'll have professionals advising them, too, I'm sure, and they always err on the side of caution, in my view.

I'm just hoping, because her name was on the lottery ticket, that Heather gets her way when the money is handed out. A holiday is lovely, but years of being her best friend must be worth more than that, mustn't they? I even started thinking of diplomatic ways to ask for more before I realized what I was doing. I stopped myself right there: it's not a good look, being seen as grasping by your best friend.

Joanna wasn't helping. "I bet that's it, you're getting a nice holiday out of it, and no more. They'll close ranks on you, you mark my words. I'd have something to say about that. You know who your friends are, when they come into money, that's for sure."

I kept my mouth shut. She subsided a little after that, but she had set in motion a train of thought in my head that I couldn't seem to bring to a halt.

* * *

I'm going to be travelling with James's sister, Liz, her husband, Steve, and their kids. Heather's mum's not coming, which is a shame, since I like her, but she's getting on a bit and doesn't like flying.

A car will collect me from home and take me to the airport where I'll meet them at the BA desk. That's a first for me: I'll feel special before I've even got there! I've met Liz and Steve once before, only briefly, but I've heard all about them from Heather. I know she's not all that keen on Liz, and is worried about spending so much time with them, so I'm hoping I can help with that, perhaps add something to the group to divert the pressure from Heather. I suppose it will be easier once Miles and Charlotte arrive too. It must be a huge villa, to fit us all in comfortably.

Then, thinking about it, it occurs to me that I'll be a bit of a spare part, especially if Heather's mum's not going. I'll be there with two, then three, couples. That's not my idea of fun. It's not that I object to having men around, not at all, it's just that the dynamic changes for us single people when we mix with couples. There's an unspoken bond between individuals in a couple. There are unwritten rules of engagement, so to speak. While I resent not being invited to dinner parties and events because I'm on my own, I've always hated being the odd one out. You can't win, really, when you're on your own. You go to bed on your own, you get up on your own, you're the odd one out on the walks, at the table in the restaurant, at the New Year's Eve party. You have no choice but to walk into gatherings on your own, hoping you'll find someone you know before people realize.

Then I get to wondering if there's a chance that Nick could come. I do like him a lot, and I know he likes me. We don't have a lot of time together when we're working, and it would be lovely to relax together, all expenses paid, no pressure. And we're both adults, both realistic. I'm sure we could have a lovely time, even if it doesn't lead to anything.

Then I get to wondering how much space there really is in the villa: it certainly sounds enormous. Maybe we could even start with separate rooms, and let things move on gradually. Then there really would be no pressure — except, I suppose, that he'll know nobody. But he seems the kind of person who would take that in his stride. He's well travelled, a man of the world. He might even have been to this place, Zahara, before. Would it be too much to ask Heather if he could come?

CHAPTER TWENTY-SEVEN

Heather

"Mum, this is the most brilliant holiday ever." Harry plumps himself down on the lounger beside her, his pale body glistening with water from the pool. "I like being rich!"

"It is fabulous, isn't it?" she says, looking up from her book. She's taking the opportunity to read some of the books she's wanted to read for years. "But be careful, don't get too used to this. You and Ben will have to go back to school at the end of the summer, and you don't want it to be too much of a shock. And remember—"

"'Don't go around saying we're rich'. I know, Mum, don't worry, we have got the message. But there's weeks to go before we have to go back. I'm going to be an expert kite-surfer by then! Can we come here for every holiday, Mum? It's the best place."

They've booked daily lessons for the boys at nearby Tarifa. The teacher is a lean, tanned Spanish lad called Miguel, with curls reaching to his shoulders and interesting taste in surfing shorts. He collects the boys every morning, drives them to the beach and spends two hours giving them instruction before dropping them back. Though they're both still finding it hard, battling the massive winds of the Atlantic coast, they are already in love with the waves, the speed of the kites and the spectacle of watching the experts twist and jump and fly. They come back full of enthusiasm, tired but happy. Heather and James have watched them a couple of times, but they both prefer the peace of the villa, with its crystal-clear pool and its shady spots on the terrace.

The boys arrived at the end of last week with their bags and their noise and their mess. With the nucleus of her family together again, Heather feels immediately more settled, safe and anonymous in this beautiful environment. The social media onslaught, the threat of the newspapers, the stress of having that pile of money in the bank doing nothing: all this has taken on a dreamlike quality. The boys are so solidly themselves, unchanged in their reactions, delighted by what they're doing, she's beginning to believe they can keep the money in perspective. Now that some of the decisions are made, too, she feels more secure, as if the ground is more solid under her feet and she can start to walk with confidence again.

Her plan to do something special with the rest of the money is still there in the back of her mind, to be brought out in quiet moments, mulled over and embellished. It brings a secret thrill to know that there's so much possibility, opportunities just waiting for her to grasp them. She has yet to discuss her idea with James, but she's already begun to research online. By the end of the summer, she hopes to have a concrete plan, so that once the boys are back at school she can start putting it all together in earnest.

She watches as Harry dives into the pool with a yell of delight, all bony legs and arms. Ben is already lounging there on a huge plastic rubber ring, looking cool in a peaked cap and sunglasses. She was quite extravagant at the local shop, buying armfuls of pool toys, parasols, chairs for the beach, sun hats for everyone including the guests, and piles of brightly coloured towels. But for once she was happy to indulge her children, and it was a good feeling not to have to worry about the expense. All this would be well-used in the weeks ahead, she told herself as they carried their unwieldy haul back to the villa. They can afford to be extravagant once in a while.

James, too, laughed at the piles of purchases, only saying mildly: "The money'll run out sooner than you think, guys, if you go on like this." But he didn't mean it. The boys just laughed.

* * *

When she invited Natalie to Spain, Heather began to understand how little Natalie had to look forward to.

"That's . . . wonderful." Natalie's voice broke with emotion at the end of the line. She sounded close to tears. "Thank you so much. I can't tell you what it means to me. I was dreading the summer . . ."

"Oh, Nat, why? I thought you loved the long holidays."

"I do. Well, I did. I love not having to do my bloody boring job. But I have nobody to go away with, and all my money seems to go on rent. It's great having six weeks off when you can do something with it, not so good when you can't. So this is brilliant! Now I can really look forward to it."

"I'm so glad. You deserve a holiday. You can stay as long as you like — the whole of the summer holidays, if you want to. You'll love it here. The villa is just fabulous, with a gorgeous view, right at the end of a long, sandy beach. You can swim in the pool or the sea within minutes, if you want to. Bring all your summer kit — it's very hot indeed. You won't need a hat, we've bought lots, there's one to suit everyone."

"I'm not sure I've got much in the way of summer clothes," Natalie said. "They're all up in the attic. Last summer was so bad I barely got my shorts out! Perhaps I'd better get some new ones . . ."

Heather imagines Natalie already worrying over what she should pack. "Listen, don't buy anything. Or at least, buy some things if you want, but I'll pay for them. I know money is tight for you, and I'd like to help. Please let me. You wouldn't have to buy anything if you weren't coming, after all."

A muffled sob at the end of the line. "Thank you, Heather, I'm . . . I don't know what to say. Perhaps I will get a couple of things."

"I'll reimburse you, okay? Just let me know what it costs. And we can get more when you're out here. The shops are lovely, quite different from at home."

"Brilliant. Can't wait, Heather, thank you so much."

This is all such new territory. While Heather has always tried to be generous, giving to charity, to the homeless girl at the Tube station, dropping her coins in the collection boxes until she has none left, she's never had this kind of money. Will people think she's patronizing them if she offers to pay for summer clothes, or for everyone's meals in restaurants? Perhaps they'll resent it if she doesn't. Perhaps from now on she and James will be expected to pay for everything. They'll have to learn new boundaries, set new rules, or risk making terrible mistakes.

CHAPTER TWENTY-EIGHT

Before

"There's nothing to eat," he says, looking at me as if it's my fault.

"I know. I went to the cashpoint, but it didn't work. I tried three times, and then it swallowed my card. So I couldn't do any shopping."

"Can't you use your credit card? Just for the moment . . ." His eyes slide away from me, and I know he's avoiding telling me. My credit card is not an option; I don't even know if I can pay the monthly minimum.

"It's maxed out. Please, tell me what's going on?"

"What do you mean? There's nothing going on."

"The joint account's overdrawn, but I've barely spent anything this month . . ."

He controls the joint account, as he does everything else. He must know what kind of state it's in.

"I told you, I'm waiting for payment. If there's nothing in the joint account, it's because you've spent it. You'll just have to use your credit card." His voice is harsh, his shoulders hunched as he turns away from me.

I bite my lip. I'm frightened of him now, after the last time. It was hard to hide the bruise on my cheek, and I was lucky not to have a black eye. I know he's under enormous pressure and I want to help, but he won't let me go to the bank; he says I'm hopeless with money. I *might be hopeless, but he can't talk about it without losing his temper. Perhaps it's true, I'm not good with money, but everything we had went into his business, including my dad's inheritance. All of it. Every time I think of it, I feel sick.*

There's no one to talk to. My parents are gone and my sister is three hundred miles away and has no idea we're going through this. He won't let me tell anyone. He's so proud.

What am I going to do?

CHAPTER TWENTY-NINE

Heather

"But we barely know him." James's reaction is no surprise. It's exactly what Heather thought when Natalie suggested they invite Nick to join them in Spain. "Why would we invite someone we don't know? Let alone pay for him."

Heather has just finished a long call with Natalie, who called late, forgetting the time difference. James is already in bed, his laptop perched on his knees. She sits on the edge of the bed and kicks her sandals off.

"She's not suggesting we pay for him. Just that he joins her for a holiday, while she's here. Not for the whole time, just a week or so. I do understand; she thinks she'll be a spare part, the only singleton with three couples. But it is awkward."

"But she's only been seeing him, what, a few weeks?" James's idea of a relationship involves years, not weeks, and in this situation Heather's inclined to agree with him. It's the damn money again, making everything so complicated.

"I think it's more like three months now. But I agree, he's relatively new, and even I haven't met him yet. I suppose it's too much to ask, that things could be straightforward?"

"We have to be careful. Are you sure she hasn't told him about the money?"

"Well, if she has, I'd be surprised, after all I've said to her. But you never know, I suppose." It's true Natalie hasn't always been good at keeping confidences, but there's a limit to how many times you can ask a friend the same thing; one more time and it will look as if she doesn't trust her.

"What does this guy do, anyway?"

"His name's Nick. He's an antiques dealer, has his own business. Beyond that, Natalie can't tell me much, except that she likes him. She hasn't said a lot more, but I think she has high hopes." Natalie always has high hopes, but usually they come to nothing. This one does sound as if it might last, though, if only because she's not talking about it much.

"Can we trust him? If everyone knows except him, it'll be pretty tricky, especially as it's the reason we're here. Almost impossible, I'd say. We'll have to agree what we can tell him."

"I know. It's so difficult, James. If we tell people we've come into some money, the first thing they'll wonder is 'how much?' It's a natural reaction. We don't know if he'll put pressure on Natalie to tell him, or how trustworthy he is."

James looks thoughtful. "How about this? We agree the story with everyone who knows the truth, tell them to say this and nothing more. We say my business is doing really well, we've had an extra-good year, and we're taking a well-earned break with some of the profits. I'm in the money business, after all. People often think we're wealthy anyway, just because I work in finance."

She pulls off her dress and drops it in the linen basket. It's good to know that the washing will be done without her, her clothes returned clean and ironed, as if by magic. At home, she'd find this one more thing to feel guilty about, but while she's here she's going to enjoy it. "Brilliant, James! That would work. It'll put people off the scent, anyway. Better than saying we've had some kind of mysterious windfall."

"Indeed."

"Shall we say yes, then?"

"Have we got the room? Are they . . . ?" James raises one eyebrow suggestively.

"Oh Lord, I don't know. Probably. I could ask, I suppose. If not, though, we won't have the space, unless we put the boys in together. Though I don't suppose they'll mind, for a week or so."

"Okay," James says. "I know you want to do it for Natalie. Let's agree that he can come for a week, at the same time as Miles and Charlotte, on condition that she only tells him the official story and no more. We'll have to brief all the others properly, so there's no way he'll get the full story. Then, if we decide he's a great person, totally reliable and good company, he can stay for longer. If Natalie wants him to, of course."

"Phew. That's great, thank you, James. I feel better about it now. But let's not have Liz and Steve stay for too long, eh?"

He winks at her. "Why on earth not?"

"I'm just not going to answer that."

* * *

Natalie, Liz and her family arrive on Friday; Charlotte, Miles and Nick, the following Wednesday. That's a few days to discuss the money with the closest family, followed by a full house for at least a few days.

Room allocation: herself and James; Liz and Steve; Natalie; Miles and Charlotte; four teenage kids; Nick possibly with Natalie, possibly on his own. Eight adults, four kids. Thankfully, there is enough room: there are seven bedrooms in all, though one is a single room on a lower level, with only a small window overlooking the garden. It's nice enough, if you don't mind a little less luxury than the others, and it has its own shower room. Nick will take this one, if he's not with Natalie. Otherwise, if the boys and their cousins are happy to share, there will be enough space. Heather decides to have all the bedrooms made up anyway. It'll be a lot of work for their housekeeper, Carmen, but no doubt she's being paid well.

She lives with her extended family, just down the hill from the villa. Her English is halting, so explanations have to be slow and precise, but she seems to understand most of what Heather says. She always has a smile on her face. She's discreet, usually arriving once the family is up and out on the terrace or in the town, doing her work thoroughly and without fuss. She keeps the house immaculate.

James is working on suggestions for 'activities' for the full group. He's planning daily outings, arranged so that people can choose to go or not, lunches and dinners at local restaurants and bars. Water sports lessons for the youngsters, every day. Horse riding in the surrounding hills, boat trips, visits to nearby Seville, Cádiz, Jerez.

An organized timetable is not something Heather would choose to do; she'd rather take each day as it comes, deciding to get up late, to stay at the pool, to walk into town when the fancy takes her. But with a bigger group she can see the logic. Hanging around the pool reading novels isn't for everyone, and the kids will certainly need some kind of routine. She hopes he doesn't include nightclubs. She hopes he leaves them some 'down time', particularly for the introverted types, like herself.

And that they won't all stay for too long.

CHAPTER THIRTY

Heather

"We're here!" Liz's voice carries round the side of the house, and despite all her plans to be relaxed about her sister-in-law, Heather's heart sinks. She'd heard the car draw up outside the gate, one of the boys running to answer the buzzer, and there was just enough time to pull her dress over her costume before figures appeared at the door to the terrace, squinting in the glare of the sun on the smooth white tiles.

She walks over to welcome them, slipping on her sandals as she goes. Liz and Steve step out into the sunshine first, in a flurry of kisses and hugs and exclamations, Joshua and Cara following, gazing around them with expressions of amazement.

"Heather, so lovely to see you, thank you so much for asking us here . . . the flight was lovely, in business class, we've never had the luxury before." Liz is in full flow, then. "We got champagne! Well, some kind of bubbly, anyway. That view is just stunning, and the villa looks fantastic. I can't wait to look around. What a fabulous pool! Are you enjoying yourselves, boys?"

"Welcome, everyone," Heather says, giving Natalie, bringing up the rear, a special hug. "I'm so happy to see you!

You're going to love it here: it's beautiful, as you can see, and we've got some brilliant things planned. Come and sit down — I think James and the boys are onto the drinks."

They've already prepared the big dining table on the terrace. Two huge umbrellas cast large squares of shade across the space while the chairs with their brightly coloured cushions are arranged so that everyone can admire the view. James leads the way with two large jugs of Carmen's home-made lemonade, while the boys bring wine coolers, champagne and jugs of iced water. It's late afternoon and they plan to stay home tonight, to allow their guests to rest after their journey. They're going to sample Carmen's excellent salted fish tonight, bought fresh from the market today.

"How the other half lives!" Liz says, winking at Heather and raising her glass, bubbles sparkling at the surface.

Heather sighs inwardly.

James takes his cue and stands, looking around the table, waiting for the boys to finish pouring the drinks. "To us," he says, picking up his glass. "And many thanks indeed to my wife, for acting on an uncharacteristic whim and buying a certain lottery ticket. Without her, none of us would be here."

"Well done, Heather — always knew you were a dark horse." Steve has changed into a dazzling Hawaiian shirt and long shorts; his legs, pale and skinny, seem out of tune with the rest of his corpulent body. "My wife spends all my money on lottery tickets, and not so much as a penny comes back. I want to know how you did it! Cheers all . . . and thanks for inviting us here." He turns to Heather and James and lifts his glass.

"To Heather!"

"To Mum!"

"To us all!"

Heather smiles and raises her glass, taking a tiny sip. The last thing she wants to do is get drunk tonight. It's stressful enough, this spotlight on the money.

* * *

Later, while the others settle into their rooms for the night, Heather and Natalie find themselves alone on the terrace, a gentle breeze stroking their bare arms. James has brought citronella candles to the table to discourage the mosquitoes and a golden glow flickers on their faces as they lean in, elbows on the table. Round the edge of the pool, silvery lights shine from beneath the water, ripples sparkling across the blue surface.

"I can't thank you enough for this, Heather," Natalie says. "It's just beautiful here, it's like a dream holiday for me. I can't tell you what a difference it's made, already."

"Will you stop saying thank you?" Heather says, laughing. "It's getting on my nerves now."

Natalie smiles. "Only after I've said it one more time, for letting me invite Nick. I really do appreciate it. I know it's a bit of a risk, but I wouldn't have asked if I didn't think we could trust him. I hope you know that."

Heather nods. "Of course. I hope it works out for you: perhaps it'll help, to be away. Our story, for Nick and anyone else we happen to meet, is that James has had an exceptional year at work and we're relaxing on the profits. No more than that — okay?"

"That's fine. I'm sure he won't question it. He's quite sophisticated . . . well travelled, easy-going. I'm sure you'll like him."

"I'm sure we will. But listen, while I've got you alone, I've got something to tell you . . ."

CHAPTER THIRTY-ONE

Heather

She wakes to the sound, through the open window, of breakfast dishes being laid outside on the terrace. Glancing at her watch, she wonders which of their guests is up and about. James sleeps on beside her, though it's already eight o'clock, much later than their usual waking time.

She loves this time of the morning in Zahara, when the light is soft and kind, the air fresh, before the heat of the day arrives. From their bed, the view of the sea is breathtaking. Tiny waves sparkle and glisten, birds wheel and call to each other, the sound whipped away by the breeze. The ocean lies in turquoise, aquamarine and grey stripes, darkening towards a razor-sharp horizon.

There's no rush: everyone here helps themselves to breakfast, arriving and leaving when they wish. The days are long, punctuated by meals that start and finish late, without formal routine. The boys will be up and getting themselves ready for their kitesurfing lesson; for once they need no chivvying along. They will almost certainly be back before anyone else is ready to go out.

Last night she told Natalie what she and James wanted to do for her. Finding the right words had been hard; she was determined not to sound patronizing. It helped knowing this was the right thing to do, that this would mean a better life, for ever, for Natalie.

She described her dream of making a difference with the money, explained that she wanted Natalie to leave her miserable job and work with her. Natalie's eyes grew wide, her mouth dropping into a perfect 'O'.

Then Heather dropped the bombshell. "And we'll buy you a place of your own," she said, watching Natalie's eyes fill with tears, a wobbly smile spreading across her face.

"What? Really? You'll actually buy me a place? In London? Oh, that's . . . it's too much, Heather, I can't accept it . . . I—"

"Of course you can. We can't promise you a mansion in Hampstead, but it will be enough to buy you a decent flat in a good area. Anyway, it's decided, we've planned it all. James agrees with me, we want to do this for you. No arguments."

"My goodness. I don't know what to say. Are you sure? I can't believe it . . ." Natalie's voice broke, her eyes brimming over. She sat back in her chair as if in shock.

"Believe it. You don't need to go back to that job after the holidays. You never need to go back."

"Oh, Heather."

Natalie opened her arms and hugged her as if she would never let her go.

"Okay, enough now, you're soaking my dress," Heather said, brushing the tears from her shoulder. "Don't you dare thank me again."

"Am I allowed to thank James?"

"I suppose so. But only once, okay? This is all down to luck, and I'm so happy I can share it with you. You deserve it, Natalie. Thanks for being my friend."

* * *

144

"It went well," she says as she climbs into bed beside James. "Couldn't have gone better, in fact. She was stunned."

"Good. I hope Liz'll be happy, too." As usual, he's sitting up, working on his laptop. He closes it, yawning.

"She should be delighted. And Steve. I bet he gives up his job."

"Probably. But that's up to them; we can't impose conditions on what they do with the money, even if we think they're going to lose it all."

Another outcome she hasn't foreseen. It's really not so simple, winning the lottery. "So if they decide to blow everything, sell the house and sail round the world in a luxury yacht, we just have to say, okay then, good luck? Hm, that could be hard . . ."

"That's why we're not overdoing what we give them," James says. "We'll be putting them in a comfortable financial position. We don't want to be constantly having to bail people out — that includes the boys — and we need to make that completely clear. We're being generous now, and what they do with the money in the future is entirely up to them. It's not our responsibility." He pauses. "I hadn't really thought about that until just now . . . being expected to bail people out when they act stupidly, I mean. There has to be a cut-off point, but I imagine that's hard when people know you're wealthy."

"I see what you mean. Oh dear . . ."

"The other thing I foresee happening, by the way, is that once it sinks in that we're giving them some money, they start wondering what other people are getting — and then wanting more. I've seen it happen with clients, when they inherit money. They're delighted at first, but when they hear that someone else is getting more than them, they start to feel aggrieved, and that's when the trouble starts."

"Please don't say that." She sighs. "For once I was feeling pretty good about the money. I honestly hadn't realized how hard it's been for Natalie, surviving in London on what she earns. She told me she hasn't saved anything for her retirement. I don't know how she thought she would survive on the state pension."

"Many people don't. Not because they don't want to, but because they can't, especially in London," James says. "They look forward for years to stopping work, and then when they do, they have all this spare time, but can't afford to do anything with it. It's tragic."

"I wish we could help more people."

"We can — you will, with your big project. But it would be madness to give money to every person we know. People have to make their own way in the world, and where we can help, we will. But if we overdo it, some people will take advantage. We have to set limits, and stick to them. We're doing the right thing by our nearest and dearest."

"I hope so. James . . ."

"What?"

"You don't think . . . do you think Miles and Charlotte will be expecting something? I mean, we've invited them to join us and the close family — perhaps they'll expect something more than just the holiday?" This has been niggling at her ever since they asked them.

"Of course they won't! They're well off, as far as I can tell. He's always saying how well his business is going, talking about huge projects they're involved in. Property's pretty buoyant at the moment, and I'm sure he's doing nicely from it. We don't want to give money away where it's not needed — anyway, we agreed, close family and Natalie only."

"We did. Only I don't want the money to cause trouble with friends."

"I'm pretty certain Miles and Charlotte aren't like that. They were thrilled to be invited on a free holiday. To my mind, that's already way beyond the call of friendship . . ."

"I'm sure you're right." But though James is always the voice of reason, she can't ignore the prickle of anxiety at the back of her mind.

"It will all work out, believe me," James says, giving her a squeeze. "Think of Natalie's reaction. She'll never need to worry about money again. And neither will we."

She turns to switch off the bedside light with his words ringing in her ears. James is always right about money, but for once she is doubtful. She has never worried about money as much as she does right now.

CHAPTER THIRTY-TWO

Heather

They've agreed on a plan for Liz and Steve. They're going to pay off the mortgage on their house; property prices are low in North Wales, so it's not a huge amount of money. They'll also give her a lump sum that, if she invests it wisely, will give her an income large enough to ensure her family is comfortable for the rest of her life. Though Steve will be part of the discussion, James will make it clear to them both that the money is Liz's, and the decisions will be hers.

As Heather and Natalie make their way along the shore-line towards Zahara, their sandals dangling from their fingers, their hats pulled low over their eyes against the breeze, Heather's thoughts are with James, back at the villa, talking it all through with his sister. How will she react? What if she feels hard done by, that they could have given her more?

From the first, they have avoided telling anyone exactly how much they won, even if they asked. But Liz was, as usual, persistent. When James first called her to tell her the news, Heather, standing next to him, could hear her shrill voice screaming with excitement.

"How much? Come on, James, how much? Millions, tens of millions? I know, I'll suggest a figure and you say yes or no. Come on, is it five? More?"

James refused to play that game, only saying patiently: "We're not going into detail about how much, for good reason. Not to anyone — not even the boys. So you'll have to stop asking. Suffice it to say, it's enough to keep us all very comfortable for the rest of our lives, and that includes you."

"A hundred million?"

"The more you ask, the less you'll get."

"Okay, okay, you've got me there! Anyway, even if you never tell me, it's brilliant news!"

So it will be interesting to see how today goes. If they turn up at lunch looking happy, Heather will breathe a sigh of relief.

As they walk along the vast stretch of sand, the sea water cool on their feet, she reminds herself to stop worrying. They can only do their best for people, and that's what they're doing.

Natalie says: "You're very quiet. Are you worried about Liz?"

"A bit. She can be . . . unpredictable. She probably thinks we're mad, not going public; you know how obsessed she is with celebrity. If it was up to her, we'd be spraying champagne everywhere, going crazy spending. She'd be posing for pictures, rubbing shoulders with the rich and famous . . ."

"She sounds just like Joanna, fantasizing about living in the pages of *Hello* magazine."

"Exactly. You didn't . . . ?"

"No, of course not. But listen, getting back to Liz — honestly, I'd leave it with James. He really is very sensible, your husband. He'll know what to say if she starts playing up. And I'm sure you're being very generous."

"You're right. James is brilliant with her, and we are being generous. He keeps telling me not to worry, but it's hard. People who worry can't just turn it off."

"Even winning the lottery has its problems, hm?"

"Stupid, I know, but it does. I must learn to enjoy it. You're happy, aren't you?"

"I'm feeling fantastic." Natalie bends and picks up a tiny white shell. "Honestly, I slept better last night than I've done since I was a child. It's like all the stress has floated away. And I didn't even know I was stressed."

"Except for your job."

"Except for my job."

"And money . . ."

"Stop it. Okay, I was pretty stressed. But now, it's just brilliant! Nothing in the world to worry about."

Heather laughs, glad to have made at least one person happy. Natalie looks radiant this morning; she can't stop smiling. She takes Heather's arm and they meander on along the beach in comfortable silence, towards the distant, glistening town.

* * *

Lunch is at Roberto's, one of the open-air restaurants known as *chiringuitos* which spring up along the beach for the holiday season. Having wandered around a peaceful town closing up for the afternoon, Heather and Natalie are led to a large table shaded by a parasol. Most of the other clientele are in swimming costumes, some of them wet from the sea, but it's a good place to meet, with plenty of space between tables and music playing softly in the background.

They order drinks and wait for the rest of the party to arrive, watching families playing in the shallow waves, throwing brightly coloured balls, falling and splashing into the water. Children run along the beach, chasing each other while their mothers watch from beneath large-brimmed hats and umbrellas, towels spread around them. A soft breeze blows off the sea, ruffling their hair, cooling their sun-browned skin.

Natalie breathes deeply, lifting her face and closing her eyes. "Bliss," she says. "Wake me up when the others come."

"I don't think I'll need to," Heather says. "They're coming now, I can see them." She stands and waves at the little group as it approaches, the children ahead of the others, running and splashing in the shallows. James is walking with Liz and Steve, but she can't yet see their faces. Harry waves back and she can see him beckoning to the others.

"Hey, you," Heather says as Harry gives her a hug. "Here, Ben, come and sit down."

Ben flops into the chair beside Heather, looking around. "This place is so cool, I love it. The food better come quickly — I'm starving."

"Nothing new there, then," Heather says, smiling. Her son's face is flushed, or maybe he's caught the sun. His skin is still smooth and clear, while some of his friends struggle to control teenage acne. She hands him some sun cream, pointing to his face. He obeys without a murmur, to her surprise. He must be tired after the morning's lesson.

"How was the kitesurfing today?" Natalie asks.

"Brilliant. We're going to try tricks in a couple of days. You should have a go — and you, Mum." Harry's grin is mischievous.

"Oh very funny," Heather says. "Because I'm such a talented sportswoman, you mean? You won't see me anywhere near a kite surfboard, or whatever they're called. I'm quite happy to let you have the pleasure while I tough it out by the pool."

"How about you, Natalie?" Ben says. "You must be pretty fit, with all the gym stuff you do."

"I don't know, Ben. It does sound fun. I'll come and watch one day, see how I feel, but I think I might be a little bit past throwing myself into the air from a seaborne skateboard. Why don't you ask your dad and Steve? I'm sure they'll have a go."

"Have a go at what?" Steve says, pulling out a chair. Today's shirt is, if anything, louder than yesterday's, stretching somewhat alarmingly over his gut.

"Kitesurfing. The boys are already pretty good, I hear," Heather says. She watches Liz's face as she approaches, still in conversation with James. She looks happy, smiling as she speaks. James gives Heather a discreet thumbs up as he joins the group.

She can barely contain her sense of relief. He was right; it's all going to be okay.

"Kitesurfing? You thinking of joining the experts?" James slaps Steve on the back. "You'll have some catching up to do, that's for sure. These lads are already super-proficient."

"Dad, will you come too?" Harry looks hopefully at James. "Please?"

"I'll go if you do," Steve says, laughing. "Can't make a fool of myself on my own."

"Why not? It'll give you plenty to laugh at, that's for sure," James says.

"Really? Is this my husband speaking, or has he been kidnapped, and you're a clone?" James, exercise being a foreign land to him, has never taken up such a challenge in his life before. "Seriously, I don't want to spend all the money on hospital bills, James. Do you think it's wise?"

"I won't overdo it, I promise. Perhaps we should wait for Miles to join us, though — then the men will have another partner in crime."

"Miles will show you up, Dad," Ben says, with the unkind confidence of a teenager. "He runs most days, I see him on the way to school. He's way fitter than you."

"Thanks for your support, son. Now I've got to rise to the bait, haven't I? Come on, let's order before we all starve."

* * *

"More drinks, Senor, Senora?" The young waiter clears the table of the detritus of a good lunch, topping up glasses.

"I don't know if I can take another drop," Heather says. But James, in an expansive mood, nods and gesticulates at the empty bottle.

"Yes, go on — one more."

Liz and Steve agree. "We've got all afternoon, haven't we?" Liz says. "Nothing to do except enjoy ourselves. Fantastic. We do have something to celebrate, after all, don't we?"

"Okay, some water too, then. We don't want to wreck the day with headaches and dehydration."

"Good point." James nods at the waiter. "More champagne, more water, please. *Gracias.*"

The youngsters, eager to swim, have left the table and can be seen jumping in the waves close by. They're all good swimmers, but Heather keeps half an eye on them. Zahara's winds can cause strange currents in the ocean, and she doesn't want them out of sight.

She moves to Harry's chair, next to Liz. While the men are distracted, discussing the cricket results of the day, she can have a quiet conversation with her sister-in-law.

"So, everything okay, Liz?"

Liz turns green eyes towards her, a smile lighting up her face. "Everything's just perfect, Heather," she says. "How can it not be, here? You chose well, this is a great place to spend the summer. Though it is jolly hot," she remarks, leaning forward to pull the fabric of her dress away from her damp back. A bead of sweat makes its way through a glistening sheen of damp on her shoulder.

"I could get used to this kind of heat, as long as I'm here," Heather says. "I can't imagine what it would be like in grey old Shepherd's Bush." What a contrast the image conjures up. She wonders if she'll ever want to go back there, to the drizzle of West London. "But I didn't mean Zahara, or the villa. I mean . . . your chat with James, earlier . . ."

"Oh, yes, of course! Sorry, I was being dim. I'm like that sometimes, especially after a glass or two of the bubbly." She wiggles her glass to demonstrate, the golden liquid spilling a little onto the table. "I forget what I'm talking about, misunderstand people, start talking rubbish. Steve has to shut me up sometimes, I can tell you."

Heather's beginning to wish she hadn't started this. It would be much easier to talk to James later. He'll give her a sensible account of their conversation.

"So . . . what do you think — about what we're giving you?" It's uncomfortable being specific, but Liz is making any other approach difficult.

"Oh, sorry, there I go again. It's fantastic, of course, thank you so much, Heather, you've been so generous, I can't tell you—"

"No need to thank me, Liz, that's not what I meant. I just want you to be happy with your share . . ."

"Oh we are, indeed. Very happy." She takes a large gulp of champagne. "How could we not be? We'd never have been able to pay off the mortgage, let alone have a pot of money in the bank. We're so grateful."

"I'm glad."

Liz leans forward with a conspiratorial air, keeping one eye on James. But he's turned the other way, watching the boys jumping through the surf. "I couldn't believe it when I heard. It must have been amazing when you found out — I would have wet myself with excitement! Did you realize straight away?"

"Not straight away — I'd never done it before. I didn't even know how it worked."

"Never done it before! Your very first ticket. How lucky is that?" There's something in her voice, the way she says the word 'lucky', that puts Heather on her guard. But Liz is smiling, her eyes innocent.

"I know, extremely lucky," Heather says. "I never expected anything to come of it. It was a huge shock."

Liz moves a little closer, and Heather can smell the alcohol on her breath. "So, come on, Heather, how much did you win? You can tell us now, surely."

Heather glances at her warily. She's glad she held back on the champagne. "Liz. You already know the deal. James and I agreed early on not to say. It's best if we keep it quiet, for lots of reasons."

"But you can't keep it quiet for ever, surely? Promise I won't tell anyone . . ."

"No, Liz, I'm sorry. Honestly, it's for the best . . ."

Interrupting the awkward pause that follows, the boys reappear at the table, demanding ice cream. Thankful for the distraction, she busies herself getting them some money, hoping that Liz will give up.

But she's like a dog with a bone. As soon as the boys have gone, she says, raising her glass: "Oh well, I can always look it up online. Cheers, Heather!"

CHAPTER THIRTY-THREE

Natalie

Well, I wasn't expecting that. Never in a million years, in all my dreams, would I have thought I'd have this kind of luck.

Everything in my life, until now, has been a struggle.

Maybe not everything. As a small child, I was happy. My parents worked hard, building a successful business; there were always people coming and going at the shop, and I had plenty of attention from them. But I was often left to my own devices, and for friends I had my fantasies, my make-believe world where I was beautiful and slim and became a famous model. They made me happy for a while, until I realized how hard it was to go from fat to slender, from plain to beautiful. And I was never going to be tall enough to become a model. I was mediocre at school, at best, what with the bullying and the teenage angst. So when the family business failed, it was just another disappointment; I decided I was an unlucky person, and always would be. I would just have to put up with it.

But all that has changed now. I can leave my mundane, badly paid job for a new and inspiring one, working with Heather, helping other people. And I'll have a place of my own, no rent, no mortgage, all mine! It really is a dream come true.

The first thought I had after the news had sunk in was *I can't wait to tell Joanna.* Straight away, I realized I couldn't, and then remembered I'd already told her Heather had won the lottery, even though I promised not to. Stupid thing to do, now I think about it.

My life is about to change dramatically, though, and it'll be hard to hide something like that from Joanna. I suppose I might get away with leaving my job: I can tell her I applied for the new one months ago, and it's only just come through. But moving house as well? Joanna knows how broke I am. I could make up some story about coming into some money from an ancient aunt, or something like that, but I'm not sure she'd believe it. She'd know it came from Heather and James.

I felt terrible, lying to Heather.

Heather would be furious if she found out. I would be. She might even change her mind. That would be terrible, I couldn't bear it. So it mustn't happen. I'll have to warn Joanna about it again, make sure she understands that I'll be in big trouble if she tells. And I'll keep her at arm's length until it's all settled down. I'm going to text her now, make it crystal clear she's to keep it quiet. Then I'll cross my fingers.

* * *

I love everything about this place. The weather, the beach, the swoosh of the sea breaking on the sand. Even the wind, which messes up my hair, but makes me feel fresh and alive. The town is delightful, with narrow streets and cafés spilling out over the pavements everywhere. Little boutiques with beautiful clothes, jewellery shops, gift stores, everything so different from back home. The restaurants are brilliant, the food delicious — at least in the ones we've sampled. We're eating so well — fresh, healthy salads and lashings of fresh tuna. I can't imagine ever getting tired of it.

And the villa! It's the most beautiful place I've ever stayed. My room, as I sit on the bed right now, has a fantastic view of the ocean, all the way to Africa. I'm about to call Nick, who I've spoken to almost every day. I can't wait for him to see all this.

I am only slightly concerned about the sleeping arrangements. Heather, bless her, has tactfully had an extra room prepared in case we want to sleep apart. We've had sex, of course — I don't believe, at my time of life, there's any point waiting around, if you fancy someone — but we've never slept the whole night together. It would be nice to think he'd like to, but if he snores . . . Perhaps I've lived on my own for too long.

Since I texted Joanna to remind her to keep quiet, she hasn't stopped sending messages asking me all kinds of questions about the money. The first one said:

How much did she give you? Promise I won't tell . . . xx

I was shocked. Hadn't she got the message? I texted back: *I'm sworn to secrecy!* I was trying to keep the tone light, but she came back with: *House in the King's Road?* and a winking emoji. I almost dropped the phone. I decided not to text her again, not for a while, and even then, just with a bland message.

Heather's right. Some people don't know when to stop.

* * *

"Hey, honey, how are you today?"

I love it when he calls me 'honey', in his soft, sexy voice. I'm not going to tell him that, though, I don't want to come over all keen. This one's a keeper, as they say, and I don't want to mess it up.

"I can't tell you how well I feel. This place is doing me a world of good. I can't wait for you to see it."

"I'm looking forward to it. The weather here is terrible, hasn't stopped raining since you left. I'll be glad to get away from it." There are sounds in the background; he's pouring coffee. He likes his coffee black and strong; exactly how I like it.

Heather's been asking what Nick is like, as a person. I found it surprisingly hard to describe him. He's always relaxed, quietly confident, comfortable in his skin. I admire that, it's how I'd like to be. At least, that's the side I've seen of him so far. When a man meets a woman at our age and stage in life, we're both on best behaviour for a period of weeks, possibly months. We don't want to rush things; we circle around each other, learning as we go along the individual foibles of the other, accommodating them quietly. One of Nick's foibles is neatness; when I saw his flat I couldn't believe how empty it seemed. Every surface was clear, every book on the bookshelves arranged by size, no clutter anywhere. Unlike mine, which is kind of messy, filled with ornaments bought on various holidays, family photos, fairy lights round the door. His home looks as if nobody really lives there, while mine is definitely lived-in.

"Your flight's all organized, and you're meeting Miles and Charlotte at the airport. James has organized a car to collect you, so I won't see you until you get here. I'll probably be lazing on the terrace with a glass of something cold in my hand when you arrive."

"Sounds perfect," he says. "I'll be happy to join you. Should I bring a gift for our hosts?"

Such good manners.

"That's kind, but I'd say not. They're not short of money. Perhaps flowers or something, while you're here?"

"Good idea. See you then, sweetheart."

CHAPTER THIRTY-FOUR

Heather

So now they are twelve. It feels like more, with everyone gathered for drinks on the terrace before they go into town for dinner. As she helps Carmen with the drinks, Heather takes the opportunity for a long look at Nick, the only stranger in the group.

The first thing Miles said when he arrived was: "We found a loner on the flight and dragged him along with us. He's a good chap; I told him you wouldn't mind." Laughing, Nick shook hands with everyone including the boys, giving Natalie a long-drawn-out hug that made her blush.

"Showing Steve up, I see," Liz whispers to Heather, nudging her arm. Next to Steve in his usual Hawaiian garb, Nick looks the epitome of cool in neat linen shorts and a loose white shirt.

"Seems like a nice man," Heather says. "I'm so glad for Natalie."

"I bet she doesn't need a man now, though, eh, Heather?"

Heather picks up a bottle to refill glasses, leaving Liz's side without an excuse. She's already tired of all the insinuations. She's going to have to get James to have a word.

"Miles, good to see you," she says, lifting her cheek for a kiss. "Hope you had a good flight?"

"Made very pleasant by the company of Natalie's friend," Miles says, indicating Nick, who's inspecting the pool with Ben. "Do you know him well?"

"Not at all. It just seemed the right thing to do, to invite him along with Natalie. She was delighted he could come. So . . . is Zahara new territory for you, or have you been this way before?"

"I have, actually. We're involved in a development just down the coast, in Tarifa. Luxury apartments, doing very well. I might even pop in while we're here, see how it's doing. And we've had an interest in a golf and leisure development a bit further away, in Málaga. So much going on down here, it's good business."

Miles seems to have his fingers in property deals all over the Continent. Ever the salesman, he's always talking about the latest deal, asking people if they'd like a part in it. If he hasn't already done so, it will only be a matter of time before he proposes some 'must-have' deal to Nick, or even Liz and Steve. She reminds herself to have a quiet word with them. It's not that she doesn't trust Miles, only that she doesn't want her family to think that she and James endorse his business deals just because he's their friend. As James has said, it's always tricky getting into financial transactions with friends. And friends of friends.

* * *

"So, how long are you here for?" Charlotte asks Liz, across the dinner table. Charlotte, as always, is beautifully dressed, in a white sleeveless shift dress and silver sandals, her slim legs already sporting a light tan. Heather looks down at her own choice of evening wear, her favourite navy linen frock. It's showing signs of age and is already crushed, wrinkles deepening across the folds of her stomach. She tries to smooth it away from her skin, then gives up with an inner sigh. She'll never look like Charlotte.

"Good question," Liz replies. "As long as they can put up with us?" She winks at Heather.

Heather smiles but refuses to be drawn.

"But truthfully, we have to get back for work in a week or so," Liz carries on. "We can't take the whole summer, like some lucky people."

Irritation rising, Heather turns to Steve, sitting on her other side. She finds him far easier to talk to than her sister-in-law. "How long did you take off work?"

"Ten days. Although now—" he says, lowering his voice so only she can hear, "—I'm not sure I want to go back, to be honest."

She looks at him in surprise. "To work, or to Wales?" she says, hoping he means the former.

"To work. I won't leave them in the lurch, but now we have a few more options . . . I'll have to go back initially, of course, can't be too hasty. You wondering when we're leaving?" he says, lifting a questioning eyebrow. "Had enough of us already?"

"No, of course not," she says, hoping the flush of guilt doesn't show in the candlelight. They're sitting at the front of a small restaurant, in an outdoor area flanked by planters full of colourful blooms. The air is warm here, the surrounding buildings blocking the wind blowing off the sea. "Just trying to be organized. We have some trips set up for the next few days; James is going to run through what's available tomorrow."

"Great — sounds good. To answer your question, I expect we'll be here a week or ten days, if that's okay with you."

"Of course," she says. "We're delighted you could come." At least that comment is partly true. She is happy they could come, for James's sake. But she'll be happy when they leave, as well. The party has grown just a little too large for her anxiety level.

* * *

162

"So, how are we all getting on?"

Heather swings round in her seat, wondering where she's heard that voice before. Julie is standing at the end of the table, a balding, smiling man hovering behind her. She waves at Heather and James, grinning around the rest of the table as if she's found a group of long-lost friends.

"This is my husband, Roger. I'm Julie, for those of you I haven't met. And you must be Heather's sons — Ben, is it? And Harry." Ben and Harry half-rise from their chairs, awkwardly shaking hands with the new arrival. The others, somewhat bemused, raise their hands one by one and introduce themselves. Julie flutters around the table, offering her tiny, limp hand to those closest to her, an enthusiastic wave to the rest.

She has swapped her shorts and flip-flops for a figure-hugging dress in a luminous pink so bright it dazzles. Huge silver loops dangle from her ears, her blonde hair piled high. If it weren't for the sun-lined skin on her face, you'd take her for a teenager. But you could scarcely imagine a more conventional-looking man than Roger. Dressed in a short-sleeved shirt tucked into neatly pressed beige trousers, with what looks like a golfing jumper draped over his shoulders, he looks more like Julie's father than her husband. He stands awkwardly, smiling from one person to another, as Julie shimmies round the table to hug Heather.

"So glad you found this place — did I recommend it? It's one of our favourites. Not for every night, of course, bit pricey for that, but lovely for the odd occasion. I see you're celebrating — I don't blame you, who wants to be in rainy old England right now! Zahara is such a welcoming place, I'm sure you'll all love it . . ."

Heather smiles and lets her chatter on. She catches James's eye. Should she ask Julie and Roger to join them? Would it seem rude if she doesn't? She shrugs her shoulders at James, hoping he gets her meaning, and is relieved when he rises from his seat to rescue her.

"It's great to see you, and nice to meet you, Roger," he says, shaking hands. "We'd invite you to join us, but tonight we're together for the first time, so there's lots to catch up on . . . a bit boring for you."

"Oh, no worries, we're not staying," Roger says. "We're eating somewhere else, anyway. Julie just spotted you from the street. Eyes like an eagle, my wife."

"Tell you what, when you're settled in, come for a barbecue at ours," Julie cuts in. The skin on her shoulders gleams with some kind of glitter. "We love entertaining, don't we, Roger? It would be great to get to know you better, and your family and friends, of course—"

Heather smiles weakly. "Thank you, that's very kind. We're not sure yet what we're doing for the next few days, but that sounds . . . lovely." It's the last thing Heather wants to do, and she's pretty sure James will hate the idea, let alone the kids.

"And listen," Julie says, undaunted, "if you're planning to explore or get the kids doing activities, do let me know. I can help with contacts if you need them, I know everybody round here. Might even be able to get you discounts . . . Not that you need them, of course!"

"Better get back to our guests, eh, Heather?" James says, ushering Heather away. "Good to meet you, Roger, we'll be in touch. Bye, Julie . . ."

Heather sits, a prickle of anxiety at the front of her mind. But before she's had time to catch hold of it, she's drawn back into conversation with Charlotte and Steve.

CHAPTER THIRTY-FIVE

Heather

Everyone appears for breakfast in various states of undress. James is fully clothed, the kids are still in nightwear, and a couple of the others have opted for bathing gear. The table groans with jugs of fresh orange juice, baskets of *tostadas* — large toasted bread rolls, served with olive oil and a tomato paste —fresh tomatoes, cereals and yoghurts. The aroma of coffee drifts around on a gentle sea breeze.

"So," James says, tapping his water glass with a spoon. "Ladies and gentlemen, welcome to breakfast and I hope you all had a good night's sleep. We haven't planned anything formal for your first full day here, so you can get to know the place a little if you want to. This morning, I can offer a relaxing option for those who want to chill out, and an activity option for people who prefer to throw themselves on the mercies of the Atlantic Ocean. Or you could try the compromise and go and watch those who like to throw themselves . . .

"The relaxing option is to stay here at the villa for the morning, take in the view and enjoy a gentle dip in the pool. Read a book, doze in the shade, chat to your friends and family, it's up to you. You could even stroll down to the sea and take a gentle paddle. For the more energetic of us, the kids will be demonstrating their kitesurfing skills, and we can join them and their cool dude teacher, Miguel, either to watch or to sample a starter lesson on the beach. That'll all be at Tarifa, about forty minutes' drive from here. I'm joining the action party, and we'll be leaving here at nine o'clock sharp. Who's with me?"

A forest of hands goes up, including Joshua and Cara.

"You'll love it, it's brilliant," Harry says with a grin.

Nick looks at Natalie. "Fancy going to watch your god-son? I doubt I'll be trying it myself, but I'd like to see how it's done. I've heard Tarifa is quite a place."

"Sure," Natalie says. "Though I'll be at a safe distance, on a nice relaxing chair on the beach. Are there taxis there, so we can get back if it's all a bit too much?"

"Of course. You can order one at any time, they'll be delighted to get your custom," James says. "Everyone, be warned: it gets very hot towards lunchtime so take hats and sun cream — and keep applying it. Sit in the shade if possible, the first couple of days. Especially you, Josh and Cara, we don't want you getting sunstroke on the first day."

"I'm staying put," Heather says. "Kitesurfing's far too energetic for me, even watching it. Anyone with me?"

Charlotte and Liz both put their hands up and Heather feels a jolt of relief that she won't be left on her own with Liz. She's not sure how much more she can endure, fending off those probing questions.

"That's great," James says. "We'll all meet back here around two o'clock and go for a late lunch in the town. It's all booked. You'll get used to a new, relaxed schedule here: nobody eats lunch before about two, and they often stretch it out for the whole afternoon. Kids, if you're going to be hungry before then, grab some snacks to take with you. And plenty of water!" The youngsters pile into the bread rolls, filling them with cheese and jam until the baskets are empty.

"Tonight I will announce the activity options for the rest of the week. All pretty flexible, no need to do anything if you don't want to, but there are some great trips for those who'd like to explore."

"Such as?" Miles asks.

"Such as whale watching, paddle boarding, horse riding, mountain biking, sherry tasting, and lots more I can't remember."

Murmurs of "Cool!" "Fantastic" and "Sounds good!" around the table. Heather smiles. James is in his element, never happier than when he can please others.

"My friendly local trip organizer, Antonio, will arrange anything we want, at short notice if necessary. Come on then, kitesurfers, let's get to it!"

* * *

At an extended lunch the morning's kitesurfing is the main talking point.

"Mum, it was so exciting — you should see how high they go," Cara says. "Please can we have lessons for the rest of the holiday?"

Liz smiles at her. "You need to ask your dad."

The adults are less keen to go again. James and Steve both tried their hands at it, with mixed results, James declaring that he'd had quite enough exercise for the entire holiday. "I'm glad I gave it a try, but it's not for me. I'm not as fit as I was."

"Dad, let's face it, you were never fit." Harry grins at his dad, who gives him an affectionate dig in the ribs.

"You'll carry on, though, won't you, Dad?" Josh asks Steve. "Come on, you've got to do a railey before we go home."

Steve laughs. "I think that's unlikely, Josh. I don't want to end up in hospital."

"What's a railey, Josh?" Heather asks.

"It's when you jump in the air and swing the board over your head . . ."

"Okay, I get the picture, but I don't want a demonstration. Sounds far too scary even to watch."

Back at the villa, some people rest in their rooms or in the shade, while the youngsters play a raucous game of tag in the pool. Heather places herself well away from them, so their screams and yells are muffled by the sounds of the sea beyond.

"I'm sorry we weren't able to help you find your place for this summer," Miles says, joining her in the shady part of the terrace.

She lifts the brim of her hat and watches as Miles places a jug of iced lemonade and some glasses on the table beside her.

"Thanks, Miles, I was just getting thirsty. I'm so relaxed out here, it takes me half an hour to decide to move."

"Here you go," he says, pouring the drinks and settling into the lounger next to Heather. "How did you come across this villa? It's a great find."

"It is perfect, isn't it? Thanks for your suggestions, by the way, we appreciate you put some work into it. In the end, I found this through a little travel agent in Shepherd's Bush. They were so helpful, really seemed to understand what we needed. Not that you didn't, of course . . ." she backtracked quickly, wishing she'd been more tactful. Miles had tried his best to find what they were looking for. Still, they'd paid him well for his time.

"It's a perfect spot, and the quality of build is fantastic," he says. "I can't tell you how disappointing it is sometimes, looking at developments out here, some of them very expensive. An awful lot of the supposed top-quality villas are jerry-built, won't last a minute in bad weather. But this one looks as if someone used a good architect, put some thought into it, and built it to a very high spec. It's discreet, too, which is great for people buying in this area. Quite modest at the front, and secluded, but opens up into a great amount of space."

"I'm pleased I found it. It would have been pretty frustrating to find it didn't work, after booking it for the whole summer."

There's a pause as a huge roar reaches them from the pool. Someone has thrown the ball right out of the garden. They'll have to retrieve that later, she thinks.

"So what now, Heather? Have you and James thought about what you're going to do next?" Miles lies back on his lounger, his eyes hidden behind dark sunglasses, a discreet Chanel logo on the arm closest to her.

"In what sense?" A flicker of irritation threatens her relaxed state. But it's a natural enough question, from a friend who knows.

"I was wondering if you're thinking about buying over here. I reckon a house like this would be a pretty good investment, and you could spend plenty of time here while the boys are still young. You'd get lots of use out of it."

"Honestly, Miles, we haven't talked about it." That statement, at any rate, was honest. They haven't discussed buying property in Zahara; it feels like they've only been there five minutes. "That's why we're here really, to decide what to do long-term, but we've got the whole summer to think about it. Though it's not a bad idea, buying here. This villa, even. What would something like this be worth, do you think?"

"A good few million, I'd say. It depends if you want something in Europe, close to home, or if you're prepared to go further and put up with jet lag. Like the Caribbean, for example. I can put you on to some beautiful properties there . . ."

She laughs and reaches out to put a hand on his arm. "Thanks, Miles. Ever the salesman. As I say, we really haven't thought about buying anything yet. But we'll let you know if we do decide to go that route."

"Just saying. Let me know if you want any help."

"Of course."

CHAPTER THIRTY-SIX

Heather

"What are we going to do about Julie?" Heather says.

The scorching heat of the sun has weakened, a few cotton-wool clouds hanging close to the horizon as they walk into the town for dinner. The group is spread out along the shoreline, James and Heather leading the way, the kids mostly behind, kicking a ball to one another as they progress slowly towards Zahara. The beach is quiet now, with only a few stragglers dozing in the late sun, dog walkers strolling along the edge of the water.

"What do you mean?" James bends to pick up a shell from the water's edge.

"I mean, she wants us all to go for a barbecue. She dropped a note in today, she wants us to go over on Saturday night. I'm really not keen, and I know the kids won't be, but it seems rude to say no."

"I see what you mean. Do we know where they live?"

"Yes, it's one of those town houses in the little row of seven or eight, on the way down to Zahara. You know, with the beautiful pink bougainvillea spreading over the balconies.

She says they're mostly owned by Brits, and they have a wonderful social scene going on."

"Sounds dreadful. I don't think a barbecue with people we don't know is a good idea at all."

"No, I'm with you on that. It could be really awkward. So what should I say? She's left a mobile number for me to call or text."

James thinks for a moment. "It's kind of them to ask — we're not a small group, after all. But I think it's out of the question. Tell you what, let's use that as an excuse and invite them — just the two of them — to come to us. It's no hardship for us, and that means we won't be surrounded by strangers. What do you think?"

"Brilliant — that's a great idea. Carmen can do the shopping and get everything ready, and we'll do the barbecue. That means the kids can come and go as they please, swim or go to the beach. Everyone will be happy."

"And — don't tell me you weren't thinking it — we can keep a closer eye on what people tell them."

She smiles, flicking a small spray of foam at James with her foot. "Do you know, sometimes it's irritating, how well you know me."

* * *

It's all organized. Saturday is the day for their whale-watching trip, and they're aiming to be back around six o'clock. A barbecue will be the perfect end to a day of being buffeted by wind and waves, swimming in small bays, and spotting whales and dolphins, if they're lucky.

In the end, they decided to invite Julie and Roger for the whole day.

"That's so kind of you — are you sure you haven't got enough people to cater for, without us tagging along?" Julie had said, when Heather called her to ask her. "Is Carmen helping you out? I thought so — she's lovely, isn't she? She and her family do lots of work for summer visitors. I've heard she's a great cook. Did you know her husband does the gardens here? He probably does yours too, perhaps you haven't seen him yet. You'll have to come to us later in the summer when your guests have gone back, then you can meet our little group — we're all ever so friendly, the men play golf together, the women go to Pilates . . ."

Eventually, Heather was forced to make an excuse to stop her talking, and was left wondering if they really wanted to invite her at all. She'll have to watch out for Liz, who seems determined to pump everyone for their darkest secrets, though probably they'll suit each other. Both seem to ask hundreds of questions and think up their own answers.

Heather narrowly missed having an altercation with Liz yesterday. It's left her with a new worry, that Liz is now determined to find out what other people are getting from what she calls 'the spoils'. Heather hates the term; it sounds as if they've wrestled it away from others, people who deserve it more than they do.

She pointed this out to Liz in a quiet moment in the kitchen. Liz said: "So what else are you going to do with the spoils, Heather, assuming there's some left over from the gifts to family and friends? Go on, I bet you've got some great plans . . ."

Heather made a determined effort to keep her voice level. "Do you think we could not call the money 'spoils', please, Liz? It sounds like we've stolen it, or come back from a war with a shedload of people's valuables."

"Really? I didn't realize you were sensitive about it," Liz replied. "I thought it was just a light-hearted way of describing money. I'll try not to call it the wrong thing in future. What's a better word: loot?"

"No!" Heather said, horrified.

"Only joking, keep your hair on!" Liz grinned.

Heather managed a weak smile. She really didn't want to fall out with Liz. Luckily, at that moment, Harry and Ben ran through the room in their swimming trunks, yelling. The interruption was enough for her to compose herself.

"'Loot' sounds like we're pirates. Or bank robbers. It's all just a bit . . . negative. Can we just call it money, do you think?"

Liz made a placating gesture with her hands, which had the opposite effect on Heather, who had a sudden urge to slap her. "Okay, I'll modify my vocabulary."

There was an awkward pause as Heather prepared a tray of coffee. But Liz wasn't ready to give up.

"So I'm assuming the others know what they're getting now, and we can talk about it freely? I don't want to cause any kind of offence, obviously, but just so I know, so I don't put my foot in it — are we getting similar amounts? Natalie and I, for example?"

This was too much for Heather. She took a deep breath, placed the coffee pot on the tray and faced Liz.

"Liz, I—"

"Hey everybody, come out here, quick!" Harry called, from the open doorway. "Come and see our new trick — hurry, we can't keep it up for long."

Brushing past Liz, Heather hurried to the terrace to see the four teenagers with Miles and James in the pool, the three tallest in the water, the others standing in a pyramid on their shoulders, wobbling alarmingly. She was just in time to see Cara, the smallest and lightest, in position at the top before the whole thing collapsed into a heap of laughing, spluttering bodies.

She didn't forget the conversation with Liz, though. Later on, James, with a sigh, agreed to talk to her.

CHAPTER THIRTY-SEVEN

Before

He can't look at me anymore. Not that he's home very much — he spends all day at the office, leaving before I'm awake and arriving home late in the evening. Sometimes he smells of alcohol. I don't say anything. I pretend to be asleep when he climbs into bed, the chasm between us worse than the empty, echoing space when he's not there.

There's no money left. I know he's borrowed more; I see the envelopes arrive, take the phone calls. I know we're on a horrible downward spiral and there's nothing I can do about it. The house is mortgaged to the hilt; my salary goes nowhere near it. I doubt we'll be given much more time here; the bank will foreclose soon and we'll lose our home. We should have sold up long ago, but he wouldn't hear of it.

The other day, they took the car away. His pride and joy. I hated that car; it smacked of showing off. But it seemed to bolster him. He's always been less confident than he seems; in many ways he's quite fragile. When we first met, I found that attractive — I liked the vulnerability; I wanted to look after him.

But he didn't want to be looked after. He wanted to control everything, and, at first, I was touched when he wanted to take care of me. I thought it was sweet of him to manage the house, the money, our holidays. He even chose our friends. Eventually all the people I knew and loved before we were married drifted away. You can only tell people you're busy so many times before they get the hint.

I got used to him taking charge, though I did sometimes worry that I'd be helpless if he died before me. Like my mum. By the time my father died, she'd lost the ability to make out a cheque or fill the car with petrol. At the time, I thought it was her mistake, that she should have stood up for herself more, but now I wonder if he had that controlling gene as well. Perhaps there are many men who treat their wives like fragile dolls, incapable of anything that needs a functioning brain.

I don't love my husband anymore. It's sad, but it's gone on too long, and he's a different person from the one I married. All I see now is the obsessive need to manage everything, even me, to the point where only he is right and everyone else is wrong. The anger that boils over if he's challenged. That part of it is frightening, it's so close to the surface. When he's in the house, I tiptoe around, not daring to speak.

I live in fear of the bailiffs coming. If they come when he's out, I'll have to let them take everything, and he'll be incandescent with rage when he gets home. If he's in when they knock on the door, I fear he'll become dangerous and violent, and end up in prison.

I've got to get out of here, even though I've got nowhere to go, no money, no friends or family I can turn to. Nothing.

CHAPTER THIRTY-EIGHT

Heather

They're welcomed onto their gleaming boat by a captain, a smiling cook and their guide, Antonio, a good-looking Spanish lad with immaculate English. The boat is large and luxurious, with comfortable vantage points for viewing and cushioned, shady areas for relaxing. Already, a mouthwatering aroma of fresh coffee emanates from below. They settle in straight away, looking forward to the day.

Almost as soon as they reach open sea, they spot a pod of killer whales, their distinctive white markings clearly visible through the waves, sleek bodies curving up and down in perfect harmony with each other, never seeming to waver or adjust their speed, even as the boat changes direction to give its passengers a better view. The children, who have never seen any kind of whale before, shout in excitement, pointing and taking pictures. To Heather, the creatures look benign, smaller than she expected, but Antonio describes them as some of the deadliest, most intelligent creatures in the sea. Later, a group of dolphins plays alongside them for a while, the lithe, glistening creatures showing off their acrobatic skills to everyone's delight.

They stop for lunch in a small, deserted bay surrounded by craggy rocks and sheltered from the wind. When they drop anchor, the sea is clear and turquoise. Encouraged by Antonio, they all swim, the kids jumping from the deck, the adults lowering themselves gingerly into the water from a short ladder, their sun-drenched skin flinching from the chill of the Atlantic.

After a brief but invigorating swim, Heather wraps herself in a towel and finds a comfortable corner to sit. Soon Charlotte joins her, looking slim and relaxed in a white swimsuit. Heather decides to keep her towel round her until she has the chance to dress properly; she's painfully aware of the contrast between their two bodies. Nonetheless, she's glad of the chance to talk to her.

"How are you doing, Charlotte?" she says. "I've barely had a chance to catch up, it's been so busy with everyone arriving and settling in. It's a bit different from Shepherd's Bush, isn't it?"

Charlotte smiles. "It certainly is. I'm having the most wonderful time," she says. "It's gorgeous here, and for me, not having to cook and clean and do all the drudgery is such a relief."

Heather is surprised. Charlotte always looks as if she's never lifted a duster in her life.

"I thought you had help at home."

"I don't have a job, so I've got the time," Charlotte says. "Miles earns the money, so it's only fair I do the rest. I'm getting into gardening, too — not that the garden's that big, but it's another thing on the list, isn't it?"

"It is, that never-ending list. It's the cooking that gets to me," Heather says. It occurs to her that now she can choose never to cook again. It's rather a pleasant thought, if she were that kind of person. Even knowing it's possible is reassuring.

"With kids, it must be non-stop," Charlotte replies. "Even for me, with only Miles to cater for, it's brilliant not having to think about what's for dinner while we're on holiday. Carmen is a fantastic cook, isn't she?"

"Thank goodness for Carmen," Heather says. "She puts me and James to shame, with our cobbled-together pasta and risottos."

"Does James enjoy cooking?"

"I wouldn't say he enjoys it. But neither do I, so we share it."

For a moment, Charlotte looks wistful. "I doubt Miles would know what to do with a packet of pasta. He doesn't want to, either. Anyway, he's always working."

Julie appears behind them, stepping down from the deck to join them in the shaded seating area. "What does Miles do, Charlotte?" she asks curiously.

"He's in property — has his own company," Charlotte replies.

"Sounds good," Julie says. "A great business to be in at the moment, I'd think?"

Charlotte is silent for a moment, and Heather, thinking she's missed the reply, glances at her face. In that instant, a look of profound weariness seems to pass across Charlotte's face. Or it could be Heather's imagination; it's hard to see her eyes behind the dark sunglasses.

But the next moment Charlotte looks across at Julie and smiles. "Sure."

Somehow, that draws a line under the subject, and Heather's left wondering what just happened. Julie sits back in her seat and sips from a bottle of water while Charlotte gazes across the water. But when Heather looks down at Charlotte's hands, she notices her slender fingers picking away at the skin around her nails, leaving tiny red trails where the blood has seeped through.

Later, she joins Natalie and Nick on corner seats at the back of the boat, while James and Miles climb to the front to take pictures. A canopy shades them from the glare of the sun.

She has never seen Natalie look happier. In the few days they've been here her face has relaxed, the stress lines on her forehead seem to have faded and the skin on her cheeks has

taken on a healthy glow. She and Nick sit close to each other, their shoulders touching.

"You two look pretty relaxed," Heather says.

"How could we not?" Natalie smiles, sipping from a glass of iced water. "This is just lovely, Heather, a perfect boat ride on a perfect day. Whales and dolphins appearing on cue. We couldn't ask for better."

"Everything okay for you, Nick?" Observing Nick over the last few days, Heather has the impression that he's a calming influence on Natalie. He always seems comfortable in his own skin, fitting in smoothly with the rest of the group, joining conversations deftly, never taking over.

"More than okay," he says, lifting his sunglasses onto his head. "This is a great spot, Heather. I'm looking forward to seeing more of it."

"Do you know the area at all? Natalie says you travel a lot."

"I do, but not so much in Spain. I'm in France quite often — I like their style, it's what I deal in, mostly. Sometimes further afield, but I've never really got into Spanish antiques. Bit too heavy and ornate for my liking, and a lot of religious artefacts. I hear you were in the museum business?"

"I was, mostly in marketing, but I loved getting involved with the exhibits. It's fascinating, if you like history, of course."

"Thinking of going back at all, when the kids are grown?"

She glances at Natalie, wondering fleetingly if she's given Nick a hint about the money. "No, I've got something else in mind, actually."

"Heather's setting up an anti-bullying charity," Natalie says, smiling at Heather. "It's okay to tell Nick, isn't it? We're going to work together on it, it's really exciting."

"Really?" Nick says, turning to Natalie in surprise. "Well, that's got to be good. So, you'll be leaving your job?"

Natalie nods. "I can't wait."

"That's quite a swerve, with your background," Nick says to Heather, putting his sunglasses back on as the boat turns. "Any particular reason, for the bullying part of it, I mean? Not your own kids, I hope?"

Heather and Natalie look at each other. "No, not my kids — well, only a hint of it, and the school has dealt with it well," Heather says. "But Natalie and I were both victims of it at school, and it wasn't a good experience. In fact, it took us both a long time to get over it."

It's not something she usually discusses with strangers, but there's something about Nick that makes her feel she can trust him. It's the quietness, maybe. He seems able to listen without judging.

He looks from one to the other, his eyebrows raised. "Really, you surprise me. You both seem so . . . well balanced."

"Yes, well," Natalie says, raising her eyebrows at Heather. "It's not a good subject for a day like today, is it, Heather? I'll tell you properly some time, Nick, if you really want to know."

"I agree," Heather says. "Let's enjoy the day. Looks like lunch is on its way — something smells delicious."

Antonio, leaning over from the upper deck, beckons them to a table groaning with dishes of food. But before they help themselves, he insists they taste his favourite sherry, pouring small glasses for everyone — including the children.

Harry smells his, crinkling his nose. "Ugh. I'll stick with the lemonade, thanks."

After lunch they doze in the sun or sit quietly watching the constant movement of the sea. Even the youngsters seem overtaken by the heat, seeking out the shady parts of the boat, prostrating themselves on long cushions. The heat and the wind seem to have slowed everything down, as the boat's rhythm rocks them gently towards Zahara.

* * *

It's an unusually sleepy group that arrives back at the villa, where Carmen is already preparing the evening's barbecue. Everyone heads for their room, or the shade of the terrace, for the rest of the afternoon.

Heather, leaving James to take a quick swim with the boys, washing off the salt from their afternoon dip, goes to their bedroom, where the air conditioning makes her shiver after the warmth of the outdoors. She showers and relaxes on the bed in a robe, gazing at the view from the window. Within moments, she's asleep.

She's woken by the soft sound of water from the shower, and is surprised to see that she's slept for almost an hour. She checks her mobile. She's been enjoying the freedom of having most of her closest family and friends right here, knowing that not many people have her new number anyway. But because of her mother, she needs to keep an eye on her messages.

When she opens the screen, she gasps. The words leap out at her like poisoned darts. She throws the mobile onto the bed and stares at it, aghast.

How can this have happened? Only the small group she's with, the school, the lottery people and her mum have her number. Nobody else. Who is this and why are they hounding her, stalking her as if she's some kind of criminal?

She hears the shower stop. Sounds from the bathroom warn her that James is about to emerge. She sits up, tries to compose herself.

But he knows her too well. "What is it? You look as if you've seen a ghost."

She picks up the mobile and hands it to him.

"You need to unlock it," he says.

With shaking fingers, she keys in the code, brings up the message and holds it out to him.

Rich bitch. You think you can escape. But I know where you are, you and your precious family. I know everything. The money can't help you. There's nowhere to hide.

CHAPTER THIRTY-NINE

Heather

She steps onto the terrace, shaken and unnerved. James's words ring in her ears — "Ignore it, it's just some joyless idiot" — but she can't shake the feeling of dread. Someone knows where she is, someone is watching her — and that person means her serious harm.

Everyone is here. The barbecue is smoking, the table filled with salad bowls, baskets of bread and drinks. Spanish music plays in the background; Carmen hands round aperitifs. From a distance, everything looks normal: people talking, laughing, enjoying the beautiful weather.

Is it possible that one of these people, the people closest to her in the whole world, is threatening her? Surely not. Why on earth would they want to, when all she's trying to do is be generous, and fair, and to make people's lives better? She sees their smiling faces from the doorway, tries to imagine who it might be — but each one looks open, guileless, incapable of being so cruel. Granted, there are people here she knows less well than the others, but even they have the trust of people she knows and loves. What could be their motivation for threatening her family?

The money, of course. She shakes her head, berating herself for being so naive. Since the moment the money arrived, her life has changed irretrievably. Has been forced to change.

People kill for a lot less . . .

If it isn't one of these people, then who can it be? She searches her memory. She has given her number to so few people. Perhaps her phone's been hacked: she's heard of clever people who can access almost any gadget they want. But if that's the case, it could be anybody, and she'll never be able to trust anyone — or a mobile phone — again.

She slips her sunglasses over her eyes. The last thing she feels like doing is socializing. What she really wants to do is find the biggest plate, pile it with delicious food — preferably cake — and eat it all as fast as she can. But that's not something she can do here, right now.

She pours herself a large glass of wine and sets her face into what she hopes is a neutral expression. Fortunately, the first person to approach her is Julie, perhaps the only person who's beyond suspicion. And Julie doesn't know her well enough to notice her mood. Roger hovers at Julie's shoulder like a benevolent shadow.

"Heather, today's been wonderful, so kind of you to have us. We brought you some flowers — Carmen is putting them in a vase right now. I love your dress! Everyone's looking flushed and healthy, aren't they? It was fabulous — last time we did that whale-watching trip, we weren't so lucky, it was all a bit disappointing, and we never tried again, I'm so glad we came along . . ."

"You're very welcome, and thanks for the flowers — there's really no need. Come and join us . . ." Glad of the distraction, Heather takes them over to the group, eventually manoeuvring them towards Liz and Steve. This gives her the chance to excuse herself, hoping they'll stay together for a while. Hopefully, Julie will talk Liz under the table.

She searches out Natalie, sitting by herself under an umbrella, slightly away from the others.

"Is everything okay?" Natalie says immediately.

"I — yes, fine," she replies. "It's just — oh, it's nothing. I should ignore it."

"Ignore what?"

They both look up as Carmen approaches the table with a plate of nibbles. Heather waits for her to leave.

"Do you remember at school?" she says quietly. "The bullying, the little notes, the whispering, the sly glances?"

"Of course I do. Why on earth are you thinking about that now?"

"I don't know how you did it, but you always seemed less bothered than me. You let it wash over you. Perhaps you were more resilient than I was." She takes a large gulp of her wine to mask the shakiness in her voice.

"Listen, Heather. I've never told you this before — or anyone, really," Natalie says, her eyes invisible behind dark glasses. She takes a deep breath, letting it out slowly. "As we're harking back, I suppose now is as good a time as any to tell you. I lied all the way through school. Probably these days, you'd call it compulsive. I lied to my parents, told them I was popular at school, had lots of friends — I even pretended I had boyfriends when I didn't. I told lies constantly, about where I was, who I was with, how I was doing at school. I told them I was happy, and in my little made-up world, I think I was. Beautiful, slim and happy. I lied to you, too, quite a lot, about the bullying. I pretended it didn't bother me, but it wasn't true. I don't know why I did it, but perhaps it gave me some kind of armour against all the nastiness. But I was just as hurt, just as miserable as you were."

"Really? I had no idea. I thought you were much better at handling it than me. I admired you for it."

"No, I was just better at hiding how bad I felt. I'm really sorry. It's not something I'm proud of, but I've lied all my life. At work, too. I've made up some brilliant stories, though I say it myself. It doesn't help sharing an office with someone like Joanna. It's too tempting not to make up stories for her — she's so gullible."

"What kind of stories?"

"Mostly my supposed love life," Natalie says, with a wry smile. "I've concocted some brilliant dating fantasies — I should put them in a book. Joanna's a great target, she'll believe anything. It's mean of me, I suppose. I've persuaded myself it doesn't do any harm, but it's not kind." She looks down at her hands.

Heather, shocked into silence, begins to wonder what else her friend has lied about.

But Natalie interrupts her train of thought. "Anyway, what's brought this on?"

Heather watches as the children help themselves to food, returning to the shade to eat, joshing each other, chattering like a gathering of little birds.

"I've been thinking about it a lot, because of the charity idea. Bullying then, when we were at school, was different, it was more . . . obvious, more face-to-face. Now, the bullies have gone online, where they're anonymous. They can say anything they like. It's devious, and in a way much more hurtful. It'll be a huge part of what we do, dealing with the fallout from unpleasant behaviour on social media. We'll have to be prepared for that. We — or at least I — have got a lot to learn."

Removing her sunglasses, Natalie gazes at Heather, her eyes narrowing. "Of course we will, I realize that. It will be a lot of work, but so worth it. I'm looking forward to it. But come on, I've told you one of my innermost secrets, aren't you going to tell me what's happened to make you feel like this? You seemed fine earlier, the day went really well. Something's bothering you, isn't it?"

"It's stupid. James says it's to be expected. But I honestly thought once I'd changed my phone number, it would stop. I had a lot of unpleasant messages at the beginning, when it looked like the news was getting out about the lottery — I probably didn't tell you, everything happened so quickly. I hoped it would stop, and a lot of it was on social media, which I've cancelled now. But someone's got hold of my number. I've just had a really nasty message. It was a shock."

"I knew there was something — I'm so sorry."

"Only a few people have this number, Nat, I've been really careful. I can't think how it happened."

"Listen," Natalie says firmly, "don't let it bother you. It is weird how people find your contact details, but it happens. And it probably doesn't help that you've disappeared. Perhaps that looks suspicious to these idiots, makes them more determined. They're sad and pathetic, with nothing better to do than be nasty and cruel. Honestly, James is right. Forget it and enjoy your holiday. I hope you didn't answer it?"

"I'm not that stupid. No, I deleted it straight away." She massages her temples. "Honestly, sometimes I wonder if the money is more trouble than it's worth."

"What? Now you're making things up. Believe me, it's the best thing that could have happened to you, and to your family — and to me, too. It's fantastic, in fact, and don't ever think otherwise."

Despite herself, Heather laughs.

"That's better," Natalie says. "Hold that thought and don't let it go. Now, let's join the party and forget all about the sick bullies."

* * *

Some time later, Heather finds herself sitting with Steve and James by the pool, watching the youngsters splashing around as the light fades on the horizon. Though she's known Steve for many years, she's never felt close to him, probably because he's always with Liz. But James has a number of times pointed out that on his own, Steve is good company: he loves storytelling, enjoys making people laugh. Right now, though, they're discussing his job. The last time Heather asked, he was working for the local council, looking after the parks and gardens, but that didn't last, like many of his previous endeavours. Now he's selling kitchens for a small company based near their home, and he's not enjoying it.

"It's okay, I suppose," he says, his Welsh accent lilting. "I like meeting the customers and helping them work out what they need. But I get paid a very basic salary, the rest is on commission. For most people, a kitchen is a big outlay, so it can take months to get them to commit. And then they change their minds, fiddle about with the design, nitpicking, wanting discounts, asking for changes where they're not needed. It's a frustrating business."

"What about the people you work for?" James asks politely.

"My boss is a pillock. Sometimes I want to smash his stupid face in, know what I mean?" Heather watches as his huge hand curls into a fist on the arm of his chair, his chin jutting with anger. Then, seeing the look of alarm on James's face, he grins. "Only joking, of course. He is a mean bastard, though. Until I get a sale, I'm earning the minimum wage, pretty much. I wouldn't say it's the best way to live. That's why this . . . your generosity has come along at just the right time for us. Liz likes her work, mind, but she doesn't earn a lot. Plus, we've got a few debts to pay off, so the money will definitely come in handy. It'll be nice to leave something in the bank for the kids, not just an overdraft!"

"Debts?" James flinches. "What kind of debts?"

Steve laughs, waving a dismissive hand. "Nothing much, really, just a couple of credit cards maxed out. Soon get rid of that, now you're helping us out. It'll be a big help. I was beginning to wonder how we were going to last out until retirement."

"Surely you're not close to that yet, are you?" James says.

"Not as close as I'd like — and it's one of those milestones that seems to get further and further away. I don't actually know when I get my state pension, and I don't have a private one."

"Honestly, Steve, don't rely on the state pension," James says. "It won't be enough to keep you going. It's much better to keep earning now, and save as much as you can. Are you thinking of stopping work, then?" Heather can see the internal struggle on James's face. He's longing to tell Steve not to spend all Liz's money, not to give up work. But he has promised himself to leave it up to them.

"Of course I am! Now we can party, party, can't we?" Steve says, with a grin.

James's forehead crinkles. He opens his mouth, closes it again. Heather tries to catch his eye to give him a sign. But Steve goes on: "No, really, don't look so worried. I want to start my own business — it's just a matter of what."

"I always think of you as multitalented," Heather says, giving James a chance to rearrange his face. "You must have loads of different skills, with all the jobs you've done."

"Jack of all trades, master of none, that's me," Steve says, cheerfully. "But I can't think of a single job I've enjoyed, not properly. That's the problem."

"For what it's worth, and you may not want my advice—" James holds up a hand as Steve starts to object "— but I would say, do something that inspires you. Something you're passionate about. Running your own business isn't easy, it needs lots of commitment and time, and now's your chance to do something you really enjoy. Heather's thinking of doing the same, aren't you, my love?" He turns to Heather, tapping her on the knee.

"But surely you've got enough to sit back and do nothing, haven't you?" Steve says, sweeping his arms around at the beautiful setting, the luxurious furniture, the table laden with food. "I mean, just look at all this. This is what I'd do, all the time, if I won the lottery. It would be champagne and holidays all the way, for me."

For a moment, he looks wistful. There's an awkward pause, as if he's expecting a response. But James just nods. Heather studies her hands, hoping someone else will speak first.

"Not that we're not grateful for what you've done for us, of course," Steve says at last, to her relief. "We're amazed at how generous you've been. I don't think I've seen Liz as happy for a long time."

He nods, looking from James to Heather and back. "But I'm sure you've got a bit left over, haven't you?" He winks at James, his elbow twitching. If he were closer, he would dig him in the ribs. "Keeping some millions in the coffers, eh?"

Like someone's pressed a panic button, Heather's guard shoots up. But James's hand is on her leg, a reassuring squeeze.

"Even if we have, we'll carry on working," James says. "I have a responsibility to my business partners, as much as anything — but also, I genuinely enjoy my work. It makes me feel I'm doing something worthwhile. I don't think I'd last very long, doing nothing." He watches Steve's eyebrows rise in an unspoken question. "Yes, really. Heather's keen to go back to something, too, now the boys are older."

"Not go back, actually — I want to create something new, like you, Steve."

"Really, what sort of thing?"

Cautious now, she keeps her answer vague. She doesn't want to give any impression that they still have a huge stash of money in the bank. Even if they have. "A charity, probably. But there's plenty of time to think about it. For now, I just want to enjoy the summer with my family."

She turns to see Liz and Julie approaching. Hurriedly, knowing she can't face any more interrogation, she gets to her feet. "Any more drinks, anyone? Coffee? More champagne? There's plenty of dessert left, by the way — can I get anyone anything?"

As she leaves the table, her feet heavy on the cool marble of the terrace, she feels the unwelcome flurry of panic in her chest. She busies herself clearing the table, taking care not to break the delicate wine glasses with her trembling fingers.

CHAPTER FORTY

Natalie

I don't know why I chose to tell her. Why now, why here. I surprised myself. It must be a reaction to the money. Perhaps it's because she has been so generous. She's proved to me that I'm worth her . . . love, yes, love. Heather and James have given me so much more than money and a house. They've shown me how much they care. Heather has proved to me that she values my friendship, and that's the best thing anyone has ever done for me.

So maybe I wanted, finally, to be honest with her, to repay her in some way for that heavenly boost to my self-esteem.

It's odd. Right now, I'm happy in a way I've never experienced before. It's almost a feeling of euphoria. For once, I'm looking forward to the future, a future that Heather and I will create together, a worthwhile cause that I can be passionate about and proud of. Something that might even last into the future, beyond our lifetimes — imagine that. It is the most brilliant feeling.

And for once, incredibly, I'm in a relationship where I feel relaxed. I'm not wrecking it by being overanxious. By overthinking it, overdoing it, being desperate, worrying constantly that I'll let myself down — or more likely be let down by someone else. Perhaps it's to do with the new self-esteem, or perhaps he's just the right person for me. With Nick, I feel that I can be myself without being scared of the consequences. It's a bit of a revelation, actually. Because he's good-looking, confident, well balanced, I expected that I would be even more anxious than usual about messing it up. But so far, so good. He's not using the extra room in the villa, he's with me every night and it's . . . well, it's very good indeed.

They're an interesting lot, this group. I thought at first it would be weird having someone here who wasn't quite in the loop, about the money I mean, but it doesn't seem to be a problem. Nick isn't the kind of person who delves into people's backgrounds. He just seems to accept that Heather and James have money and are happy to pay for everything. Probably he mixes with wealthy people more than I do, and has got used to how people with money behave. But it's another reason it works with him here. He seems very happy to live in the moment. Perhaps I'm learning to do the same.

I see now why Heather finds Liz difficult, though. Though she seems scatty and a little immature, there's a hard edge to her. Sometimes she watches people's faces as if she's evaluating them. Then she'll chip away at them until they tell her something personal, and she seems to file these snippets of information away for future use. I've noticed, too, that when she's had a drink, she tends to be a little sharp — bitchy, even — with people. It can be hurtful, and I know Heather's borne the brunt a couple of times. I wouldn't trust Liz either, if I was Heather.

I wonder who is sending Heather those texts. She seems really shaken by it. But when you think about it, if you really wanted someone's number, and you were connected with them in some way, however distant, it wouldn't be too difficult to get hold of it. You'd find a way, if you were really determined. Some people just set out to be cruel.

* * *

I'm up early for breakfast, though we were up quite late last night. I leave Nick asleep and throw on a robe, tiptoeing from the room to get myself a coffee. There's nobody else around, not even Carmen, as I creep around the kitchen trying not to make a noise.

We cleared everything last night before we went to bed; Heather was determined not to leave it all for Carmen. She's a great find, Carmen, she seems to enjoy catering for us all, and though sometimes communication breaks down, it works pretty well. Good food and wine, beautifully presented, and a spotless house. She seems to flit in and out like a zephyr, her presence so light you'd hardly notice her.

I take my coffee to a chair on the terrace, where I can sit in the sun before it gets too strong. I stretch, letting the wind ruffle my hair, and breathe in the delicious sea air. I close my eyes and drift.

A voice from behind startles me.

"You're up and about early." It's Miles, looking rumpled, his hair sticking up as if he's just fallen out of bed. He sees me looking, runs his fingers across his scalp. He's balding, the bare patch pink and shiny after a couple of days in the sun. "I wasn't expecting to see anyone looking so fresh after last night. I think I might have had a couple too many." He takes a chair at the table, a steaming mug of coffee in front of him. "Thank goodness for strong Spanish coffee."

"I don't know why I woke up so early. I think it's the light. But I'm not tired, anyway, I feel so relaxed here, I just wake up naturally. I love the mornings, too, before it gets too hot. Everyone still asleep?"

"Far as I know." He stretches a leg out, retrieves a mobile from his shorts pocket and punches in a code.

"Not working, I hope?" I say into the pause while he scrolls, his finger flicking.

"Not really, just doing a bit of checking. Nothing really stops for a holiday in my business, except at Christmas."

"Property market going well, is it?" I'm a little vague about what precisely Miles does, but feel I must show an interest, to be polite.

"Yes, pretty good. Summer's quiet in the UK, but some other countries, like here, are quite lively. Golf developments, holiday complexes, shopping centres. All relying on the tourist market. As long as the European economy continues to grow, there'll still be demand."

"Do you know much about this area? I'd like to see more of it, while I'm here." Now that we've settled in, I'm keen to explore, and I'm looking forward to James's schedule of trips.

"Parts of it." He stops scrolling, puts his mobile back in his pocket.

"Jerez sounds interesting."

"I haven't been there for a long time, but I remember it was fun. Sherry tasting and all that. I don't know the area too well, though there is a development in Tarifa we've got a finger in."

I wonder what he means by that, but don't want to encourage him. In the mornings, I prefer to take in the view, read the paper, wake up gradually. I'd rather not get into long and involved conversations about people's jobs. But I realize I'm not going to get the luxury this morning. From the sounds and smells drifting through the open kitchen window, someone else is up and around and making more coffee.

Soon Charlotte appears, holding a pot of coffee in one hand and a basket of fresh bread in the other.

"Morning," she says, sitting down. "How are you today, Natalie? Sleep well?" She places the coffee pot in the centre of the table and breaks a chunk off one of the bread sticks.

I'm about to answer when Miles says abruptly: "No milk — where's the milk?" I close my mouth, taken aback by his rudeness. I glance across at Charlotte, but her face is in shadow. If I were her, I'd be embarrassed, if not angry, at Miles's behaviour, but murmuring an apology she jumps up and hurries back into the house, soon to reappear with a jug of milk and some plates.

"I wasn't going to set up a full breakfast, but I saw the bread had been delivered and suddenly felt really hungry," she says, settling down again beside me, leaving Miles on his own at the end of the table. "Do have one, they're delicious."

Without acknowledging his wife, Miles grunts and leans over to pour the milk into his newly replenished mug. I wonder if he's really hung-over, or if he and Charlotte have had a row. His demeanour towards her is palpably unfriendly.

"Just don't eat them all, darling," he says, staring at Charlotte. "You don't want to ruin that bikini body now, do you?" His tone is smooth, but it's clear he's not being kind.

Charlotte's dark glasses conceal her eyes, but from the set of her mouth I can tell she's not taking it as a joke. I wonder if they're always like this when they're together. If they are, then the rest of their stay could be fraught, to say the least. But surely Heather and James wouldn't have asked them here if they thought there would be tensions?

To my relief, the awkward moment is interrupted by Carmen, calling from the kitchen door. "*Buenos días.* You want breakfast now?"

I jump up to help, glad of the excuse. Perhaps I'll take Nick a coffee. Thankfully, he always seems good-humoured in the mornings.

CHAPTER FORTY-ONE

Heather

A sound, outside — no, inside. Unsure if she dreamed it, Heather lies in that strange, floating place between sleeping and waking, listening. Nothing. She leans over to check the time: 5.15. The morning light is pale and weak through the blinds, casting an eerie glow onto the bed. James's form lies peacefully beside her, his chest rising and falling with his breath.

There it is again, a tiny scratching noise, outside the bedroom. This time more certain, she grabs her robe and creeps silently to the door. It doesn't sound like a person, it's too small a sound. Perhaps there are mice in the house? Unlikely, with all this marble. Or a bird has flown in and can't find its way out. It certainly doesn't sound like an intruder. Gently she turns the handle, opening the door a crack. Straight away, a dark shadow brushes past her ankles.

A cat. In one smooth, effortless movement, it settles on the bed next to James, gazing at her as if to say: *Come on, then.* Even in the grey light of the early morning she can see it's well fed, its coal-black coat smooth and glossy, its eyes shining.

195

"How did you get in?" she whispers, tickling its ears. It answers with a deep rumble. "Okay. You're right. It's far too early to get up."

But she's wide awake now, and thirsty. Silently she slips through the doorway and makes her way to the kitchen. When she gets there, she's startled by a touch on her leg. The cat has followed her in. Opening the fridge, she pours a saucer of milk and sets it down in the shade just outside the open door to the terrace. Somebody must have forgotten to lock up. It's not surprising, given how late they were up last night, how much they'd all had to drink by the time they drifted off to bed. But it gives her a jolt of fear. If the cat can get in, then so can a person.

The cat sips delicately, its pink tongue flitting in and out between sharp white teeth.

She returns to the fridge, where the remains of last night's spread fill every shelf. There are salads in plastic boxes, cold meats and fish under kitchen foil, fruit salad in a large bowl and the remains of the boys' favourite, Eton Mess, on a plate on the bottom level. One entire plateful of it was consumed last night, and this is what's left of the second one.

With a furtive glance over her shoulder, she takes everything out, spreading the dishes over the worktop beside the fridge. She works quickly and silently, starting with the cold meats and fish. Her fingers take on a life of their own, grabbing whatever they can, stuffing slices of smoked salmon and ham into her mouth. There are a couple of leftover *tostadas*; she butters them liberally and fills them with a huge pile of egg salad, chicken and lettuce. Great gobs of mayonnaise squeeze through her fingers, falling onto the worktop as she shoves the makeshift sandwich into her mouth. She pours water into a jug, gulping directly from the lip, the liquid splashing onto her robe, the skin of her chest. Her belly begins to stretch and gripe, but she's not finished yet. Returning the leftovers to the fridge, she takes the dish of Eton Mess to the breakfast bar, finding a spoon in the drawer beneath. She pours a great pool of cream over the pile of fruit and meringue and demolishes it, wiping juice and crumbs from her chin with her spare hand.

At last, it's gone. Crouching over her bursting stomach, she washes and wipes, putting everything back in its place. The cat is long gone — inside or out, she's not sure — but she washes up its bowl too, and puts it away.

She checks the floor for evidence, and, satisfied that all is as it should be, heads for the washroom by the front door.

* * *

"I think we need to increase the security here."

James glances up in surprise, in the process of dressing, his chest bare. The tan on his arms ends abruptly just above his elbows, making the rest of his body look whiter than ever, bar a triangle of brown at his neck.

"Why, what's happened? Not because of that silly text, surely?"

She turns away, steps towards the window. "Not just that, no. Though it has really unsettled me. It's scary, James. I know it's just words, but words can be deeply hurtful. It's bringing up all sorts of stuff that I thought I'd forgotten. And actually, that message was intentionally threatening — *I know where you are, you and your precious family* — that's a downright threat, not just to me, but to you and the boys as well."

"It is pretty threatening, but in our situation . . . you're not thinking we should involve the police, are you?"

"No. Yes . . . I don't know. I'm feeling suspicious of everyone. We have to do something."

James sits on the bed, patting the space next to him. She sits, tense and miserable.

"Listen, I'm sorry," James says. "I know you're worried and frightened. I'm sorry about my clumsy efforts to reassure you, I should have thought more carefully about it. It is horrible, and we'll do our best to stop it happening. But has something else happened, to make you want to look at the security here?"

"I was up in the night, I heard a noise. It was a cat. A sweet little thing, scratching at our bedroom door. I got up for a drink and gave it some milk. The door to the terrace was open. If it wasn't for . . . Normally, it wouldn't bother me, it all seems pretty safe round here. I realize with a house full of people, it's difficult to make sure everyone is careful, especially the kids, but honestly, anyone could have got in."

"If they got past the alarms around the house, you mean."

"They weren't on. And if they were, wouldn't the cat have set them off? We haven't tested them, have we? Perhaps they're only there for show . . ."

Heather hates the idea of alarms and security companies. It's exactly what she doesn't want, now, here, at home or in the future. But perhaps the risk is too great. If someone genuinely means them harm, if someone were to get into the house — who knows? She remembers a newspaper story about a bank manager, woken in the night and forced at gunpoint to open his bank to robbers while his family was kept prisoner, tied up and threatened.

"Perhaps you're right," James says, standing and slipping his feet into leather flip-flops. His legs still look remarkably pale despite their time in the Spanish sun. "We are probably being a little too relaxed. I'll check with the agents today, get the alarms tested. But if we decide to ramp up the security, we'll have to get everyone to take responsibility. The kids included, which might be difficult."

"I know, but it's worth the effort. We'd be mad not to do it, when you think about it." She thinks of the windows left casually ajar, the sliding doors open while they're out for dinner. They would never do that in London; it would be out of the question. This isn't London, and crime is nowhere near at that kind of level, but just because everyone else here is relaxed about security doesn't mean they should be.

"I'll get on to it as soon as they open. As a precaution. I don't think we're being threatened, seriously, but I think it's wise to be careful. Then will you promise me to stop worrying?"

"I'll try." She smiles at him. When he says he'll do something, he rarely lets her down. "Once it's done. Oh, and James?"

"Something else?"

"Let's try not to make too big a thing of it with the others. I don't want people to feel frightened here, especially the kids."

"Of course, no worries. It'll still be less frightening than London, I promise you."

But the words keep buzzing round her mind, like an angry wasp at a window: *People kill for a lot less* . . .

CHAPTER FORTY-TWO

Heather

The town of Jerez nestles in a fold in the dry hills of Andalucía, its blonde stone glowing in the bright sunlight. To Heather, even from afar, it has the look of an ancient city, full of contrast, like an old man's face. Around it the land is scorched and barren, the few hardy trees and bushes stark against a desert backdrop.

"So," James says from the front seat of the minibus, a guide book in his hand. "As your self-appointed guide, I'm going to run through the options for today. Those of you who like museums—" he nods in Heather's direction, "—have a treat in store. There's a thirteenth-century palace for you, called the Palacio del Virrey Laserna, which apparently is filled with antiques, art and family heirlooms. One for you too, Nick, I think. If you don't fancy that, it's a pretty town to wander round. There's a Moorish fort — which is well worth a visit, the guide says, if that takes your fancy — and I've booked us all onto a sherry-tasting tour—" a cheer from the back "—followed by a long lunch tasting all the local tapas, in various bars. That should take us most of the afternoon. Then, if we're still awake and halfway sober, we might get to see the famous Andalucían horses. Or not, if we choose not to. The sherry tour is at one thirty, so I suggest once we're in the town we find a good place to meet up, so we can split into groups for the first couple of hours, then meet up for the tour and lunch. We'll keep in touch by mobile. Okay, everyone?"

At supper last night, James had proposed this trip to Jerez, a town some forty miles to the north of Zahara, beyond Cádiz. Most of the adults were keen, but the youngsters declared the proposition 'boring' and announced they would much rather go to Tarifa for their morning's kitesurfing lessons with Miguel and spend the rest of the day there. Neither of the mothers were keen on their children spending the entire day on their own on Tarifa beach, so when Miles and Steve said they would go with them, everyone was happy. Once Miles decided to go, Charlotte said she'd go too. Julie and Roger were invited to join the Jerez party.

Heather finds herself sitting in the centre of the bus with Julie. James has taken himself up front with the driver, while the others are settled into small rows of seats behind. Though the journey's only around an hour, Heather's relieved not to be sitting next to Liz. She wants to enjoy the day without any tensions.

"Heather, this is so good of you, inviting us along," Julie says immediately as she sits down. "We tend to get rather lazy, living here. We rarely do anything like this. In fact, I can't remember the last time we went to Jerez. Can you, Roger?" She cranes her neck around to get Roger's attention from the back seat. He nods and smiles, though Heather is certain he hasn't heard what Julie said. "Don't forget to tell us what we owe you," she says, turning back to Heather. "We've already enjoyed so much of your hospitality; you couldn't have been more generous."

Heather, seeing her opportunity, says: "It's up to James, really. Perhaps ask him what he'd like you to do. It's because of his business we're here — they've done rather well this year. He's sharing his success with his nearest and dearest."

She hopes this will be enough to put paid to any unwanted speculation from Julie.

"How lovely, what a great thing to do," Julie replies. "I'll have a chat to him later. I think we'd feel more comfortable if we could contribute, as we're hangers-on . . ."

"Not at all," Heather says. "We're glad you could come along."

"So how are you enjoying Zahara? This is your first visit, isn't it?"

"It is, and we're loving it. We're lucky to have found the villa. How long have you been coming here?" She wants to turn the conversation round before the questions get awkward.

"We started coming years ago, just for summer holidays. Then we bought a small apartment nearer the town and let it for part of the year. When Roger retired, we decided to come here full-time, so we bought the town house. We love it; we've never looked back. It's cheaper to live here, too. We couldn't live like this on Roger's pension back home."

Heather's attention drifts as Julie chatters on. She wonders if they'll feel the same some day. They could decide to live here or elsewhere in Europe, or almost anywhere in the world. She can sense her mindset changing because of the money. But she's still not sure she wants it to.

* * *

It's three o'clock before they're ready for lunch, by which time those who opted to take the tour have tasted enough sherry to give some of them a headache. A slight hitch in James's schedule was caused by the discovery on arrival in the town that the mobile signal was weak, and for some of the group, non-existent. So everyone had to be given the address of the restaurant and find their own way there. Unsurprisingly, with a few muzzy heads after the sherry tasting, it took longer than expected for them to gather.

They sit at the long table, where fresh bread and unidentified tapas have already been served. Bottles of wine have appeared as if from nowhere, along with jugs of water and olive oil.

"Did we order this?" James is surprised, about to question the waiter.

"I took the liberty," Nick said. "We're all starving, so I ordered straight away."

"Nick speaks fluent Spanish, it seems," Natalie says, smiling at him. "He's a dark horse. I had no idea."

"Great — thanks, Nick," James says, pulling out a chair. "I'm hungry. You might regret letting your secret out — your skills could prove jolly useful."

"Glad to be of help," Nick says, as the party settles down and the wine is poured.

"Any news of the surfing party?" Natalie asks, helping herself to bread and dipping it in a small bowl of pureed tomatoes.

James digs out his mobile. "I can't get a signal. Can you?" He glances over at Heather.

"I got a weak one earlier," she says. "I sent Miles a message, to see how they're getting on. I haven't had a reply yet." She checks her phone. "No, nothing. And the signal's gone, I've got nothing now."

"I'm sure they're having a brilliant time," James says. "That picnic looked delicious. The kids would have been bored here, though I'm sure Miles and Steve will be sorry to have missed the sherry."

"They'll make up for it later," Liz says from across the table, indicating a pile of shopping bags in the corner. "We've bought enough to keep us going for months. Lots of presents, too."

"No need to worry about them, they'll be fine," James says, as two waiters arrive with huge trays laden with tapas. "Now, let's eat, before the hangover sets in. I don't know about you, but even sipping that stuff made my head spin."

It's only later that Heather wonders why she felt so reassured. Perhaps it was the alcohol, though she'd been cautious, unwilling to let her guard down. Or perhaps it was because Steve, Miles and Charlotte were with the children. Three responsible adults with four teenagers; it should have been foolproof.

* * *

It's a sleepy group of people who return to the minibus late in the afternoon. On the straight road back to Zahara they fall quiet, the conversation dampened by food and wine. Some rest their heads on windows, others doze sitting up, so when the buzzing starts in pockets and pinging noises begin, they all start, their simultaneous half-slumber interrupted.

Heather looks up, all her senses tingling. It's a similar feeling to that first ominous text, back in her kitchen in Shepherd's Bush. She knows immediately that something's wrong. Her heart starts to thump. She fumbles with her mobile, but it still has no signal. She leans over the seat in front, her arm outstretched, trying to get James's attention.

He is the first to open his phone. "Five missed calls from Steve, two from Ben, and a load of texts . . . wait a minute—" His face, normally so sanguine, drains of colour. "Stop the car. Stop, please, right here. Please . . ." The startled driver nods and pulls over into the side of the road. James scrabbles at the door handle and jumps down, already dialling.

"What's happening? Can you let me out, please, Julie? I need to get out . . ." Heather, suddenly claustrophobic amid all these people, starts to clamber over Julie's legs.

Julie struggles to get the door open and the last thing Heather hears before she jumps down is Liz's gasp, immediately muffled by her hand. "Oh my god . . ."

"What's going on, James?" She puts her hand on his shoulder and leans forward in a vain attempt to hear what's going on. But the rumble of heavy lorries and cars passing them drowns everything out. James walks quickly away from the road, climbing over a barrier into a patch of scrub to get some distance, the phone glued to one ear, his spare hand to the other. "James!"

She follows him, coarse grass scratching at her ankles, her sandals scrabbling and slipping on the dry, stony slope beyond the barrier, her toes soon covered with yellow dust. But she doesn't care. Something's happened, it must be the boys. It's her worst fear, and it's coming true. As she reaches James, he cuts the call and looks up with a look that chills her heart.

"What is it, tell me!"

He runs a hand over his head. "It's Harry. He's missing."

CHAPTER FORTY-THREE

Heather

She gasps, her eyes fixed on his, the shock hitting her like a punch in the stomach. "What — what do you mean, missing?" For a moment, she doesn't understand the word. Missing. What a strange word to use.

James stares at his mobile, then drags his eyes back to hers. "He left the beach just for a few moments, to go to the toilet. It's not far, they use a café bar, just on the front there. They were all playing football, apart from Steve, who was looking after their stuff, watching. He just . . . didn't come back."

"When? What time was it? How long has he been gone?"

"It was mid-afternoon, around three fifteen, they think." The hand that holds the phone is shaking. She's never seen him like this before.

"Or rather, Steve thinks," he says, a stunned look on his face. "He's the one I spoke to. They're all still there, looking for Harry. Luckily, Miguel's there and he's going to take the other kids home; we don't want them wandering around on their own."

"No . . . no, of course." Her voice sounds calm, practical as she speaks. But the one in her head says, over and over: *This can't be happening, it can't . . . not Harry . . .*

"Are they sure he didn't go into the sea? Oh, my god, James . . ." She has a sudden vision of him struggling in the windswept waves of the Atlantic Ocean. "What if he went swimming, got dragged out to sea?" The wind, whipping her hair around her face here, inland, can be vicious out at sea, and though he's a strong swimmer, she knows he'd have little chance if he got pulled the wrong way by the current.

"He didn't go that way, Steve said. And they were told not to swim on their own; they all know how dangerous it can be. I doubt he would have wanted to, anyway, not while they were playing football."

A hand on Heather's shoulder startles her. "Heather, we've just heard," Natalie says, putting her arm around her. "This is awful, I can't believe it . . . Listen, we should get back, go and help. We can stop by the villa on the way, drop people off. Come on, James, let's get everyone back on the bus."

The rest of the group is gathered at the side of the road, gazing at them with shocked expressions. The driver stands at the front of the minibus, looking agitated, as the traffic roars by.

"Let's go!" Natalie calls as they scramble up the slope, their feet slipping and catching on the rocky surface. "Let James and Heather sit together . . . I'll sit with you, don't worry." She whispers the last part in Heather's ear as the group parts to let them on.

Heather's vaguely aware of Julie and Liz clutching each other as she passes, of Nick muttering to the driver. The shock has sent her into a daze. As she sits with James and Natalie, it's all she can do to hold her head up. Natalie hands her a bottle of water and tells her to sip it slowly. She obeys, but swallowing is hard, there's something growing in her throat. What was it she needed to say?

James is back on his mobile, talking to Steve. She's vaguely aware of his voice, stronger now, and calm. She hears isolated words. *Police, search party, road block . . . helicopter.* James seems to be agreeing to everything. There's something nagging at her, something she needs to say.

"James," she says, urgently now, tugging at his sleeve. But he's listening intently, giving her a sign to wait.

"What is it?" Natalie asks.

"Natalie, the police . . ." She clutches at Natalie's arm, trying to think.

"The police?" She drops her voice. "What is it, Heather?"

"I don't know," she whispers, breathing deeply, forcing her brain to function. "Natalie, what if he's been kidnapped? We can't just tell everyone about the money, we can't. We can't tell just any old local police, they'll have to know . . ."

It's Natalie's turn to gasp. "Kidnapped?" She closes her eyes for a moment, then leans across Heather's body to grab James's arm. "James, stop. We need to talk about this. Heather needs to talk to you, can you call him back?"

* * *

James turns a devastated face to Heather, holding her eyes with his. "Listen, I'll call you back," he says into the handset. "Don't do anything for the moment. I need to talk this through with Heather. Two minutes."

James, Heather and Natalie form a huddle in the middle seat where they speak in low tones, the rumble of traffic outside muffling the sound of their voices.

"We have to act quickly, Heather," James says urgently. "The first few hours are crucial. Why did you stop me?" He seems to have aged by ten years in the last fifteen minutes, the skin of his cheeks grey with shock.

"Steve has called the police?"

"Of course he has. He's with them now."

"We can't just go with the local police, James!" Heather says. "We have to talk to somebody senior, tell them about the money! If he's been kidnapped, the money makes all the difference. There could be a ransom demand, and, and — the local police could be completely out of their depth. They'll need to get negotiators, and . . ." She's not sure what she's saying; all she knows is that this isn't a job for the provincial police.

James nods slowly. "You're right," he says. "If this is a kidnap . . . We need a Spanish speaker. We'll have to tell Nick about the money — are we okay with that, Heather?"

"You can trust him," Natalie says. "I'm sure of it. Tell him."

They nod at each other and James cranes his neck around the front passenger seat to talk to Nick. Luckily, the engine noise drowns out James's voice; even Heather, sitting right behind, can't hear what he says, but she can see Nick nodding.

Nick talks to the driver in fluent Spanish; there's a swift and urgent discussion before Nick turns back.

"He says the local police will be useless. He thinks we should talk to the *Guardia Civil*. Call one, one, two — ask for them," Nick says. "If they don't speak good English, put them on to me."

James dials, leaning forward over his knees, the handset pressed tight to his ear. "Yes, it's an emergency," he says. "Can you put me through to the Guardia Civil? Tarifa. But I must speak to a senior detective, please. Yes, a—" His eyes flit towards Nick, who's now kneeling up in the front seat, watching James's face. "*Un* — Nick, can you say it, please? We want the most senior man possible — tell them it's of the utmost importance."

Hurriedly he passes the mobile to Nick, who speaks rapidly into the handset. He listens for a moment, then becomes more insistent. There's a pause while he waits to be connected to someone, then he speaks again. He seems to be arguing with the person on the other end. His voice rises; the driver throws a sideways glance at him, nodding and raising his hand in a 'thumbs up' gesture.

A longer pause, then Nick puts his hand over the mouthpiece. "They wanted us to call the local police, make it a missing person report. I've said no way. I think they got my gist." He raises a hand and listens again, then he nods and passes the mobile back to James, staying in his kneeling position, his eyes on James's.

"Who am I speaking to, please? Capitán Martínez. Good. My name is . . ."

Heather leans back into her seat, her eyes closed, Natalie's hand in hers, comforting and warm. She listens as if in some nightmarish dream to her husband describing how their younger son has disappeared, is missing, hasn't been seen for almost three hours, in an unfamiliar town in a foreign country.

When he talks about the money and the strong likelihood of kidnap, she feels as if her heart will break.

CHAPTER FORTY-FOUR

Heather

When she looks at her watch, she realizes how fast they've been driving. At the villa, the gates are open. Ben runs into Heather's arms, his eyes red and swollen. "Mum, it's awful, I'm sorry . . ."

"It's okay, Ben, we'll find him. We're going on there now."

"I want to come with you. He's my brother — please, Mum."

"Okay, you can come. But you must stay with one of us, preferably Dad. James, Ben is coming too." She can see James is about to object, but a glance at Ben's face changes his mind.

The group splits, most staying at the villa with the other children while the driver takes the search party on to Tarifa. Everyone wants to join them, but James insists it's too many.

"Please, I want to help," Natalie says.

"Thanks, but my guess is, the police won't want us searching," James says. "Heather, Ben and I will go. And Nick, would you mind coming? It could be useful to have a Spanish speaker with us . . ."

"Of course."

"We'll call you straight away if we need more hands, Natalie."

Natalie nods. "Go on, go! Good luck. I'm sure you'll find him, safe and well."

* * *

"Tell us exactly what happened, Ben," James says as the minibus makes its way onto the main road.

"There's not much to tell," Ben says, shaking his head, his eyes filling. "We were playing football, and he needed the toilet. He went up to the bar on the front there. We always use it, it's fine, it's not even very far. We carried on — we were playing some stupid chasing game with the ball, and we got carried away. The time just seemed to go. I didn't think, Mum, I'm so sorry — I didn't notice how long he'd been gone."

"It's not your fault, Ben, really. You weren't in charge of him." She gives him a hug, even now surprised that he lets her; he stopped hugging anyone a few years ago. His thin body seems so fragile in her arms. She tries not to think of that other young body, so much more vulnerable.

"Go on," James says. "Everything you can think of will be important. The police might want to interview you. Try to think."

At the mention of the police, Ben flinches. Heather gives him a reassuring squeeze.

"I don't know, Dad, there's nothing I can think of."

"What was he wearing? Did he have his mobile with him?"

"A grey T-shirt, his blue swimming shorts. Flip-flops, I think. He doesn't like going barefoot into the toilets. No, his mobile was with Steve. We put all the valuables together when we were surfing, so that one person could look after them."

"What about money?"

"I doubt it. He wasn't going up there to buy anything. And he wouldn't keep money in his swimming shorts. Oh, Mum . . ."

"It's okay, Ben, we'll find him. This is useful stuff, you're doing really well."

"Who noticed he'd been gone too long?" James prompts. "Was it you?"

"No, it was Miles, I think. He'd gone up to get ice creams for everyone, and when he got back, we realized Harry was missing."

"Any idea how long he'd been gone before that?"

"No idea. I'm sorry, Mum, I should have been looking out for him. I should've . . ." He dissolves into tears, while Heather, her own eyes filling, stares in anguish across his head at James's desolate face.

* * *

Tarifa is at one end of ten kilometres of golden sand. At the other is a beach called Punta Paloma, where Miguel and his kitesurfing school are situated. Here the beach hooks round the shoreline into a massive sand dune, which is where many schools are located, as even in the strong *Levante*, the infamous offshore wind, the dunes can pick up any students who drift off downwind.

As they approach the shoreline, panic rises in Heather's chest. How on earth are they going to find Harry here, where the beach stretches for miles in either direction, where people come and go all the time? They've already lost more than three hours. He could be anywhere by now, miles from them, in any direction — where will they even start? She can only hope the Guardia are quick to act. She has no idea of their reputation, how efficient they are, what level of technology they have to help them. Her only hope is that because Harry is a child, they'll work fast, clamp down on the area, put everything into the search.

At last they reach Punta Paloma. They have no idea how long they'll be here, so James lets the driver leave. Their eyes are already searching the beach, the car park, the streets behind them. Almost immediately Heather spots two black and white Guardia Civil vehicles, their lights flashing, uniformed men milling around them.

"There, James, over there," she says, grabbing his hand. She can make out Steve and Miles, talking to a gesticulating policeman. He looks more like a soldier than a police officer in his grey uniform, a gun at his hip. Charlotte hovers around behind them, a pile of beach bags around her.

"I hope they have more cars than that," James says as they hurry towards them. Miles turns, leaving Steve with the uniformed man, his face grim.

"I'm so sorry," he says immediately, a hand on James's shoulder. "I feel terrible . . . we all do. He just . . . didn't come back."

"It's nobody's fault, Miles."

"Come and talk to this guy," Miles says. "He seems to be the boss man."

James beckons to Nick to come with them. "Capitán Martínez? I'm the father, James, this is Harry's mother, Heather, and his brother, Ben. Nick here speaks good Spanish. Thank you for coming to meet us."

"Please, come with me," the man says curtly. The four of them hurry behind him towards a large four-wheel drive vehicle parked alongside the police cars. They climb in, the policeman in the driving seat, James in the front passenger seat, Heather, Nick and Ben behind.

The Capitán, as it turns out, speaks good English. His approach is confident and businesslike. He reaches for a clipboard from the dashboard and pulls a pen from his top pocket.

"You did the right thing to ask for the Guardia Civil," he says, after he's taken their names and the Zahara address. "I understand you suspect kidnapping?"

"Yes, we do," James says, looking at Heather, who nods, not trusting her voice. Ben's hand creeps into hers, and she clasps it with both of hers gratefully.

"This is because . . . there is a great deal of money in the family, I understand?" He speaks softly, politely, with the confidence of seniority, making notes all the time. Heather feels at once reassured and terrified.

"It is," James says.

"In the order of?" he says, without glancing up from his paperwork.

"In the order of many millions of euros," James says firmly. The Capitán glances up, as if to ask for more detail, but seeing the look on James's face, seems to decide against it.

"Right. We'll finish the paperwork as fast as we can." James opens his mouth to object, but the Capitán holds up his hand. Heather notices the neatly trimmed nails, the wedding ring on his fourth finger, wonders if he has children of his own.

Nick leans forward to speak to the Capitán. Heather's not familiar with Spanish, but it seems to her he's putting particular emphasis on certain words, repeating them to make sure his meaning is completely understood.

The Capitán looks up at him, his face grave. "I can assure you," he says in English, "my men are searching right now, along the beach and in the streets. We have set up checks on the roads out of the area. I have twenty men on this job, a major crime team; a helicopter will join them. We are giving it the highest priority."

It seems Nick has made the situation clear.

"Thank you," James says. "That's reassuring."

"And no publicity," Heather says, urgently. "The media mustn't get hold of this. No journalists, no reporters." James nods in agreement.

"This I cannot guarantee," the Capitán says, shrugging his shoulders. "My men will not talk, but other people . . . who knows? We may be able to hold it for a couple of days, but after that . . ."

Heather closes her eyes. She can hardly bear to think about it. Right now, she'd give anything not to have bought that ticket.

CHAPTER FORTY-FIVE

Heather

Things progress frustratingly slowly. Each person in their party has to be interviewed separately, so they split off one by one to sit with an officer in a Guardia vehicle. Heather tells them as much as she can about Harry, his personality, his habits, how he's likely to respond, what he was wearing, his health. She responds in a daze and, when they ask if he has any medical issues, almost breaks down.

Then, despite their protests, Capitán Martínez sends them back to the villa to wait. He is adamant. They have to concede defeat and, exhausted, return to Zahara.

A family liaison officer will arrive soon, and the rest of the group will be interviewed this evening. Moreover, the Capitán wants the villa searched, top to bottom. It's normal procedure and an important part of their intelligence work, but the thought of having men rummaging through their things isn't pleasant. It's getting late, they're all tired, and surely the men should be out looking for Harry? On the journey back to Zahara, she bites her lip until it bleeds.

This evening they will be joined by a negotiator and a technical officer, who will set up monitoring equipment and stay with them at the villa for as long as it takes. The Capitán had wanted to set up a 'negotiation centre' at a nearby hotel, in case the perpetrators were observing the villa. But when James heard that they would expect the family to stay there, he was adamant; they were not going to leave the villa, none of them. The Guardia could set up in the massive dining room, he said. It would make a perfectly good centre of operations. The Capitán frowned and spoke rapidly to Nick, gesticulating wildly. Nick responded calmly and firmly, and eventually the Capitán shrugged his shoulders and gave in.

All they can do now is wait. For a text message, a phone call, an email demand for money. Or for a call from the Guardia. Whichever one it is, it will be terrifying.

It's still light when they get back to the villa, though the sun is on the horizon. The onset of night is horrifying to Heather, as she imagines ghastly situations, unable to help herself. Harry tied up and gagged in the boot of a car racing away from them across Spain; Harry in some dark and dismal basement, without food or water.

Everyone gathers around the table on the terrace, their faces white with shock in the fading light of the evening. Natalie places dishes of food on the table, but Heather can hardly bring herself to lift hand to mouth. The 'what ifs' are gathering in her head like a swarm of wasps, pestering her, returning again and again. What if, unbeknown to anyone, he went for a swim? The police aren't searching the water; perhaps they should? What if he's being taken across the short stretch of sea to Africa, where he'll disappear without trace? What happens then? What if the police stop looking once it's dark?

James puts a hand on her arm. "Try not to think too much," he says. "You'll make yourself ill. We need to stay strong, in case we're needed."

"I know," she says, shaking her head. "I just can't help wanting to be out there, looking for him. I feel so helpless, James — I know it's stupid, but it feels as if we're giving up. Isn't there something we can do?"

Everyone looks at James, who shakes his head. "I don't think so. Capitán Martínez seems to know what he's doing, and we mustn't get in the way. But we must keep our phones on and with us, in case we get a message. Where's yours, Heather?"

With a start, she realizes she hasn't checked her mobile in a while, which is charging in the bedroom. She makes a move to retrieve it, but James says: "No, let Ben get it." Ben rises immediately from his seat.

"On the table by the bathroom door," Heather says. She can't bear the thought of looking at her messages, not after the last time. Now, though she knows she must, the thought is even more horrifying. She leans over to James, her voice low. "Could you check it for me please, darling? I can't face it . . ."

He nods, taking her hand.

For a moment, they're all silent, then Liz, who has been abnormally quiet since they arrived back, says: "Can you bear to fill us in with what the police said, James? What are they thinking has happened?"

"They're pretty much going on the assumption that it's a kidnapping. Well, we insisted, really. As soon as they heard about—" His eyes flick to Nick "—the money, the whole thing went to another level. A specialist team, a helicopter, road blocks — they don't normally come out."

Liz's eyes widen. "But who could it possibly be? Who knows we're here, apart from us?"

"Hardly anyone." James shakes his head. "Heather's mum. She won't tell anyone, or at least not about the money. The lottery people, the school, the newsagent . . . We tried our best to avoid publicity, but the news got out at home, we don't know how. Social media, wagging tongues, we have no idea. But we didn't expect it to follow us here."

"We should have realized. We were complacent. How could we have been so stupid?" Heather puts her face in her hands.

"Heather, you can't think like that. Beating ourselves up is not going to help," James says softly.

"If it's anyone's fault, it's the adults who were there," Steve says, his voice breaking with emotion. "I'm so sorry. I'm his uncle, I should have gone with him . . ." He looks exhausted, his skin grey against the garish colours of his shirt.

"Absolutely not," James says firmly. "Nobody is to blame anyone."

Heather's heart flips as Ben hands her mobile to her. "Here, James." Time stops for her as James taps in the security code and flicks through her messages.

"Nothing significant," he says, and she can breathe again. "You deleted that last message, didn't you — the threatening one? I wonder if the police can retrieve it."

Nick looks up in surprise: Natalie clearly hasn't told him. "I imagine they probably can," he says. Heather's glad he doesn't ask.

"We'll ask them tomorrow," James says, placing Heather's mobile and his own in front of him on the table. They lie there, small but significant, the whole table gazing at them as if willing them to ring.

"So is this it, this is all we can do?" Miles says into the silence. "We just sit and wait, do we, for a call, or a message?"

"That's what the police advised." James looks around the concerned faces. "Look, there's no point everyone losing sleep over this. I'm going to stay up; I won't get much sleep anyway. The rest of you should go to bed, you included, Heather, you need at least to try. You look shattered."

She shakes her head, but knows it's the right thing to do. Though she can't bear to think of waking up to find Harry's still missing, her head feels too heavy for her neck and there's a throbbing behind her eyes, as if she's had too much sun. "Perhaps I'll lie down for a bit," she says.

"I'm going to stay up with you, James," Steve says. "It's the least I can do."

Gradually people drift away from the table, Ben giving Heather a hug when he goes. "He'll be fine, Mum," he says softly in her ear. "He's tougher than you think."

She gives him a wobbly smile. "Thanks, darling. Try to get some sleep."

It's only when she reaches the bedroom and closes the door that she gives in. Her tears stream onto the pillow, her mouth open in a silent howl of agony.

CHAPTER FORTY-SIX

Before

He's gone. It's been days now, and I can only assume he's left me. His mobile isn't working, there's no answer at the office. Time is running out and he knows it. I think he's fled before they catch up with him.

The other day I rang work and resigned. There doesn't seem any point anymore. I'm too tired to deal with small children, too ashamed to explain what's wrong. I've stopped answering the door and the phone. The post lies on the mat unopened, the bills piling up. I can only assume it's a matter of time before the bailiffs come and kick down the door. They'll take everything, and even then it won't be nearly enough.

For the last week, or it could be longer — I've lost all track of time — I've spent all day in bed. It's been too cold to get up with the heating off, so I've moved the TV into the bedroom. All day I stare blankly at shows I don't understand. It's the only company I have now. I have no appetite for food, even if there was any.

But today is going to be different. I'm out of bed and dressed. When I look in the mirror I see a waif, a small girl with an old woman's face. I've lost so much weight my clothes hang off me; I have to wear a belt to keep my jeans up. My hair has begun to fall out, and even when tied back it looks thin and patchy, all its beautiful shine dulled. My neck is wrinkled, like an old woman's, the skin on my face mottled.

Dark smudges lurk beneath my eyes. When I turn sideways in the mirror, I fade into the background.

I am literally a shadow of my former self.

But today I'm going to make an effort. I dig around in a drawer until I find my favourite silk scarf, draping it around my throat, its delicate pattern of pinks and blues falling in gentle swirls. It's long — long enough to go twice around, the ends trailing down my chest, soft and warm against my skin. I've heard that silk is stronger than steel, so I know it won't let me down.

Carefully, I apply eye pencil, shadow and mascara. I dot foundation onto my cheeks, smoothing it into my flaking skin, making sure the edges don't show. The blusher is too bright, making me look like a china doll, so I scrub at it until it fades. The lipstick feels soft and creamy on my lips, and I add layer after layer so that it lasts. I stare at my face in the mirror again. That will do.

I leave the bedroom, walking through the house to the garage, which connects via the laundry room. It's even colder in here, damp seeping in from outside. High above me the bare wooden rafters are draped with cobwebs, clumps of fluff and dust clinging to the trailing ends. I gaze at them for a moment, choosing my spot.

The garage is empty except for a few boxes of tools on shelves along the back wall, a broken bookshelf, and the stepladder. It's aluminium, and when I lift it and place it carefully in the spot where his car should be, it feels remarkably light. It's the perfect height for me to reach the rafters.

I place my foot on the bottom step and start to climb.

CHAPTER FORTY-SEVEN

Natalie

It was a nightmare. I was praying they'd find Harry safe and well in Tarifa, playing football with some locals, perhaps, or asleep in the sun somewhere close by. Though in my heart I knew. I've watched too many police dramas on TV, read too many crime novels, not to be suspicious. When large amounts of money are involved, things have a habit of going badly wrong.

Harry wasn't the kind of boy to wander off. Friendly, yes, but quiet, home-loving, even. He was more often to be found in his room, playing computer games, than out on his bike or hanging out at friends' houses. Sensible, too. He knew why there were rules and guidelines, and he was never any trouble for Heather and James. Not that Ben was, either; they were both good boys.

But he was small for his age, and vulnerable. Possibly a little too trusting. If someone befriended him, he wouldn't suspect them. I could imagine situations where he would agree to help someone, and he wouldn't suspect their motives. It wouldn't be difficult to persuade him to go with you, if you needed help. He was a lovely boy, but that innocence could be a problem if someone had bad intentions.

So when they came back from Tarifa without him, looking exhausted and defeated, their faces aged with worry, I started to think the worst.

I didn't say anything, of course. This was the most awful situation imaginable, without me making it worse by speculating. Nobody deserved this, least of all Heather. I was lost for words. All I could do was hug her and sit with them and share as much of their pain as I could.

We sat together on the terrace, all the enjoyment of the day gone, forgotten. I put the food out in silence, hoping, if not to raise the spirits, to fortify the bodies. But barely anyone ate, only the kids making a half-hearted effort. As I looked around the table, the people that stared back at me showed all the signs of shock. Grey-white faces, mouths downturned, foreheads crumpled. Even Nick, the one who knows the family least well, seemed shell-shocked. I was glad he knew about the money now; it was beginning to feel wrong for him to be the only one not to know.

Nobody spoke at first. Liz sat close to Steve, her lip trembling, her daughter's head on her shoulder, while Steve, normally ebullient, hung his head. Miles sat at one end of the table, Charlotte at the other, next to James. Her hand shook alarmingly when she sipped her drink.

Ben stayed close to his parents, Josh next to him, offering silent, boyish support.

My mind was in overdrive. There'd been no ransom demand as yet — no contact, even — and I wondered how long it would be before we knew. It made sense to assume it was a kidnapping. He wasn't just missing; that would have been hard to believe. So if it was a kidnapping, then it was somebody who knew about the money. And who knew about the money? All of us here.

If this had been a detective novel, the police would start close to home. Which meant that we were all under suspicion.

* * *

224

I'm not a melodramatic person. I'd describe myself as rather cynical, in fact, the world having given me my share of knocks. I don't even have a particularly vivid imagination these days, the fantasies of my youth having faded with the passing years. I'm not one to overdramatise a situation.

Yet as I walk to my room with Nick that evening, my mind whirs with possibilities.

Of all of us here, I'm probably the closest person to this family. Heather is like a sister to me, James has become like a brother; the boys are the nearest I will ever get to having children of my own. So their problem is my problem. I'm going to think this one through logically. Even if I don't get anywhere with it, I will feel as if I've tried.

Minutes later, Nick is asleep, snoring gently, his arm thrown across my hips. But I am wide awake, half-propped on the pillows. There's no question of sleep; I'm fizzing with nervous energy.

I try to think like a detective would. A private detective, not revealing his identity. I run through the list of people who know about the money. But it's no good doing it in my head, I need to write it down. Carefully moving Nick's arm so as not to wake him, I step out of bed and retrieve a notebook and pen from my bag. The air conditioning is on, chilling the skin on my arms, so I climb back into bed and turn the bedside light on, thankful that it's one of those silent, touch-sensitive lamps. Nick doesn't stir.

Who knows about the money? I go back to the beginning: Heather at the newsagent's. Sanjay knows, of course, because they went back there to get the ticket checked. But he's so far removed from the south of Spain, I can't bring myself to put him down as a suspect.

Could there have been someone in the shop who heard, by accident, the exchange between Heather and Sanjay? They said the shop was empty when they went back, and Sanjay checked the CCTV, but it's possible, though unlikely. I write '*ANO in the shop*' on the list.

Heather's mum: Harry's grandmother — she knows. Ridiculous thought. She could have mentioned it to someone else, though. I'm pretty sure she wouldn't, but it's always a possibility. So I add: '*ANO: Heather's mum's contact*'.

The lottery people. Of course not. But they know, so their names must go down. I don't know their names, so I put: '*Lottery people*'.

James mentioned they were ramping up the alarm system at their house in Shepherd's Bush. Security people are already checked and approved. But this is a lottery win, and could be a huge amount of money; certainly, many people assume it is. I make a note.

Who else? Surely not the hotel they stayed in; there's no way they would know. The car driver? Extremely unlikely. I don't include them. The travel agent? Possible, though unlikely. I add them to the list. The school: anything's possible, and Heather did get some strange messages from people she scarcely knew when it first happened. '*School +++ ANOs*' goes down. The media? They were on to the story, and they must have got it from somewhere. I add '*Media*', even while wondering if I'm taking things too far.

I start to think about here, in Zahara. The security firm knows the house is occupied. They're used to being called out to the bigger villas; no reason to assume they'd pick this family, if they had bad intentions. But I add them anyway. The boys' kitesurfing teacher — I forget his name, but I make a note. The boys could have said something to him by accident. Carmen? Surely not. I flinch from the thought — she seems such a lovely person. But it's possible; there might be someone in her family who has been speculating about the sudden influx of British people to this huge, luxury villa — people who seem to have plenty of money. I add '*Carmen's family?*' to the list. The question mark somehow makes me feel better, as if I'm not accusing her. Julie and Roger — yes, definitely they need to go on the list. Julie has made a couple of remarks that have got me wondering, though at the time I thought I was imagining things.

Everyone in this party goes on the list, bar Heather, James and the three children. For the other children to be involved is simply unthinkable — impossible, and Heather and James have no reason to extort money from themselves. I shake my head at myself: I know it's late, but now I'm getting ridiculous.

But the others. They're the ones I'm interested in.

* * *

I stare at the list, my heart sinking. It's much longer than I thought it would be, even though there are many people on it who are really unlikely. But any one of these people could have spread a rumour that could have spread to others. If you work out how many connections each person might have, you can soon see that for just one of the list, there could be hundreds, if not thousands, of possible connections. Hence the success of social media, I suppose.

But I can't think like that. I have to focus on the probabilities, the most likely candidates. It will take my mind off thinking about poor Harry.

Julie and Roger? We don't know them at all; we've welcomed them into our group without any kind of checking. And Julie seems to be a dreadful gossip; she never stops talking. Roger never gets a word in edgeways, so I have no impression of what he's like at all. We have no real grasp on their backgrounds, their values. I might be doing them a disservice, but they are candidates.

Liz and Steve? I can't believe James's sister would arrange the kidnap of her own nephew, but you never know. She does seem obsessed with the money, asking constantly how much they've won. It's a horrible thought, but as I know from all the crime dramas, it's not unusual for a family member to betray a parent or a sibling for personal gain. Steve, too. I don't know him at all well, and I don't think Heather and James are that close to him, probably because Heather and Liz don't always see eye to eye. He seems nice enough,

227

but can't hold down a job. Perhaps they're in some kind of financial trouble. But surely, if that's the case, James would help them out? They wouldn't need to go to such lengths as to kidnap a young boy, and a family member to boot. It's hard to believe.

This is really hard. I'm not sure I'm making any sense of it at all. But I've got no hope of sleeping so I keep running down my list.

Miles and Charlotte. There's a couple I've met a few times, but I have no idea what they're really like. Miles seems nice enough, if a bit thick. He's loud, and sociable, and friendly. He seems focused on his business. Perhaps it's not doing so well? Charlotte seems . . . downtrodden, and my one glimpse of friction between them raised questions. It's possible she's under Miles's thumb. But that doesn't make them kidnappers.

I sigh. I'm not enjoying this, and I don't even know if it's going to do any good. But it has to be done. I'm only speculating, I tell myself. The list is for me, for my eyes only. Nobody else needs to know, not even Nick.

I take a deep breath. Nick. I glance across at his sleeping form, his face open and calm. Asleep, he looks much younger than his years, the lines smoothed out by his state of deep relaxation. Even though I know he's fast asleep, I turn my shoulder as I write his name. Nick. I've known him, what? Three or four months — these days, I don't count the days. In that time I've seen absolutely no reason to suspect he's not who he says he is. He seems kind and honest and I've seen no evidence that he's short of money. But when I think about it objectively, as a proper detective might, I admit that I've probably seen him at his best. We haven't been subject to the pressures of daily life, or seen each other in a crisis. Except for now, of course, but this is why it's crunch time. I have to include him on the suspects list, whether I like it or not.

CHAPTER FORTY-EIGHT

Heather

She wakes into that blissful moment before awareness hits. The morning light filters gently through the blinds, promising another sun-filled day, and for an instant she feels her spirits lift. But in a single heartbeat, the memory of last night's horror hits her. She sits up suddenly, reaching out for James with a frantic hand. But he's not there, his side of the bed staring at her, cold and empty. She scrabbles on the bedside table for her watch. Five o'clock.

As she swings her legs to the floor, a wave of nausea flows over her, her stomach clenching. She leans forward, holding her belly, waiting for it to pass. Yesterday, she had nothing to eat after lunch. She's not hungry, but she knows this feeling. The nausea won't settle until she eats.

Throwing on a robe, she walks barefoot on the cold marble through to the living room, where the sun is already blazing through the wall of glass overlooking the sea. James sleeps on the sofa, still in yesterday's clothes. She crouches, gazing into his face, where the shock still shows in the lines and shadows. Waking him would be a cruel thing, while sleep muffles the horrible reality of the day.

Their mobiles lie before him on the coffee table like twins, their charging leads attached, waiting to be woken by the first person who touches them. It won't be her. She's lost the courage to even touch her phone. It's taken on an evil aura, repelling her, and she recoils even from the idea of checking the messages. She knows she should, but tells herself it's only five in the morning; even the police won't be up and about yet.

Unless they've been up all night, like James. She wonders where the negotiator has gone. Probably to the spare room downstairs; there's no sign of her here. Perhaps she went home, having heard nothing; perhaps they heard something but there was nothing to be done until the morning.

Last night the Guardia came to carry out the search, looking for any kind of intelligence. They already had Harry's phone, which revealed nothing. They needed his DNA, so his room, shared with Ben, was the one they focused on. All the other rooms were subject to a going-over too, even the unused ones.

Though they had been warned to expect them, it still felt like an invasion when they arrived. A swarm of uniformed men went from room to room, their presence huge and threatening. Once inside, they asked the family to stay outside on the terrace while they searched. They departed about forty minutes later, leaving behind them a strong scent of body odour and a feeling of violation. Everyone returned to their rooms, subdued, to replace their belongings in drawers and cupboards.

Looking down at the two mobiles, so innocent on the glass surface, she suffers a paroxysm of indecision, her hand hovering. She bites her lip, but she just can't make herself look. She needs the solid, grounded presence of James, conscious, beside her to face the grim messages that might await her. Or perhaps as bad, the empty screen.

All night long images of Harry tormented her. Harry alone, in the boot of a car, travelling fast, miles ticking away with the road beneath him. Harry locked in some horrible metal container on a boat, rocking, seasick . . . His soft hands, those stick-thin legs, the tousled head. These, and worse, kept her tossing and turning into the small hours. She must have slept for less than a couple of hours altogether.

Now the anxiety rises again, her stomach clenching as she counts the hours he's been gone. Fourteen hours, more. That first crucial period is gone, revealing no clues, no suspects. Last night before she lay down, she'd insisted James wake her if there was any news. He didn't come into their room once in the night, and she daren't think what this means. With shaking fingers, she fills the kettle and searches in the cupboard for instant coffee. The machine's too noisy; it will wake the entire household. When she opens the fridge, the shelves beckon her, full of last night's meal. But she can't do this now. She just needs to fill a hole so as not to pass out, to relieve the continuing growl of her empty gut. In the bread bin, she finds the end of a French stick. She eats standing up, shoving the hard crust into her mouth while the kettle boils behind her.

When her coffee's ready, she wraps her robe around her, curls up on the sofa opposite James, and waits.

* * *

The harsh buzz of a mobile startles her, coffee spilling down the front of her robe. Ignoring the spreading stains, she reaches out, almost dropping the mug — but James is ahead of her, galvanized into action.

"I've got it," he says as he grasps the handset, tearing the charging lead away. Heather sits beside him as he punches in the code, his fingers clumsy on the smooth surface. For a moment, he glares at the screen, then closes his eyes.

"This is it," he says, holding the mobile out for her to see. "The ransom demand. I need to get . . . the negotiator. What's her name? Quick . . ."

"Paola." Her eyes are glued to the message.

10 million euros for boy. 2 days.

The words jump out at her, as if they're alive, filling her eyes. An avalanche of questions crashes through her head.

Who are you — where is Harry — is he okay? Are you being kind to him?

The message says so little. She has an urge to shake the handset to make more words appear. Ten million euros — does that mean the kidnappers are Spanish? Perhaps it just means they're trying to hide their Britishness. Two days . . . and then what? Is Harry in danger? Is he even alive right now? How will they know? She closes her eyes, lost in a maelstrom of ever-more-unanswerable thoughts, until she feels the warmth of James's arms encircle her.

"It's okay," he says softly. "Now we have something to work with. It will be okay."

Within seconds, Paola is there, fully dressed, her dark ponytail gleaming. "Please, let's go," she says, leading the way to the dining room. There, an array of equipment has been set up, waiting for this moment.

Paola, a thirty-something woman with a brusque manner, arrived last night with a colleague. She shook hands with them, asked to be shown the room they would use, nodded and got to work. When she spoke in English, her accent was so strong Heather could barely understand her, and worried immediately that there might be problems. But Nick, listening to the conversation, volunteered immediately to help with the communications, both with the Guardia team and with the kidnappers, if they proved to be Spanish. Paola accepted his presence as soon as James and Heather agreed. Though the thought occurred to Heather that they were putting their trust in the person they knew least well, she pushed it to one side. Nick was turning out to be intelligent, calm and reliable — exactly what was needed in a crisis. They had to trust him.

"Do you need us to wake Nick?" Heather says as Paola connects the mobile to her equipment.

"No, that is not necessary yet," Paola replies, without raising her head.

"Are we going to answer the message?" James asks.

"Yes, as soon as we have the information we need," Paola says. James looks as if he's about to answer, but thinks better of it, raising his eyebrows at Heather.

Heather looks at her watch. It's past seven o'clock, and she can hear sounds of other people moving around the villa.

"I'm going to get dressed," she whispers to James, not wanting to disturb Paola as she works.

"Yes, go ahead. See who else is up," he says. "I'll stay here, just in case. I'd love a coffee, please, love . . ."

"Of course. I'll be back."

She closes the dining room door behind her just as Natalie appears in the corridor. She looks as if she's been awake for some time, her eyes ringed with darkness. She's dressed and carrying a mug of coffee. She puts an arm around Heather and holds her for a moment. "Coffee?" she says. "I've made enough for an army."

This is what Heather loves about Natalie. There's no need for small talk; she already knows what Heather is feeling.

"I'll just get changed. Be with you in a minute," she says.

When she returns she finds Natalie and Ben in the kitchen. Ben hugs her silently. "Has anything happened?" he says.

"A text asking for money. Nothing else. Nothing to say how Harry is . . ." Her voice wobbles and she stops before she loses control.

Ben's eyes widen. "Really? How—"

"There's nothing more to say, really. Just we have two days to get the money. Not where it should be left, or how it will be paid . . . I'm sure that will come nearer the time. Paola's working on it now. Dad's with her."

Natalie pours coffee into a large mug and hands it to her. Heather takes it in both hands, breathing in the heady aroma. It seems to clear her head a little.

"Is Nick up and about yet?"

"He's having a shower, he'll be with us shortly. Is he needed?"

"Not right now, but it would be good to have him available. What about the others?"

"Miles was up really early, went for a run," Liz says, appearing in the doorway, startling them. "I saw him leave. I don't know about the kids, but Steve's still out cold. How did we all sleep?" She looks around the grim faces. "Sorry, wrong question. Is there any coffee going?"

"Here," Heather says. "I'm about to take some to James and Paola. How about you get the breakfast things out, Ben? We should all get something to eat — it looks like it's going to be a long day."

She starts to prepare a tray to take to the dining room, grateful for the excuse to get away. She can't face the third degree from Liz, not this morning. Today is going to be hard enough without any added drama.

* * *

In the dining room, everything's quiet. The technical officer from yesterday evening has appeared from nowhere and is sitting with earphones on next to the equipment, fiddling with the dials. Paola seems to be making notes, while James and Nick wait silently.

Heather places the tray in the middle of the table.

"What's happening?" she asks James, keeping her voice low.

"We're deciding how to respond," James says, nodding towards Paola, who stands, stretching. She pours herself a generous mug of black coffee and turns to Heather and James.

"Okay," she says. "We're all here. This is what we need to do. First, we need proof of life."

Heather gasps. "Sorry," she whispers, biting her lip.

Paola ignores her. "No money until we have proof Harry is alive and well."

"How will we get proof of life via text?" James says, his voice breaking a little.

"We ask a particular question that only Harry can answer. You need to think of something, the parents." She looks intently from one to the other. "This is very important. No proof, no money."

"But—" Heather's about to say she doesn't care about the money. But James's restraining hand is on her arm.

Paola ignores her again. "Then, when we have proof, we delay payment."

Heather opens her mouth, but closes it again when she sees Paola's expression.

"We say we can't get it all, we might get some of it in the next two days, but not all. The bank won't release more, there's a delay in the UK, anything to give us more time. We send messages from the same mobile, and if there is a call, you take it—" she nods at James, "—but you will take over, Nick, if it's a Spanish person. Understood?"

"Understood," James says. "Okay, so we need to think of something to ask Harry."

Heather's mind goes blank. "Like what? I can't think straight . . ."

"I know — what about the colour of my eyes?" There's a family joke about James's eyes, which he thinks are grey, but his new hairdresser called them 'violet', to the amusement of the boys. They have never let him forget it, but nobody else would understand the reference.

"Yes, that would work," Heather says. "You'd better explain . . ."

Paola looks sceptical at first, but after James explains the family joke, she nods. "Good. Let's send the response."

She writes a few words down and turns the page towards them. They exchange glances and nod.

CHAPTER FORTY-NINE

Heather

It seems wrong to sit in the sun this morning, surrounded by the beauty of the Spanish morning, the glistening ocean, the trailing bougainvillea. By unspoken agreement, they gather in the cooled air of the spacious living room, appearing one by one, sitting silently for the most part. Steve appears with fresh croissants from the local *panadería,* enough for everyone and more. They help themselves mechanically, Natalie taking a plateful to the dining room for the negotiators.

Leaving James and Nick to deal with Paola is a small relief for Heather. She's too anxious to be close by, waiting for news. The strain of watching others doing their work, using technology that is opaque to her, is too much. But sitting around with a group of people who can only look at each other, helpless, or stare out, unseeing, at the sea, doesn't help her either.

"I'm going for a walk." Eight white faces look up immediately. "No," she says firmly. "I need to be on my own. Sorry . . . Natalie, can we talk?"

Natalie follows her to the corridor. "Can you get the kids to go for a swim, please?" Heather says in a low voice.

"Or maybe go down to the beach with them, let them kick a ball around? They don't need to be sitting around with us."

Natalie nods. "Of course."

"Don't let them go on their own, though."

"No, no, I'll go with them. Perhaps someone will come with me."

"Thanks so much. They'll go nuts if they stay in all day, but I can see they feel as if they have to," Heather says. "See if Charlotte will go with you — she looks as if she needs distracting, too."

Natalie nods. "Of course. Yes, I agree about Charlotte. She looks right on the edge this morning, and Miles is pretty useless. I'll see what I can do."

"Thanks, Natalie, you're a star. I'll just tell James I'm going. I won't be long — my mobile has to stay here, so I won't be in touch. Twenty minutes, half an hour, maybe. I'll check with Paola first, make sure she knows what we're doing."

"Okay, I understand."

As she leaves the villa on the path that snakes down to the sea from the gardens, Heather has the strange sense that she's abandoning Harry, her feet faltering on the sandy gravel. She almost turns back, but after a moment of indecision, carries on. She needs this time alone.

She walks away from the knots of holidaymakers enjoying the sun and the foaming waves, staying on the part of the beach where the wind is strongest and the people sparse. The breeze ruffles her hair, cooling the back of her neck as she walks. Her sunglasses protect her eyes from the worst of the glare, but even so it's hard walking into the sun, against the strong *Levante* wind from the east, so she lets herself sink down onto the sand, ignoring the dampness that soaks through the seat of her dress.

The feeling of nausea she felt when she awoke hasn't left her. It won't go while her son is missing, she's sure of that now. She gazes out at the vast sea, breathing in deeply. The ocean is beautiful, endless, powerful — and cruel, changing from benign to malevolent with a whirl of the wind. Dangerous, horrifying. Like the situation they're in.

This is about the money. Not for the first time she curses the whim that made her buy the ticket that set this all in motion, that won them a fortune but — possibly — lost them something infinitely more precious. If she'd known in that moment that the small slip of pink paper she held in her hand that day in the newsagent would lead to this, she would have torn it up in a heartbeat.

* * *

Refreshed by the wind and the tang of the sea air, she walks slowly back to the villa. On the path, she comes across Natalie, Charlotte and the three teenagers, carrying a football and a couple of beach bags, towels spilling from them. There's no news from the villa.

"I'm going back up anyway," Heather says. "I want to give James a break."

"Do you want me to come back with you, Mum?" Ben says immediately. "I can come to the beach later . . ."

She smiles at him. He's taking this hard, though he tries to hide it. "No, darling, it's okay. You need to let off a bit of steam. Try not to worry."

"Take care of him for me," she says to Natalie as she turns up the steep path.

"Of course, don't worry about him."

At the villa, she puts her head round the dining room door. James and Nick sit together at one end of the table while Paola and her colleague talk in Spanish at the other, huddled over their equipment. "Anything?" she says to James.

He stands and leaves the room, closing the door behind them. "No response yet. But they have the location of the mobile when the text was sent. They were able to track the number to a place not far from here, about ten kilometres further down the coast towards Tarifa."

Her heart leaps. Surely this is good news? "Ten kilometres? Does that mean they're still here, then? Have the police gone to find them?"

James makes a placatory gesture, his palms towards the floor. "We can't assume anything. The mobile they used is not responding now, it could be a pay-as-you-go phone. They've probably ditched it already."

"But they know it was sent from somewhere nearby . . . surely that's good news?" She feels like she needs something to hold onto, some tiny scrap to give her hope.

"Honestly, love, we don't know. I'm just leaving Paola to do her job, hoping she's getting somewhere. They have sent someone to the location, but it's doubtful that's the place they're holding Harry. No self-respecting kidnapper would be that stupid, unfortunately for us."

She feels her body sag. She puts her hand out to the wall for support. James takes her by the hand and leads her away from the living area to their bedroom. Closing the door, he makes her sit down.

"So they have nothing?" she whispers.

"Well, they have a little. They know the kidnappers were still in the area when the message was sent. That must be a good thing for us."

"What are we doing about the money?"

"I've asked the bank for an urgent transfer to Gibraltar; that's the nearest branch. We should be able to do it in time. But we won't tell them, not until we know Harry is okay."

"No!" She almost sobs the word. "No, James, we should give them what they want! I don't care about the money, I wish we'd never won it! They can have it all — I just want Harry back, that's all I care about!"

"It's okay, Heather. It's okay. We'll get him back, we will."

She knows James is doing his best to comfort her, but his words do nothing to relieve the terrible feeling of emptiness in her heart.

CHAPTER FIFTY

Heather

"Julie called," James says, as she splashes water onto her reddened eyes.

She pauses in surprise, water dripping from her chin. "On your mobile? How did she—?"

"Jerez. I gave everyone my number in case they got lost."

"Oh. That's all we need," she says, reaching for a towel.

"Indeed," he says with a wry smile. "Caused a bit of a stir in the room, we jumped out of our skin. We had to ask her not to call again."

"What did she want?"

"Just to see if there was any news and offer to help."

"We don't need that number blocked by anyone. But I suppose it was nice of her to check. Do I look any better?" She looks at herself in the mirror, knowing the answer already. She looks terrible, her eyes underlined with dark shadows, her cheeks sagging. But it doesn't matter now, nothing does except Harry and finding him.

"Julie and Roger have been questioned by the Guardia, you know. It doesn't mean anything—" he says, as she glances up, a question on her lips. "They have to question everyone in our party, and they were with us that day."

"You know, it did seem to me, before, that she knew a lot about us. She certainly seemed to assume we were rich . . ."

"I know she did. But think about it: we're renting a huge, luxurious villa, no expense spared, for the whole summer, inviting a big party of people and pretty obviously paying for everything. You don't have to be a member of Mensa to work out we're not short of money."

"You're right, of course. I can't help wondering, though. Could it really be someone close to us? How could anyone else know, here, in Spain? It's horrible, suspecting our friends, even our family, but it's the logical conclusion, isn't it? You know all those crime dramas Natalie watches, all the thrillers she reads — the family and friends are always the prime suspects. And in real life. So where does that leave us?"

It leaves them with the group that's gathered in this villa. They have to suspect everyone around them: Nick, Liz, Steve, Miles, Charlotte. Even Natalie, her best friend. It's a horrible thought, but Natalie has admitted lying to Heather many times. Perhaps even she's not the person Heather thought she was.

It's horrible, unthinkable, but it's true. Here, right here, are the prime suspects.

She shakes her head; she can't deal with this now. "I should call my mum," she says, brushing her hair, punishing it with the hard bristles. "She'll worry if she doesn't hear. What am I going to tell her?"

"Don't call her," James says. "Send her a picture of the boys on the beach, the one we took the other day. Just tell her we're all having a great time. She'll be happy with that. There's no point upsetting her."

"You're right. But — I can't use my phone . . ."

"Get Natalie to send it — your Mum won't think that's strange at all."

Her brain must be slowing down with the stress; she would not have thought of that.

"Have they traced those other texts yet? I told the Capitán about them . . ."

"I don't know. I mentioned it too, so they should have done. I'll remind them — it could be important. You know, I'm beginning to think they're not great at communication. And Nick saw one of the reports they'd written down at the beach. He said it was pretty patchy, but when he tried to give them more detail, they waved him away. He's going to try to keep on top of them, talk to the Capitán for us . . ."

She looks up at him, panicked. "I hope we're doing the right thing, James. How do we know if the Guardia are any good? What if they're missing things? It's already been almost twenty-four hours . . ."

"Listen, they're doing their best. We have to trust they know what to do. They have the experience, this lot, and we don't have a clue between us about how to deal with a kidnapping. Nick and I will stay on top of it, don't worry."

She massages her forehead. "Please stop telling me not to worry, James. I simply can't stop. You must feel the same as me — the waiting is just awful, the hours ticking past, nothing happening . . . I want to do something, anything, to get him back. Throw money at them, send an army . . ."

James takes her by the shoulders, turning her towards him. "Look at me," he says. She looks up, her eyes filling again. "I know. I feel exactly the same. It's horrible, heartbreaking, deeply frustrating. But we must follow the advice. If we don't, we risk messing up the negotiations. We have no choice. Do we?"

"I suppose not. You're right, I need to pull myself together."

"I wasn't saying that. You're doing really well, anyone would feel desperate in this situation. But we need to keep our heads, for Harry's sake."

"Yes, I know. I'm okay, really. I'll be fine."

"Good. Look, I mustn't leave Nick for too long. Could you get us all some cold drinks? It's going to be a long haul today."

"Of course. I'll just take a few minutes . . ."

As the door closes, she takes a deep breath and closes her eyes. She has to get through this.

* * *

She finds Liz and Steve by the front door, about to leave.

"We thought we'd walk into the town, if that's all right with you," Steve says. "We're feeling a little useless."

"We are allowed out, aren't we?" Liz says. "We're not under house arrest or anything?" She seems to think she's said something amusing, looking at Steve for a reaction.

"As long as the Guardia haven't said you should stay, you can go, of course. Are you taking a mobile with you?"

"I've got mine," Steve says, patting his shorts pocket.

As they leave, he turns back to her. "Will you be okay? I don't want you to think we're deserting you."

"Not at all," she says, touched. "I'll be fine. James and Nick are here."

As the front door closes, she wonders if, if she says it often enough, she will begin to believe it.

It's good to have the rest of the house to herself. She can only take so much of the intensity in the dining room, and she can't bear the speculation that must be going through the minds of the others, the unasked questions. It's hard enough coping with her own imagination.

Looking in the fridge for cold drinks, she tries to ignore the food that fills every shelf.

But when she returns from the dining room, having left James and the others with fresh lemonade and iced water, she's drawn back to the kitchen, to the tempting contents of the fridge. She'll just have a small plate, to stop the nausea.

Nobody needs to know.

Afterwards, the guilt hits her harder than ever. She lies on the bed, her throat aching with the effort, the muscles of her stomach stretched and sore. Her hair stinks, her breath must be worse. Vomiting is disgusting, demeaning. Why

243

does she do it? Especially now, with Harry lost, alone, possibly hurt. What a terrible, selfish woman she is, comforting herself with food while her son suffers. She thumps her forehead with her fist until her head pounds with it, punishing, hating herself.

But there's nothing she can do about it.

CHAPTER FIFTY-ONE

Heather

"We've had a reply." James dips his head around the bedroom door and is gone. Startled, she sits up suddenly, her head pounding after the punching she's given it.

She jumps up, runs to the bathroom, hurriedly washing her face, scrubbing at her hair, anything that might give her away. She squeezes a blob of toothpaste onto her finger and rubs it on her teeth. Throwing the towel on the floor, she races barefoot to the ops room, stubbing her toe on the doorjamb in her hurry. "What did they say?"

"Violet. The message says: *Violet*. He's okay, love."

She sinks into a chair. "Thank god. Anything else?"

"They sent bank details for the money. They're looking at that now."

Paola is jabbering into a phone in rapid Spanish, turning her back. More uniformed officers have joined her and the room is beginning to look crowded. They sit away from James and Nick in a huddle, some slumped in dining chairs, a couple leaning against the wall, their backs to the door.

"The rest of the text said no to delaying; the money must be transferred in two days," Nick says. "Paola's conferring with the Capitán, deciding what to do next."

There's a sudden flurry of activity as Paola disconnects the call. She gives rapid instructions to two of the men, who leave the room immediately. The slam of the front door is followed by the revving of a car engine and the click of the gate.

"Where are they going?" James says, standing, Nick close behind him.

Paola shakes her head. "They have to go into the town," she says. "Another job."

"Another job? But what's going on? Have you tracked the latest message?"

"Please." Paola frowns and starts to punch numbers into her mobile. "Let us do our work."

As she starts to talk again, James and Nick retreat to the other end of the table. "Something's going on, isn't it?" Heather says. "What aren't they telling us?"

* * *

"We're going to speak to the Capitán," Nick says firmly, going up to the group of uniformed officers at the other end of the room. Paola tears her eyes from the screen in front of her and stares at him, frowning, her dark eyebrows almost touching.

"*¿Por qué?*" she says, and carries on in rapid Spanish. Nick replies, eliciting a shrug and some expressive hand gestures. From her tone of voice, Heather guesses the idea hasn't gone down well with her. Paola turns back to her laptop, her shoulders hunched.

"I've told her we need to know what's happening," Nick says. "She says we know everything, but I don't think we do. I'll give him a call. Tell me what you'd like me to ask."

The list is long: did they track the original threatening texts on Heather's mobile; was there any information from

246

the café bar where Harry was last seen; were Guardia officers sent to the locations of the first and second messages; did any of the interviews raise suspicions; have they completed the house-to-house search in Tarifa . . .

What is their plan?

"We have to know what they propose to do about the handover," James says. "That's what really worries me. They seem determined that we should offer them only part of the ten million. I'm not sure about that — surely it will just annoy the kidnappers?"

"Maybe offering part of the money is one of the ways to entrap the perpetrators," Nick says. "But how are we to know? We have to trust they know what they're doing."

"The money's not important," James says. "We can give it to them as soon as we've got it, for all I care — they can scarper as soon as they've given Harry back. But if we give them the money, how will the Guardia know that they'll hand him over? Is it done simultaneously? Or do we give them the money first, risk losing Harry and go right back to where we started? I'm worried the Guardia might care more about catching the kidnappers than about Harry."

"I agree, they must tell us how they intend to do the handover," Nick says. "It's so tricky when the kidnappers aren't speaking to us directly. If we could talk to them, we might be able to get some kind of rapport, show them we're being reasonable. Dealing with them by text makes it much more difficult."

"There could be good reasons for it from their point of view, though," James says, throwing a worried glance at Heather. "Gives them more anonymity, less chance to be caught out."

Heather knows he's not saying what she's thinking, to protect her.

Especially if it's one of us.

"Right," Nick says. "I'll go and do this in our bedroom. I'll take lots of notes, don't worry. Best if Paola doesn't listen in. Let's hope I can get hold of the Capitán. If he won't speak to me, I'll insist he comes and talks to us properly, personally."

"Should I come with you?" Heather asks, keeping her voice light, though what's going through her mind is far from light-hearted.

"It's okay, it'll all be in Spanish, anyway."

But what if Nick's part of this? If he is, are they giving him everything he needs? She catches a look from James, who shakes his head at her, out of Nick's line of sight. "Right, Nick, thank you," he says. "Good luck with the Capitán."

She just has to hope that James is right and Nick is beyond suspicion.

CHAPTER FIFTY-TWO

Natalie

This is a good idea, to let the children work off some energy, to give them some sense of normality.

I'm worried about Ben. I'm going to look after him so Heather and James can focus on finding Harry. On the way down to the beach, he hangs his head, speaking to nobody until we come across Heather on her way back up. He wants to go back with her and has to be persuaded to stay with me. But to my relief, once he's on the beach he cheers up, running in and out of the waves with the others, chasing the ball.

It's heartbreaking not being able to offer any real help to Heather and James; I wish I could do more.

Thank goodness for Nick. He barely knows them but he's proving to be heaven-sent — without his knowledge of Spanish, we'd feel even more helpless. The Guardia may know what they're doing, but their demeanour verges on the abrupt, and though they seem to understand English well enough, their accents are so strong I have trouble deciphering what they're saying. If they say anything.

I can only pray they're right to trust Nick.

Though his name appears on my list, I've looked at it every which way until my brain hurts, and I can't see why he would want to extort money from my friends. Unless I've been taken in by an extremely clever fraudster — which I suppose is possible, but it does stretch the imagination. He has plenty of money — or at least, I haven't seen a scrap of evidence that he's struggling financially, in any way; he owns his own home; he has wealthy clients who give him regular work. I've seen the evidence at his flat. I suppose if you really wanted to hide your financial position, it would be easy enough, but nothing I've seen points to Nick being that sort of person. And he's being so helpful. If this is for some horrible, twisted reason to further his claim on the money, then that's beyond my understanding. Anyway, how can he be texting from an anonymous mobile from some distance, when he's sitting in the room with the Guardia? It stretches belief to think he's working with an accomplice, when he didn't even know until the last minute that he would be coming to Spain with Heather and James. No, he has to come off the list.

It's a relief, and it makes my list one name shorter.

That leaves, among others, Liz and Steve, who don't seem, either of them, bright enough to do something like this. I'm not being patronizing, and I would never openly express this to anyone, but they're not sophisticated. They haven't travelled much, they don't seem to know how things work here. And really, why would Liz extort money from her own brother, threaten her nephew? She seems so fond of them both, it's hard to imagine she's putting on an act. And James and Heather have been generous with them; I'm sure they have. I suppose it could be that Liz wants or needs more — but surely all she'd have to do is ask for it? James and Heather are not the sort of people to close down a discussion like that — in fact, I've always said it, Heather is generous to a fault, she's always giving things away.

I'm going to take Liz off the list. Should I remove Steve as well? He'll surely benefit from anything Liz gets, so he's an unlikely suspect.

So, I'm left with Julie and Roger, Charlotte and Miles. And while I'm with Charlotte, I have a small window of opportunity.

She walks ahead of me, her head hanging. She's barefoot in the shallow water, but seems in a daze, stumbling once and almost falling.

I increase my pace to catch up with her. "Are you okay?" I say, startling her a little.

"I'm fine," she says, though her voice betrays her. Her eyes are hidden behind dark glasses, so I can't read her expression.

Of all of us, she seems to be taking this the hardest. Or perhaps she's always like this, and it's just because I don't know her well that she seems unusually upset. She could be a nervous type, have panic attacks regularly, for all I know. All I do know is she's cried more tears than the rest of us put together, or at least it seems so.

I'm about to ask her gently, diplomatically, if there's something else bothering her, but at that moment Cara appears at my elbow.

"I'm hungry," she says. "Can we go back?"

My opportunity is gone.

"Is everyone else hungry?" I ask.

"Boys, are you ready for lunch?" Cara yells against the wind, waving an arm.

The boys, jumping waves at the water's edge, look up. "Yes, we are!" They run back to us, sending sprays of golden sand from their heels.

I nod to Charlotte and start to head back, hoping we can continue to talk on the way.

But she hesitates. "I'm going to keep walking," she says. "I need some air. I'm not hungry, so don't worry about me. I'll be back soon."

There's not much I can do but usher the children back towards the path. Perhaps I'll get the chance to talk to her properly later.

* * *

251

Back at the villa, the atmosphere is tense and hushed. Even the youngsters feel it, their banter fading with the closing of the door behind them. It's almost as if the house is shrouded in cloud, despite the brightness of the sunshine all around it.

Looking through the living area to the view beyond, I see Heather alone on the terrace, staring at the sea. There's pain in the tautness of her shoulders, the way she grasps the balustrade as if to keep herself from falling. My heart goes out to her, but I leave her to a moment of solitude. She has always needed time to herself in difficult moments.

Our little group goes to the kitchen, where I start to unload leftover dishes and salad ingredients from the fridge. I leave the kids to lay the table while I go to check with the front-liners in the dining room.

When I put my head around the door, I'm surprised to see that Nick isn't there; James sits in the corner on his own, his laptop open in front of him. A huddle of uniforms works silently at the opposite end of the table.

"I'm on lunch duty," I say to him, keeping my voice low. "Where's Nick?"

"He's gone to your room to call the Capitán. We want a proper update, and he's doing it in private so . . ." He jerks his head towards Paola and the others. "He'll be back soon. Lunch would be great. Are you going to ask them?" Another nod in their direction.

I feel it's only fair to feed Paola, who has worked tirelessly since she arrived, but there are now three more. "I suppose so. We should have enough."

But when I ask them, the men shake their heads. Paola says: "They will go soon to the station. They can eat there. I would like to eat something, though, *gracias*."

At that moment, one of the mobiles sitting silent on the table buzzes; the group is galvanized into action. Suddenly they all have something to do, two of the men putting earphones on and staring intently at their screens, the other grabbing a notebook, while Paola picks up the phone. I stand, fixed to the spot. She gazes at the screen for a moment, swipes and taps, then shakes her head. Everyone relaxes, but she says something in Spanish and they all focus on the screens once again. She notices I'm still there, frozen.

"This is the mother's mobile. Anonymous." She shrugs. "We will trace it."

I remember those texts that frightened Heather at the beginning. I wonder what makes people so poisonous to people they've never met. It must be the anonymity, the feeling that you can get away with anything. The actual phrase that comes to me, unbidden, horrifies me. *You can get away with murder.* My thoughts flit back to Harry. Please, don't let it be that.

"What does it say?" James is at my shoulder. Paola hands him the mobile without comment. I crane my neck to see.

Rich bitch!!! Are your friends really your friends? Are you sure?

James's jaw tightens, his mouth a harsh line. He hands the handset back to Paola. "Is this them?"

"We don't know. Is possible . . . or not. We are checking."

At that moment, Heather appears at the door. "What is it?" she says, seeing us gathered round.

"Another nasty text," James says. "We don't know who it's from — it might not be the kidnappers." He tries to lead Heather away, but she stands her ground.

"Let me see it," she says, holding her hand out to Paola. Wordlessly, Paola hands it over.

Heather gazes at the screen for a moment, then gives it back, her already pale face ashen. Her hand flies to her mouth and she stumbles from the room.

I follow James's anguished gaze as she leaves. "Shall I go?"

"Give her a few minutes," he says, sinking into a chair. "She's not doing well, Natalie. She thinks it's all her fault. She was always scared the money would change everything, and now it looks as if she was right." He puts his face in his hands. "Why didn't I think about this? Why wasn't I more careful? I should have . . ."

I sit beside him, my hand on his shoulder. "Don't beat yourself up, James. Please — you weren't to know this would happen, you can't blame yourself . . ." The words are inadequate, but I'm shaken by his reaction, and it's the best I can do. James is the one person who always keeps his feet on the ground. If he can't cope, then none of us can. I have to support him, help him take the strain for both of them. Otherwise, Heather will fall off the edge of a cliff.

"No, you're right," he says, letting out a long breath. He squares his shoulders. "Heather's doing enough beating herself up for all of us. It's the inactivity, the waiting. She keeps imagining the worst."

I stand up. We need to get out of here. "Come on then, let's go and see if Nick's finished. You need a break anyway." I look at Paola watching James. "We need ten minutes, okay?"

She nods, and I imagine I see a flash of empathy in her steady gaze. "Stay close."

CHAPTER FIFTY-THREE

Heather

Heather stands alone in the corridor, her breath coming in short gasps. She leans against the wall, but her legs buckle and she slides down onto the tiled floor. She closes her eyes, listening to the sounds from the kitchen, the comments of the children, their sandalled feet padding in and out, the clink of crockery, the clash of cutlery on the worktop. A male voice, perhaps Miles's, filters through from outside, muffled. She doesn't know who else is there, but she needs this quiet moment to calm herself. She removes her shoes and sits for a moment with her hands and feet flat on the cool marble, her head against the wall, allowing the chill to flow through her.

She's still in that position, calmer now, when Nick appears from further down the corridor, a notebook in his hand.

"Hello," he says. "Are you okay?"

"Just taking a moment." She smiles weakly.

"Mind if I join you?" To her surprise, he sits beside her, his back against the wall, in a mirror of her own position. There's a long pause while they both gaze, unseeing, at the blank wall opposite.

"It's a different perspective, isn't it?" he says at last.

"Mm."

They're still sitting there in comfortable silence when James and Natalie emerge from the dining room.

"There you are," Natalie says, surprised. "Is this a private meeting or can we come and join you?"

"Actually," Heather says, shifting her legs, "it's getting rather uncomfortable. Let's go through."

"Lunch is ready, if you're hungry," Natalie says. "The kids want to get started."

"Thanks. Tell them to tuck in. We'll be there in a moment," James says, leading them to the furthest seating area in the spacious room. Through the shaded window, Heather can see Miles in the pool, swimming up and down, his head bobbing. The kids sit at one end, still in T-shirts and shorts, their feet dangling in the water, their faces shaded by baseball caps. A garish pink lilo is propped against the balustrade, water pooling around it.

It could be the image of a normal, happy summer holiday.

When Nick speaks, she has to drag herself back into the present, her mind reluctant to return to the nightmare they're living through.

"I'm not sure what I think about this," he says. "The Capitán is going ahead with the plan to transfer half the money before the deadline. He wants to prevaricate, say it's impossible to get the rest by tomorrow. The idea is to get more messages going to and from the hostage-taker, get a closer handle on the location, so they can pin him down."

"Don't they have an idea yet?" Heather says. "I thought they could track the texts to within a few hundred yards . . ."

"They can. But if the phone is a pay-as-you-go, which is likely, and it's been dumped, that doesn't help us find the person — or Harry. They think he's probably an amateur, and they'll have more chance of tracing him if they play for time."

256

"An amateur? What makes them think that?" This could be good or bad. An amateur might be unpredictable, a madman. But professional criminals might be even more dangerous.

Nick shrugs. "I don't know. I didn't get his logic."

"Where did the texts come from? Did they get an address?" James asks.

"Sadly not. They both came from nearby, a few kilometres from here, but from different numbers."

"And the other messages? The nasty stuff on my mobile?"

"Probably unconnected."

Heather glances at James, unsure what this means.

"Probably? But — they were there, in the room, when the last message came. Couldn't they — track the phone, or whatever they're doing in there?" Heather can hear the near-hysteria in her voice.

"Seems like the messages you got came from London, including the last one," Nick says.

She sinks back into her chair. "London? How did that happen?" Her mind's whirring, thinking who she's given her new number to. The school, the lottery company, the travel agent . . . who else? But none of these would want to threaten her, surely? Someone else must have got hold of her number . . . but how?

"I don't understand," she says. "Can mobiles pretend to be in more than one place at a time?"

Nobody seems to know. She feels as if she's floundering, helpless in a world she can't fathom.

"Did you ask if they have any suspects?" she says.

"I did," Nick replies. "It appears not. I'm sorry."

Heather can hardly bear the silence, the sagging shoulders, the eyes avoiding hers. She gets to her feet. Her body seems slow, unresponsive, her mind numb.

James's anxious gaze follows her. "Heather . . ."

"I'm going to get some lunch. We need to eat."

* * *

The negotiating team is back in place in the dining room; the kids have retreated to the shade with their phones. Every so often, one of them emits a yell that makes her jump. She walks over to them. Sunbeds look out over the sea, shaded by swathes of bougainvillea draped over a wooden pergola. Vibrant pinks and purples contrast with an immaculate blue sky beyond. She wishes she could just lie down and sleep in the shade, without a care in the world.

"Hey kids," she says, perching on the end of Ben's sunbed, pushing his long legs to one side with her hand.

"Whoa, Mum, you made me jump," he says, glancing up from his mobile.

"Can you pause whatever it is you're doing, just for a minute, please?" Three serious young faces lift to gaze at her.

"Thank you, sorry to disturb your game. Listen, you will tell us, won't you, if you see anything from your friends online that might help us? None of the adults are much good on social media, or the other apps you all use."

"Mum, of course we would, we're not stupid," Ben says, indignant.

"I know you would, really — sorry, Ben. It's just . . . I'm clutching at straws here." Feeling the tears welling up once again, she turns away, squinting into the sun.

"That's okay, Mum."

Cara bites her lip while Josh stares unseeing at his bare feet, tongue-tied in Heather's presence.

"We will find him, won't we, Mum?"

She pats Ben's legs, summoning her best smile. It's a weak affair, but it is a smile.

"Of course we will. Okay, I'm off. I'll be in with Dad, in the dining room, if you need me."

The day drags on. To Heather, clock-watching, painfully aware of the deadline approaching, the hours seem interminable. As the evening approaches, nobody seems inclined to gather for supper, though Carmen has delivered a series of dishes. People drift around, helping themselves when the mood takes them, and it's not long before the living areas are empty. Even the kids disappear early to their rooms.

Unable to settle, Heather moves about in a daze. Finally, around mid-evening, Paola starts to pack up for the day, ready for an early start tomorrow.

"I'm done in," James says, stretching. "Shall we have a quick walk? I could do with some fresh air."

As they head for the beach, the light is fading fast, leaving a narrow strip of purple sky close to the horizon. There's enough reflection from the dipping sun and the rising moon to light their way along the sand. For a while they walk in silence, each deep in thought, until James says: "Tomorrow, Heather, we'll get him back."

"How can you be sure, though?" Before her floats an image of Harry, all alone, sitting on a cold concrete floor, hungry and bewildered.

"The money's all there, ready to be transferred before the deadline. If the police are right and this is an amateur job, the kidnapper will wait for the transfer, grab the money and run, as fast as he can. He'll tell us where Harry is, leave himself some leeway and hope to get away before the Guardia are on to him."

It sounds straightforward, but they both know that anything could go wrong. There are a hundred different scenarios, only one of which is the one they want. It's all down to chance, in the end.

Like winning the lottery.

CHAPTER FIFTY-FOUR

Heather

After a tortuous night of lying awake, her body aching with exhaustion, her mind unable to slow down, Heather's relieved to hear early sounds of movement around the villa. She fumbles for her watch: it's five fifteen. At home she'd be asleep for another two hours. She feels as if she's been punched in the head. A lump seems to have taken shape beneath her ribcage.

James takes a short shower and is gone from the bedroom; she hears the buzzer go in the hallway and a flurry of footsteps. The Guardia are here. She dresses quickly.

In the kitchen, Natalie and Nick are making coffee.

Natalie hugs her, studies her face. "You look terrible. Any sleep at all?"

"Barely. But it doesn't matter."

"Here, this is for you." Natalie hands her a large mug of coffee.

"The Guardia have arrived in force," Nick says. "I'm about to go in. Come with me, Heather? Let's see if they have a plan for today."

The Capitán is already there, more uniformed men with him, everyone sitting around the table. He stands to greet them, his handshake firm, his expression grave.

"What's happening?" she says, as she slides into the chair next to James.

"No more messages as yet. We're talking about the deadline and when to transfer the money," he says. "They're going to try to get agreement from the kidnappers on getting Harry's location."

There's a heated discussion going on in Spanish over the table, Paola and her colleagues clearly in dispute over something. Nick listens intently, then says something to the Capitán, who raises his hand. Everyone falls silent.

"*Gracias*," he says, his voice throaty, a whiff of cigarette smoke drifting from his direction. "Today we have decisions to make. The kidnapper demands we transfer the money before ten o'clock this morning. All ten million. But this morning, we have offered half — five million euros."

Heather is about to protest, but James is ahead of her. "Hang on a minute. We can give them all of it. We don't care about the money . . ."

"We need more contact with the hostage-taker. He wants ten million, we hope he will push for that. So he will have to negotiate with us. We assume this will also be by text message. Officers are at the location where the other messages came from, and we're ready to track if the location is different."

"Have you had a response yet?"

"Not yet, but we hope soon."

They hope. Heather has to control a sudden rush of anger. Hope won't save her son.

"But . . . we're still no further ahead," she says, her heart racing. "Where is Harry? How are we going to rescue him?"

The Capitán shakes his head. "We don't know where he's being held, not yet. But we have a chance to catch the kidnapper if we follow the mobile location."

"But that won't lead us to Harry! The kidnapper could text from anywhere . . ."

James nods in agreement. "If he's in a car, he could be miles away from Harry . . ."

The Capitán holds his hands up.

"We don't know where he will text from. But we must be ready to track him. We can't chase the money if it's transferred straight to the bank, so we have to chase the messages. Otherwise, we won't catch the kidnapper."

"But what about our son?" James says. "We've got to be sure he's safe — before they get the money, surely?"

The Capitán glances at him with a look of cold arrogance. "It's best to give the money first. Then they give us the hostage."

Heather feels a stab of fear in her heart. "But surely they'll just run off with the money?"

She's almost screaming now, the muscles in her stomach clenching, panic bubbling up. How competent are these people? "They'll disappear and we'll never find Harry!"

Pandemonium breaks out, the uniformed officers all speaking at once, the Capitán waving his hands, Nick looking from one to the other, frowning. Then he speaks slowly, enunciating his words carefully. It's a few minutes before he's finished. While he's talking, the Capitán leans back in his chair, his arms folded, a deep frown on his face. He mutters something to the man next to him, who leaves the room.

The Capitán turns back to Nick, his voice gruff. What he says, Heather can't tell, but there's a brief interchange between the two men before Nick nods. Then the Capitán stands and stalks out of the room, two of his men behind him, while Paola and the technician shrug and turn back to their screens.

James and Heather stare at each other, stunned.

"Where are they going? What did you say to them?" James says to Nick.

Nick shakes his head in disbelief. "I said we're not at all happy with the way they're handling this. And we're expecting them to have a proper plan. They have to come back to us by nine o'clock this morning with a workable proposal. Otherwise, we will report them at the highest level."

"This is unbelievable," James says. "We're running out of time, and they have nothing. What have they been doing?"

Heather stares at James, her heart pounding. Suddenly she's terribly scared. It's clear to her now: the Guardia care more about catching the kidnappers than they do about the safety of her son.

"This is a farce, James. What are we going to do?"

She holds her head in her hands. Her forehead throbs as if it will burst at any moment, her breath coming in short gasps. Everything is slipping away from them. Her beloved, sweet son is no closer to being rescued than he was on the first evening.

"What are we going to do?" she says. "We have nothing — nothing. They have no suspects. We have no clue where he is. We're helpless — and if the Guardia have no idea either, then—" She can't bear to think what happens then.

"It's okay, Heather, we still have time," Nick says. He drops his voice, glancing over at Paola gazing intently at her laptop screen. "Listen — we could take things into our own hands. We have the money. The kidnappers want the money, so there must be a way of sorting this out, with or without police involvement. We might risk being charged with something, but that doesn't matter as long as we get Harry back."

"I agree," James says, running his hand through his hair in a gesture that Heather recognises. He's feeling the strain as acutely as she is, even if he hides it better. "Nick, can you talk to Paola, see what she's thinking? She's much closer to it than we are, and probably knows more than the Capitán. Then we'll go through the options and decide for ourselves the best way to go about this. Then, when the Guardia come back with a plan — if they come back with a plan — we'll be ready to make a decision."

"Right. I'll see what I can find out." Nick goes over to Paola at the end of the room, and soon they're engrossed in discussion.

Heather's thoughts are spinning, terror causing mayhem in her mind. "James, I'm so frightened, I can't think straight. There's so little time . . ."

"I know. But we must. Let's think logically. If the Guardia can get a response — hopefully, offering only half the money will make the kidnappers respond — then we have a more recent location to work with, and if they're quick enough they might be in the right place. We've got to know where Harry is before promising the rest of the money. If we're transferring it electronically, it's possible to do that very quickly. I think—"

At the other end of the room, Paola makes a sudden move as one of the mobiles sitting before her on the table buzzes. She stares intently at the screen, then looks up.

"What is it, Paola?" James jumps to his feet.

"We have a reply," she says, pulling her own phone from her top pocket.

"What does it say?" James says, holding out his hand. Paola gives him the handset and focuses on her own.

Heather cranes her neck to see over James's shoulder. The words leap out at her as if alive.

Transfer 5 million euros now. Boy in Tarifa. Money confirmed in account for full address.

"Give it to me, please," Paola says, holding out her hand, gesturing urgently. "We must track the message."

James passes the phone back. The technical man checks it and connects it quickly to his laptop, staring intently at the screen.

"We need proof of life again," Paola says. "What question? It must be something only Harry can answer."

They look at each other. Heather's mind goes blank for a moment. Then she remembers their holiday in Cornwall and the practical joke Harry played on her, the shock she had when he put a live crab in her bag. "Ask what he put in my handbag in St Mawes."

Paola looks blank. "In . . . where?"

264

"Here, let me type it," James says. "You can check it when it's done."

The Guardia man holds the phone out for James, who taps rapidly, then shows the screen to her. With a nod, she gives him the go-ahead. The message is sent.

"I will tell the Capitán," Paola says. "Talk to the bank, tell them to be prepared, please, but don't transfer yet. You must use a different phone."

"Of course. Should I give them the account number for the transfer?"

"Not yet. We will give it to them when we're ready."

"Okay. But I need to get the contact numbers for the bank from my phone. May I?"

"Yes. No messages, please."

James takes a pen and grabs the notebook Nick has been using, noting down some numbers as he scrolls through his contacts. He hands his mobile back to Paola.

"Nick, may I use your phone to contact the bank, please? And can I have a quick word with you both?" he adds, his eyes flicking towards Paola, who is now absorbed in conversation on her phone.

"But shouldn't one of us stay?"

"It won't take a minute, just come out here for a moment," he says, holding the door open for them. He closes it quietly, a strange look on his face.

"What is it, James, what's going on?"

James holds the door shut with one hand and lowers his voice. "I took the kidnapper's account details from my mobile. They want the money now, and we can do it."

Heather gasps. "Really? What about the Guardia? Couldn't it all go horribly wrong, if we do it without them?"

"It won't. We have the money. We don't care if we lose it. All we care about is getting Harry back. This way, we have control. We can even offer them more. Do you see?"

Nick shakes his head. "I know what you're saying, but we don't have a line of communication to them."

"Yes, we do," James says.

"My god, you got the mobile number too?"

James nods. They gaze at each other for a moment, frozen at the realization of what they're about to do.

The strident buzz of the entry phone startles them all. They turn as one towards the front door.

"Don't answer it," Heather says, but Nick is already lifting the handset to his ear, and she can hear a male voice speaking rapidly. On the video screen, she can see there's more than one person behind the speaker.

Nick frowns as he listens, then says: "No," slamming the handset back into its holder. He turns to the others, his face thunderous.

"The press," he says. "They're on to it."

"No! But how—" Heather starts to shake. So soon — how can that be? How much more pressure can they take?

"Heather — listen. Ignore them. It doesn't matter how they got the story," James says. "We can't do anything about it. We need to focus on Harry. We have to make this decision, now, while we have the chance."

Heather is the first to break the silence.

"Let's do it."

CHAPTER FIFTY-FIVE

Natalie

Sounds from the corridor alert me; I put my head out of the kitchen to see who it is. Miles's back is disappearing towards a side door. He's dressed in running gear, his sandy hair covered with a baseball cap, dark glasses over his eyes. He carries a water bottle in his hand. He doesn't see me, and I wonder for a moment why he hasn't come to the kitchen for fresh water. Perhaps he took some last night so as not to disturb people. I glance at my watch: it's still only six o'clock.

Taking my coffee and toast onto the terrace, I contemplate the view, my mind on Harry. Heather, James and Nick are ensconced in the dining room, and for a short time I'm alone with my thoughts. Then one by one, the others arrive, looking as tired as I feel.

My heart sinks when Liz appears, Steve close behind her. Today she seems particularly loud, speculating wildly about what might happen today. I'm glad of my sunglasses, because they hide what I'm thinking. Normally I would let it wash over me, but today is not the day to be melodramatic, and I'm feeling the strain. I don't want to think about Harry's body being dumped by the side of the road, or Harry starving to death in some sordid shed somewhere because the kidnapper took the money and ran.

So I'm grateful when Steve puts a stop to it. "Liz. None of us wants to hear this. Why are you thinking the worst? It's not helping, honestly. Just leave it, eh?"

He glances at Charlotte, whose head is turned away as if she can't bear to listen. "You're frightening people."

Liz follows his glance. "Oh, sorry, Charlotte, I don't mean to scare you. I just—"

"Just leave it, Liz," Steve says again. "I'm going to get more coffee. Anybody else?"

Glad of the distraction, they all reach out for their mugs. Liz goes with him to the kitchen, where I have no doubt there'll be a whispered altercation between the couple about how tactless Liz is.

"Are you all right, Charlotte?" I say, leaning over.

Abruptly, she stands, almost upsetting her chair. "I'm fine. That woman . . ."

"I know. Don't go, I'm sure she's got the idea now. She means well." I don't know why I'm defending Liz. Her lack of sensitivity is astounding.

"Maybe she does, but she has a strange way of showing it," Charlotte says, pushing her chair in with finality. "I'm going to my room."

* * *

When she returns I'm still sitting alone on the terrace, an untouched book on my lap.

"Feeling better?"

She draws out a chair and pours herself a glass of water. "A bit — thank you. Gosh, it's getting hot in the sun already. It's a good thing there's always a breeze here, or it would be too hot for me." I watch as she drinks, the muscles in her slender neck tensing as she swallows. She pours another glass.

We sit in silence for a moment. "Has anything else happened?" she says at last.

"I don't know. Nobody's been out here. I'm feeling the tension — I hate to think what it's like for Heather and James."

"Yes. It will all be over soon, though," she says. "Harry will be back and the holiday will carry on."

There's a strange edge to her voice, and I wonder what's on her mind.

"I really hope so. I can't bear to think of the alternative."

Charlotte stares out to sea, her mouth set. I notice the ends of her fingers, the torn skin around the nails. She doesn't seem a happy woman to me.

I glance around to make sure we're alone. "Charlotte, I've been meaning to ask you — is everything all right with Miles?"

As Charlotte talks, I'm aware of movement in the house. Glancing up, I'm taken aback to see the Capitán and two men striding away through the house to the front door. Soon the sound of a car leaving confirms that they're on their way. I wonder what's happening inside, and almost decide to go back in.

But Charlotte is still speaking, and though I'm listening with half my attention at first, I soon realize with a shock that what she's saying is very, very important.

CHAPTER FIFTY-SIX

Heather

The money's gone. At the click of a button, a huge payment has been made, the transfer confirmed. For a moment they stand silent, Heather gazing into James's eyes, disbelieving, shocked at what they've done.

They're about to go back in and come clean to Paola when Natalie appears, out of breath, her eyes huge.

"You must come and hear this," she says urgently.

"What is it, Natalie?" Heather says, glancing towards the dining room. "We need to . . ."

"You need to come." Natalie's voice is shaking with emotion. "Now. It's important. Both of you, come with me — quickly." Everything about her is tense, her breath coming in short gasps.

James is the first to react. "Nick, are you happy to talk to Paola without us?" he says. "She's not going to be happy — but this sounds urgent to me."

"Don't worry, leave it with me," Nick says. "You go ahead."

Almost breaking into a run, Heather and James follow Natalie onto the terrace. Charlotte sits on her own, clutching a crumpled tissue. Small shreds fall to the ground like confetti as she twists it round and round with shaking fingers. Her eyes are red and swollen, the skin of her cheeks pallid.

"What on earth is it, Charlotte?" Heather says, sitting next to her.

"Go on, Charlotte, tell them," Natalie prompts her gently. "Exactly as you told me."

Charlotte lifts her face toward Heather, a strange expression in her eyes. She bites her lip.

"I'm so sorry," she whispers.

Heather shakes her head, about to tell her not to apologise, but Charlotte doesn't wait for a response.

"I should have mentioned sooner, I know I should have," she says. "It's — it's all so dreadful, I don't know how to say it." Her voice is so low they can hardly make out what she's saying.

James brings a chair closer and sits in front of her, gazing intently at her face.

"Just tell them what you told me," Natalie says, a hint of impatience in her voice. "Tell them about Miles."

Charlotte takes a deep, shuddering breath. "All right . . . Miles, well, he has this property business, as you know."

They all nod.

"It's his own business, and he works so hard, all the hours he can, seven days a week. I know he's doing his best, but—" She drops her head. A single tear falls into her lap.

"But what, Charlotte?" Heather says, glancing towards the villa. "We need to get back, Nick's going to need us . . ."

"Just hang on, Heather," Natalie breaks in. "Come on, Charlotte, they don't need all the detail."

Charlotte takes a deep, trembling breath. "It's not his fault, but the business . . . it's failing. He's borrowed so much money — a frightening amount — remortgaged the house, sold all his shares. He didn't tell me. I had no idea until a couple of weeks ago. I was devastated . . ."

"So, is the company going under?" James says. "But — he gave the impression it was doing so well . . ."

"He's good at hiding it. But there's nothing left. The last project failed a few weeks ago, and there's absolutely nothing in the pipeline. He can't pay off the loans. We're going to lose everything . . . the house . . . everything." Her voice is breaking now, her eyes closed.

Cold dread strikes at Heather's heart. "Wait, Charlotte — why are you telling us this?"

Charlotte takes a deep juddering breath.

"Why are you telling us this?" Heather's shouting now, leaning over Charlotte, willing her to talk. She wants to shake it out of her, force the words up through her throat. "Has Miles got something to do with Harry's kidnapping? Has he?"

Charlotte lifts a desolate face to Heather's. She nods. "I — I think he has."

"Oh, my . . ." Heather's hands fly to her mouth. "*Miles* took Harry? What — how?"

"He was desperate, really desperate, he didn't know where to turn — and when you won the money, he thought it was heaven-sent, a way out he could never have dreamed of. When he asked James to help finance the business, he was completely convinced you'd support him. But James said no. He couldn't believe it — he was furious, worse than I've ever seen him, raging about it, violent — breaking things. He scared me. I told him to tell you the truth about the business, but he's so proud, he didn't want to tell anyone, he's always behaved like he's wealthy, he can't bear to be seen as less successful than anyone else. So when you invited us over here, he thought it meant . . . we would . . ."

"Get some of the money, is that it?" Despair has been replaced by rage, now, surging up from her gut to her face. She can feel the flush of it reach her scalp, tingling, stinging, uncontrollable. "We're *friends*. How could he?"

"I'm sorry, Heather, I really am . . ."

"And why didn't you tell us?" She's standing now, shaking with rage, her fists clenched, dimly aware of James beside her, frozen in shock. But she can't stop now. "You let us go through all this, this suffering, this horrific trauma, and you didn't say a thing. Harry's only fourteen — a *child*. You know him, he's innocent, and sweet, he doesn't deserve this! What the *fuck* is wrong with you?"

James's hand is on her arm. "All right, Heather, it's okay. Where is Harry, Charlotte? Do you know where he is?"

"I think so — Miles's company has a new development in Tarifa — an apartment block. I think that's where Harry must be. I don't know, I might be wrong, but Miles brought the keys with him . . ."

"Where is Miles right now?" James says, his voice urgent. They're all standing in a tight little group, Heather clutching James's arm, Natalie moving towards the door.

"He went for a run — I saw him go," Natalie says. "About an hour and a half ago. I don't know if he's back yet."

"If he's not, he'll be back soon," James says.

"Oh god." Heather can't breathe. "He could be with Harry, right now! James—" She clutches at his sleeve.

"We must be quick. Do you have the keys, Charlotte, can you get them for us? Natalie, will you go with her?"

Charlotte rushes into the house, keys in hand, closely followed by Natalie.

"We need to go there, right now, James!" Heather says. "Let's just go and get him ourselves, not tell the police. They'll try to stop us."

"You're right," James says, jumping to his feet. "I'll call a car."

"Wait — what about the press?" Heather suddenly remembers. "There's no back entrance."

"I'll tell Nick what's happening, get him to hold the press at the gate, and you and I will leave straight away. Natalie can stay with Charlotte. Where are the others?"

For a moment, Heather had forgotten there were others in the house. "I'm not sure — Liz and Steve were here earlier. I haven't seen the kids at all." It's hard to believe it's still early in the morning, that anybody can sleep through all this.

"Should we tell the Guardia?" she says.

"No. They'll be furious with us already — they'll only stop us. Nick can tell them once we've gone."

Within the hour, sooner perhaps, they could have Harry back. She sends a silent prayer in the direction of Tarifa, and Harry.

Hold on tight, Harry. We're coming.

* * *

A car arrives within minutes. Nick goes ahead to the gate, where he ushers the handful of journalists away from the taxi as James and Heather climb in. Keeping his voice low, he gives instructions to the driver in rapid Spanish.

"I've told him to put his foot down," Nick says through the open window. "Sounds like he knows the road. Good luck . . ."

They sit in stunned silence for a few moments, the shouts of the journalists fading away as the car pulls onto the main road to Tarifa. James says: "I still can't believe it. Miles, I mean. He's been such a good friend. I thought I could trust him . . ."

Heather stares unseeing through the window as the coastline whips by. "You never really know people, do you? He's always seemed so . . . straight, to me. He's a salesman, yes, but this? I'd never have imagined he would do something like this."

"He must be desperate."

"Poor Charlotte. It's terrible for her. She doesn't even have a job, what's she going to do?"

James nods. "We can't think about that right now, we just need to get Harry — that's the most important thing. We can sort the rest out afterwards."

"What about the Guardia, James? Is Nick going to tell them?"

"I imagine they'll be right behind us. They'll arrest Miles first, as soon as he appears. But I can't get my head around it now, I just want to get Harry out of there safely."

A thought strikes her. "What if Miles is at the apartment? He could have run there in the time he's been out."

"Let's hope he isn't," James says. "And if he is, we'll deal with it."

"Or he could have an accomplice . . ."

"It's possible. We'll just have to be careful."

It seems like an age before they arrive in Tarifa, the driver slowing to a crawl in the narrow streets. He seems to be checking every side street before, at last, he turns away from the sea. Blocks of apartments line each side of the road, some still in construction, some newly finished, with estate agents' signs outside. They check the address on the key fob, and at last, the driver nods at one of the buildings. Telling him to wait, James chucks some money at him, promising him more when they return, and they run towards the low-rise building he's indicated. Newly planted flower beds line a smart paved path to the entrance, but otherwise it's all quiet, like the rest of the street, no cars parked outside, no windows open, the balconies empty of furniture. It looks unoccupied.

At the door, James fumbles with the keys. At last the door opens and they find themselves in a marbled entrance hall. It's unlit, silent.

"Which apartment is it?"

"It doesn't say. Let's stay together."

They go from door to door, listening first, then knocking. There's no sound anywhere in the building; it seems completely deserted. Heather's beginning to despair, to think that Charlotte's wrong, it's all a fabrication, when there's a sound from along the corridor.

"There, Heather!"

James starts to run. She follows him, her sandals slipping on the smooth tiles. He stops towards the end of the dim corridor, listening.

"Harry?" she calls, her heart pounding.

"Mum?"

They whirl around. It came from the door behind them, muffled but definitely him. Relief pours through her, her body unable to hold itself upright for a moment longer.

As James slips a key into the lock, her legs give way. When the door opens and Harry peers out into the shadow, she's already on her knees, sobbing.

CHAPTER FIFTY-SEVEN

Heather

They must get away, right now. Nothing must stop them, now they have him. Her arm is around Harry's shoulders, rushing him away, as James follows, not bothering to lock the door behind him. To their relief, the taxi is still there.

She holds Harry's hand tightly; she has to touch him, to be sure.

"Are you sure you're okay?" she says for the third time.

"I'm fine, Mum, really." He leans into her. "Just glad you came."

"Did you have food and water?" She doesn't want to bombard him with questions, or talk too much in front of the driver, but she can barely contain herself.

"Loads. Lots of crispbread and stuff, snacks and things. The fridge was full . . . It had proper furniture — it was quite a nice flat, really. The TV worked, so I had that. I tried to get out but all the windows were locked, and I shouted and banged on the door a lot, but nobody heard. I don't think anybody lived in the building. I didn't have my mobile with me, so I couldn't do anything . . ."

"You must have been so scared."

"Only at first. I didn't know what was going to happen to me. Then I was bored, mainly, and a bit lonely. I missed you all."

"We missed you too, darling." She closes her eyes, forcing her mind to shut out what might have been.

The journey home seems long and slow as they make their way along the coast towards Zahara. The day is warming up, the heat creating the illusion of pools of water on the tarmac ahead of them. Heather rests her head on the seat back, helpless with relief, letting the air conditioning waft around her.

But this isn't over yet. There'll be Guardia, questions, interviews, Miles arrested. Dealing with the media. A trial, a conviction. It feels surreal, like a drama that's happening to someone else.

"Listen, Harry," James says from the front seat. "We need to warn you, the Guardia — the Spanish police — will be there when we get back. They're going to want to interview you, probably straight away, as long as you feel up to it. We won't be able to get back to normal for a while. Are you feeling well enough to go through that?"

"I'm okay," Harry says.

"We'll stay with you, of course — we won't let them overdo it. And hopefully they'll have arrested Miles by then, so you won't have to see him ever again . . ."

"Okay . . ."

There's a pause while they all stare out of the windows, lost in private thoughts, watching the scenery flit by, until Harry's voice breaks the silence.

"Why are they arresting Miles?"

Startled, they exchange shocked glances.

"Harry," James says, leaning around the seat to get a better view of his son, "what do you mean? Wasn't it Miles who took you?"

"No, it was Charlotte."

"Charlotte?" James sounds incredulous. "Are you sure — not Miles?"

"Yes, I'm sure. Didn't see Miles at all."

Charlotte. Helpless, submissive Charlotte. How could that be? Have they completely underestimated her? Or were they working together, and Charlotte has turned on him, putting all the blame on his shoulders? It hardly seems possible she was working on her own.

Perhaps Miles forced her into it and she couldn't bear to admit it . . .

"Are you sure?" she says to Harry, already knowing the question is pointless: of course he's sure. "James—"

"They need to arrest Charlotte too, we need to tell them—" James stops suddenly, his hand on his pocket. "Our mobiles . . . we can't call ahead. Shit . . ."

"What? What's happening, Dad?"

"The police have our mobiles, Harry, they're monitoring the texts. But we didn't know about Charlotte."

"My god, James." Heather shuts her eyes. This is unbelievable. "The money's been sent."

James turns back into his seat. "Yep. They'll be long gone." He eyes the driver's mobile, in a holder on the dashboard. "We haven't got the numbers, either — we're stuffed."

For a moment, she's furious. Furious with Charlotte, with the Guardia, with the money, the trolls and their poisonous messages, the so-called 'friends', the parasites who don't give a damn about anyone, only themselves. Then, a realization dawns.

"Actually, James — you know what? Who cares?" Heather says. "It's not our problem. The Guardia will just have to sort it out. We've got Harry now, and that's all that matters."

Harry puts his head on her shoulder, his boy-smell surrounding her. Her heart begins to mend.

At the gate, a uniformed officer stands talking to two men with cameras. They turn, startled, when the car arrives, but the officer holds them back as the gate opens. Ben is there on the front steps with Natalie and Nick, flanked by a knot of police uniforms, Paola with them.

"Harry! Oh, thank goodness," Natalie says, one hand on her heart, tears in her eyes, taking Heather's arm.

"He's okay, Natalie. He's fine. Thank goodness, indeed."

Ben clamps an arm around his brother in an uncharacteristic display of affection, ruffling his hair with his other hand.

"You're back, then," Ben says. "Your hair feels weird."

"Get off," Harry says, wriggling. "You're so annoying."

"Just glad to see you, bro," Ben says with a grin. "But you need a shower."

"Anyone know where Charlotte is?" James says urgently. "We need to find her."

"She went out soon after you'd left," Natalie says. "She didn't want to be here when Miles got back."

James curses softly and runs into the house.

Natalie, surprised, turns back to Heather. "They arrested him straight away, they didn't even question him. He didn't go quietly — he was yelling that it wasn't him, he wouldn't do that. It was quite upsetting. They didn't let him change his clothes or talk to anyone, they just took him away . . ."

Heather stops her with a gesture. "Listen — it was Charlotte who took him, not Miles. We don't know if Miles was even involved."

Natalie and Nick exchange stunned looks. "It was Charlotte? Really?"

"Really. We haven't got the detail, but she's the one who took him."

Before they can say more, Paola intervenes. "We need to talk to Harry straight away. And check for forensic evidence."

For a moment, Heather doesn't understand, but Nick says quietly: "We must let them, I'm afraid."

"All right," Heather says. "But I'm going with him."

Paola nods and leads Heather and Harry inside.

* * *

"I still can't believe it was Charlotte," Liz says, for about the sixth time. "At least, not that she did it willingly. She always seemed such a mouse."

It's early evening now, a group of them gathered in the seating area on the terrace. James has his arm around Heather; they lean on each other, giddy with relief. The children are in the pool, Harry included, glad to get back to normal. Heather has asked the others to be kind to him, to understand that he might be a little fragile for a while, though he seems none the worse for his ordeal.

The Guardia have gone for the day, their equipment packed up, though they will be back. The dining room has assumed its original formal state, impersonal, immaculate, no trace of uniformed men remaining. The long hours of questioning were brought to a halt by James, concerned at Harry's pale face, his fidgeting fingers. If they need more, they can come back tomorrow, he argued, and to Heather's relief, they agreed.

She can't help looking towards the pool every few minutes to check that Harry is still there. A wave of utter exhaustion envelops her. Slumping back into James's shoulder, she lets the conversation wash over her.

"How did she . . . ?"

"She asked Harry to help her with something, just took him straight to the flat. It wasn't difficult. He's such a willing lad."

"And he knew her."

"She was always so quiet, you'd hardly have known she was there, most of the time . . ."

"Honestly, I would never have thought . . ."

When they searched Charlotte's room, her handbag was missing, and with it, her passport. They found her mobile under a pillow. Everything else was still there. With the money in the bank she needed nothing, after all —not a suitcase, nothing of her old life. The bank account she'd used was untraceable, evidence of the planning that must have gone into the kidnapping.

The Guardia wasted no time in alerting the airport, the train services, the ferries to Africa, but there's been no sign of her as yet. She seems to have disappeared into thin air.

Border controls have been warned, but the consensus is that she could already be gone for good.

Everyone is astonished at Charlotte's transformation into a ruthless kidnapper, traitor and thief. Some in the party are convinced that she was coerced into it by Miles, only to betray him at the last minute; others think she acted on her own, for reasons they can only imagine. Miles would certainly have motive, if his business has collapsed and he's facing bankruptcy — but then so would she, with the prospect of losing her comfortable life in London.

But Heather doesn't care. Her son is back and that's all that matters. Later in their room, exhausted, they lie together, letting the cool air calm them.

"It could have been both of them, you know," James says thoughtfully. "Miles could be joining her once the fuss has all died down, if and when the Guardia let him go. They can easily start a new life somewhere like Brazil on five million — they'd be pretty well off out there."

She only has to think about this for a moment. "Good luck to them," she says. "I don't want to see or hear from either of them again. They can keep the money."

CHAPTER FIFTY-EIGHT

Heather

"Harry, Ben, we were wondering if we should go home. Back to London."

It's a few days after Harry's return, and Heather's worried that Zahara and the villa will be a constant reminder to Harry of his ordeal. They don't know if there'll be any long-term effects, or if staying here could make things worse for him.

"What?"

"No, Mum. Why would we want to do that?"

Both boys look horrified at the idea.

"We just thought . . . maybe it would be better for you, Harry. You'd feel safer at home."

"But Charlotte's gone, hasn't she?" Harry says. "I'm not in danger anymore. And anyway, we've got a security guard as well as a burglar alarm now. And a private driver-cum-bodyguard."

"London's definitely more dangerous than here," Ben chimes in "And the weather's rubbish there. Come on, Mum, Harry's fine, aren't you? We can't let Charlotte ruin our whole summer."

"Ben has a point," James says. "And our security is much better now."

"Yes, Mum, I'm fine, really. I won't go anywhere on my own, I promise. You can keep an eye on me at all times."

Heather has to admit, at last, that they're probably more secure here than in London.

In the three weeks since the others left, she has slept and slept. The silence helps, the gentle days spent reading in the shade, dipping in the pool, walking along the beach with the family as the sun sets.

She's glad they stayed on, now. Liz and Steve left a few days after Harry's return. Somehow, after sharing the night-mare with her sister-in-law, Heather found that she'd developed a fondness for her that she didn't know was possible. She even found herself inviting the family to visit them in London.

Natalie and Nick were the last to leave; they stayed on until Nick felt he needed to get back to work. Natalie left a different person. She declared herself transformed, looking forward to the future. She could hardly wait to resign from her job, start working on Heather's project and find a new home.

Today dawns the same as the other days: bright sunshine dripping shards of pure gold across the bed, the villa's windows gazing over a windswept sea. The boys no longer have kitesurfing lessons in the mornings. They join a group later on in the day, when it's quieter, so they sleep in most days, as teenagers do, a deep, undisturbed, simple slumber.

She wakes alone, dimly aware of James having left his side of the bed some time ago. Stretching, she allows herself to drift until the door clicks open and James is there, holding his laptop.

"Heather? Wake up — you need to see this." He places the open laptop beside her on the bed.

She groans and pulls herself onto the pillows, yawning. "What time is it?"

"It's gone ten. Look."

She pulls the laptop towards her, peering at the screen, where an email has been left open. Glancing down at the signature, she starts at the name.

Charlotte.

She looks up at James, who nods. "Yes, it's from her. Read it . . ."

1716.46

By now you know what I've done, and that I'm the guilty party. I'm already far beyond the reach of the Spanish police, and even if they track this email, I will be long gone.

I'm not going to apologise for my behaviour, but you've been kind to me and I believe you deserve an explanation.

It's true that Miles — we — are bankrupt. We owe amounts that would shock you. The interest alone is eye-watering, and it grows bigger every day. I was unaware of the scale of it until recently, when I found out by looking through Miles's statements. I confronted him. He couldn't deny it, although being the man he is, living in a fantasy bubble, even in the mud at the bottom of the slippery slope, he still insisted he could turn it round.

You've always known me as the quiet, submissive wife. I was happy to be that, to let Miles take the lead, earn the money while I looked after him. When we married, Miles promised me the earth, and I believed him. He was my knight in shining armour, and I was young and in love.

What you don't know about me is that my mother gave me up at birth. I grew up in a series of not very loving foster homes. I dreamed of one day being taken care of, and Miles offered me that. He believed unwaveringly that he was going to be a huge success, but it was a pipe dream. He always lived beyond his means. Whenever there was any money, it was spent on cars, holidays and champagne, as if we were millionaires, when really we were just two ordinary people with a mortgage and debts. I know that now, of course, but at first I trusted him; he was a businessman, and I was not. He understood finance, or so he said, and I did not. Stupidly, I believed him.

When I finally understood how disastrous our situation was, I urged him to talk to you, James, and tell you the truth. Perhaps if he had, you might have given him some good advice, or even propped his business up — who knows. I don't blame you for saying no. You're a financial expert, and doubtless you knew it wasn't a good proposition. Anyway, our last chance to keep our heads above water was gone, and we were sunk.

But then I found something out from Miles's sister. She called one day when he was out. He never told anyone, including her, what was going on, but she could tell from my voice that I was upset, and she pushed me until I blurted it out. Then she told me something that shocked me to the core.

He'd been lying to me all the time. He'd been married before, been bankrupt before, lost everything. And his first wife had hanged herself as a result.

He really should have told me that, don't you think?

Finally I understood I had to look after myself. You might think I've been disloyal to my husband, but it's all down to him, in the end. He deserves to take the fall. But he didn't have any part in it: I did it all on my own. As soon as you invited us to Spain, I started to plan.

You can show this email to the police and Miles will be free in no time.

It wasn't difficult: he's always got pay-as-you-go phones, pretending to need multiple mobiles for business reasons. I simply used them to text you, and I went out while he was running and took a taxi for a few miles before sending the messages. Then I dumped them. He didn't even notice they'd gone.

Perhaps if the Guardia had been better at their job I wouldn't have got away with it, but somehow it all worked out for me. I'm sorry that Harry had to go through it, but he was never in danger from me — I knew you would pay anything to get him back. And I'm sorry you suffered as a consequence, but as you said, you didn't really care about the money. Well, I did, and I'm set up now.

I won't bother you again.

Charlotte

CHAPTER FIFTY-NINE

Heather

Miles spent two uncomfortable nights in a cell before returning. No charges were made against him; there was no evidence that he was involved. The Guardia had to grudgingly accept his protestations that he'd been framed by his wife.

But the man who came back was not the same as the one who was manhandled, protesting, from the villa that day. All the ebullience was gone, and it wasn't because of the police questioning, or even because his wife had betrayed him in the worst possible way. For him, the humiliation of the truth being known was worse than his wife turning out to be a thief and a kidnapper. He spent an hour with James, alone, before ordering a taxi to the airport. He left without saying goodbye to anyone else.

"I feel sorry for him," Heather says. "He's lost everything, including his wife. Thank goodness there weren't any children. Although perhaps that explains why she was able to do what she did to Harry — I can't believe a mother would be involved in a kidnapping, not for all the millions she might make. Or, for that matter, a father."

"I'm not so sure about that. You never really know people."

"What will Miles do?"

"He'll have to declare bankruptcy again," James says. "It's the best thing, really. I thought about offering to bail him out, but the debts are enormous, and he's proved without doubt that he's incapable of handling money in a responsible way. If we gave him a loan, it would disappear down a black hole. We wouldn't see it again, and he'd be back in the same position. No, best he takes the hit and tries to learn from it."

"Poor Miles. He just wanted to be successful."

"Indeed. But don't feel too sorry for him, Heather. Look at the fallout — his first wife committed suicide, his second was driven to crime because of what he did. Not a great legacy."

"You're right. I don't suppose we'll see him again."

"Not if he can help it. He'll be long gone when we get back, I suspect."

She sighs. "It's so strange. You're right about not really knowing people. We thought we knew about their lives. Though I suppose we probably wouldn't have chosen them as friends if they hadn't been neighbours. But look how little we actually knew — about either of them."

"Or about their relationship. They hid it really well. I would never have known."

Heather nods. "Nor me. Maybe something happened in Miles's past to make him so driven. Charlotte's childhood made her who she is, and look what happened to her. Perhaps that's what drew them together; they were both damaged, in different ways."

Like me, she thinks. *I'm damaged by the bullying, the taunts. It lasted through the whole of my childhood. But somehow, I made the right choices. Perhaps some of it was instinct, some of it learning from my parents.*

But a great deal of it was sheer luck.

* * *

288

Only two weeks to go before they return to England. It's a strange feeling, as if this life will end and another begin. The life they left, but different.

Because nothing will ever be the same again. The drama is over, at least for the moment, but there will always be a risk, now. They will always have to be vigilant. Heather's still sad about that, but they have to be realistic.

They've been on their own, just the small, nuclear family unit, for many weeks now. She has at last settled into a new mindset in which there's no need to worry about money. And so much to look forward to. She's already helped friends and family, and that feels good. The charity project is getting closer. She wakes every day with a feeling of anticipation.

"Mum," Harry says, as they sit quietly in the shade around the breakfast table, watching the white tips of the waves lift and fall with the pull of the Zahara wind. "Can we buy a villa here?"

She glances up at him and he takes her look for disapproval. "That wouldn't be so extravagant, would it?" he says. "We know the place really well, now. You and Dad love it, and we love it for different reasons—" Ben nods his approval, "— and it works for Dad and the business. What do you think?"

James smiles as she takes a deep breath. "What do we think, James?"

"It's not a bad idea," James says.

"Can we buy this one, please? We could come every holiday, couldn't we, it would be so cool!" Harry's eyes sparkle with excitement.

"Let's see. Don't get too excited; we don't know if it's for sale. But we'll find out."

"Offer them millions! It is the best, isn't it? Let's get it!" Ben grins, punching the air. "You can do it, Dad!"

"What do you say, Mum?" Harry says.

Heather looks out at the sea for the millionth time, across the shimmering pool, over the glistening sea to the dark shoulder of Africa beyond. She could never tire of this.

"I think it's a luxury we can probably afford," she says.

CHAPTER SIXTY

Heather

The room buzzes as people mill around, chatting, glasses in their hands. The official speech is over, the canapés almost finished. The room they've hired in a London hotel has been busy, but not too full for comfort. Almost seventy people have come to support them.

It's been a huge success, this evening's launch of Stand Tall, Heather's anti-bullying charity. Its long-term promise: to eradicate bullying in every environment in the UK. Heather, Natalie and a small team will start by visiting schools all around the country, encouraging conversations, educating children and working with teachers. Once the schools project is established, they will expand into the corporate market to raise awareness of workplace bullying. Heather has plans to recruit a royal personage to head the charity as patron. Ultimately, they will lobby governments, perhaps even expand into other countries.

As people start to leave, Natalie raises a glass to Heather. "To you," she says. "You were brilliant. And I'm so happy to be working with you. We're going to make this a huge success, you and me."

"We are," Heather responds, looking around the room with satisfaction. "We'll make it work, I know we will. Thanks, Natalie, for joining me."

James and Nick are deep in conversation with a group of people on the other side of the room, but James glances up and raises a hand. They both raise their glasses to him.

"I was wondering," Heather says, picking up the guest list, with all the attendees' names ticked off. "Why didn't you invite Joanna? I thought you two were good friends . . ."

"We were friends — I wouldn't say 'good', particularly," Natalie says. "We were thrown together at work. She bore the brunt of my boredom with the job, that's for sure. But we're not in touch anymore."

"That's a shame. Any particular reason?"

"She went very strange on me. She seemed happy for me at first, when I told her I was leaving work and buying a new place. But then she got jealous. She started sending me horrible texts, calling me 'rich bitch' and things like that, really unpleasant. Abusive, really. I blocked her after that."

Heather puts her glass down. "Wait a minute, Natalie. You didn't — did you, tell her? About the money, early on, at all?"

A pink flush flows up Natalie's neck and onto her cheeks. Her eyes widen, her mouth opening and closing, but she seems unable to speak.

"I'm so sorry, Heather," she whispers at last, her eyes filling. "I did tell her, the day after you told me. It was stupid, a terrible thing to do, especially when you'd asked me not to tell anyone. I was so excited for you — I just couldn't stop myself. Then I was too ashamed to tell you, even when you asked. Will you ever forgive me?"

"Those texts. The ones I got. Could it have been her?"

Natalie's eyes grow wide. "Oh, my . . . She could easily have got your number from my phone while I was out of the room. I don't know what to say, Heather, except I'm more sorry than I can possibly say . . ."

For a moment Heather can't speak. Her mind goes back to the beginning, when she was so shocked by those venomous messages. All the time, it was Joanna, Natalie's workmate and supposed friend: she was the source of the leak. After everything she'd said to her, Natalie had gone and told the worst gossip she knew. It was . . . unforgivable.

"How could you?" she says at last, her voice low but shaking with anger. "I asked you specifically, in no uncertain terms, not to mention it to anyone. For a good reason — because I didn't want publicity, because I didn't want to receive horrible messages and phone calls. Did I not make it clear how important it was?"

Her words seem to strike Natalie like blows. She flinches, hanging her head like a child taking its punishment, all the colour draining from her face. "You did. It was wrong of me, I knew it at the time, but I couldn't help myself. It was . . . so stupid."

"It was. And thoughtless."

"I'm truly ashamed of myself. I let you down badly, I know."

"Yes, you did, Natalie."

There's a long pause while Heather breathes deeply, listening to the buzz of conversation that still fills the room. Natalie lifts pleading eyes to hers. "I don't deserve you as a friend, Heather," she whispers. "Even before all this, I didn't deserve you. But I'm different now, I promise. Can you forgive me — please?"

Heather searches Natalie's face. This is her friend, the person she's known best and longest in the world. Natalie has let her down: she's lied, gossiped, spoken out of turn. She's deeply flawed. But then so is Heather. She too has lied, pretended, battled with her inner demons. For a long time, she was so involved in her family, she failed to understand how unhappy Natalie had become. Her anger begins to drain away.

Knowing that Joanna was the source of the threats is shocking, but also a relief. At least she knows, now. It wasn't some stranger who'd got hold of their details anonymously. That would have been a worry that never went away.

"I'll forgive you," she says at last. "On one condition."

"Anything."

"No more lies. If we're going to make a success of this charity, I have to be able to trust you. You know that."

"No more lies, I promise. I don't need to pretend anymore, Heather. Thank you."

Heather picks up her glass, savouring the golden liquid as she sips. The bubbles prickle on her tongue, the warmth of the alcohol spreading down through her body.

"I'm glad the final mystery is solved. It was her, all the time. At least we know now. It was niggling me, that we never found out. It doesn't matter now. Let's forget it ever happened. Who cares about her?"

Natalie breathes out slowly, picking up her glass again, clinking it against Heather's. "You're right. Who needs friends like that?"

Later that evening, at home in Shepherd's Bush with James and the boys, Heather thinks back to how she felt then, when the money in the bank weighed so heavily on her heart. It had felt wrong, for one person, one family, to have so much money, when there were millions of people everywhere with so little.

Now it doesn't feel wrong. It feels perfect, the best possible solution. Her family will always be secure, well off, if not fabulously wealthy. The boys have each chosen a charity to support in their spare time: Harry working at a dog rescue centre in South London, Ben helping to coach disabled sportspeople. James supports them by lending his financial skills to their charities. Already, he spends more time with them than he does in the office — he jokes that he's a 'sleeping partner' now, though he seems to work just as hard when he's there.

The boys will finish their education. They will try a few things, perhaps fail a few times, learn and grow. She hopes they'll find work that inspires them, that doesn't feel like work, so they can get up every morning looking forward to a day of doing the thing they love the most. Like she does.

* * *

Even then, even at her age, with a husband she knew loved her, it was the hardest thing to tell him about the bulimia. She sat him down and held his hands in hers. His initial shock soon turned to understanding. Then he became angry with her parents and the school for not picking up the signals.

"How could they not know? Didn't your parents notice a pattern? What did they think was happening every evening when you left the table to go to the bathroom? And the school! Surely, with so many girls, they would be checking for things like that? It's unbelievable, Heather."

Her eyes were brimming; she couldn't find her voice.

"And I'm so, so, sorry," he said. "You didn't deserve any of that. I only wish I'd been there to support you."

She swallowed. "Thank you. I don't know about my parents. I don't blame them — they'd probably never even heard of bulimia or anorexia. And I suppose, in those days, schools weren't so aware of pupils self-harming. And their anti-bullying policies, if they had them at all, weren't worth the paper they were written on. It's good it's changing."

There was a pause. "Why didn't you tell me before? Did you imagine I'd think badly of you?"

She squeezed his hands. "I'm sorry. This illness is hideous. In the sense that it gives people — me included — such a deep, horrible sense of shame that it's difficult to bear, let alone talk about. And when it started again, after we won the lottery, I was even more horrified at myself. A woman in her fifties, who'd just won a huge amount of money, with a lovely family, everything to be happy about! I was doubly ashamed. Still am."

He took her face in his hands and she gazed into the soft greyness of his eyes. "You don't ever need to feel ashamed again," he says. "You have me, us. We will always be here for you."

* * *

November in Shepherd's Bush. It's never the best time of year, when the leaves are gone from the tall chestnuts in the square, the ground beneath slushy with decaying leaves. It's mid-afternoon and already dark, the headlights of the never-ending stream of cars flashing bright in oily puddles flanking the pavements, people huddled into coats, hoods pulled up against the drizzle of a Wednesday in West London.

Heather shakes her umbrella out before she enters the familiar newsagent's on the Goldhawk Road.

"Hi, Rosy," she says to the girl behind the counter, who smiles and gives her a wave as she passes. She's unrecognisable as the sad girl outside Shepherd's Bush Tube station. Tracking her down took a while, visiting the square, talking to the regulars on the benches and the pavements, but she found her in the end. Now, the girl has a place to live and a job with Sanjay.

Heather walks past the cakes and the confectionery, taking her time. Not even a tiny tug of desire bothers her; she's not tempted today. Not any day, these days. She knows it's still in her, the urge to purge. The sweet pull of the cake counter, the bars of chocolate whispering to her as she passes. But for the moment, it's dormant. Hopefully, over time, it will wither and die.

She places her purchases on the counter just as Sanjay appears from the door at the back of the shop. "Whoa," he says. "It's my lucky customer. Something good is going to happen!"

She smiles back at him. "Just these, please."

"Nothing else?" he says, dipping his head at the lottery machine on his right.

"Nothing else," she says, with a smile.

THE END

ACKNOWLEDGEMENTS

Heartfelt thanks to Caroline and Tim Plumptre, who introduced me to the gorgeous town of Zahara de los Atunes in southern Spain. I'm so grateful for your hospitality — and your endless patience with my questions.

To all my early readers, especially Judy Jones, who has the eyes I need to improve my books and the patience to read multiple drafts.

I'm hugely grateful to Sophie Hannah and her fantastic Dream Author programme, which inspired me to make the book the best it can be.

Many thanks to my publisher, Jasper Joffe, for taking me on, and to Emma Grundy Haigh, Commissioning and Managing Editor at Joffe Books, for her uplifting enthusiasm and support for my books. Thanks also to everyone else at Joffe who has worked on this story.

And to all my readers, thank you for reading!

ALSO BY SUSANNA BEARD

THE GIRL ON THE BEACH
WHAT HAPPENED THAT NIGHT
THE PERFECT LIFE

www.joffebooks.com

In the UK, BEAT offers support at
www.beateatingdisorders.org.uk. In the US, the National
Eating Disorders Association helpline is 1-800-931-2237.
In Australia, the Butterfly national hotline is 1800 33 4673.

FREE KINDLE BOOKS

Do you love mysteries, historical fiction and romance?
Join thousands of readers enjoying great books through our
mailing list. You'll get new releases and great deals every
week from one of the UK's leading independent publishers.

Join today, and you'll get your first bargain
book this month!

www.joffebooks.com

Follow us on Facebook, Twitter and Instagram

@joffebooks

Thank you for reading this book. If you enjoyed it please
leave feedback on Amazon or Goodreads, and if there is
anything we missed or you have a question about, then
please get in touch. The author and publishing team
appreciate your feedback and time reading this book.

We're very grateful to eagle-eyed readers who take the
time to contact us. Please send any errors you find to
corrections@joffebooks.com. We'll get them fixed ASAP.

Made in the USA
Las Vegas, NV
26 May 2022